T0282302

THE ARRANGEMENT

MEL TAYLOR
BRIAN SHEA

Severn River Publishing
www.SevernRiverBooks.com

ISBN: 978-1-64875-596-5 (Paperback)

ALSO BY THE AUTHORS

Booker Johnson Thrillers

The Exclusive

The Arrangement

BY MEL TAYLOR

The Frank Tower Mystery Series

Investigation Con

Investigation Wrath

Investigation Greed

Investigation Envy

BY BRIAN SHEA

Boston Crime Thrillers

The Nick Lawrence Series

Sterling Gray FBI Profiler Series

Lexi Mills Thrillers

Shepherd and Fox Thrillers

Memory Bank Thrillers

To find out more, visit

severnriverbooks.com

1

PARSON MANOR

He reached down to the floor of the car to make sure the secret he had in store was still there. Parson Manor pulled back his hand, smiled and looked at his son Gibby before turning his attention back to the road in front of him.

"Not long now." Manor gripped the wheel of his still-brilliant, red, 1978 two-seater 450SL Mercedes Benz. He could have driven any of his newer cars, but this was the Benz. The car was the first thing he'd bought when he came into some real money. Dirty money always bought nicer things, he'd thought at the time.

"I can't wait." Sarcastically, Gibby finally looked up from his cell phone. The sixteen-year-old was always locked into the world he held in his hand. The world of games, hundreds of texts and stupid videos with no time for anything else. Activities with his father were limited. "Never quite know where you're taking me, dad."

Today, the older Benz no longer gave a smooth ride, yet Parson Manor would never, ever sell the car. One more turn and he was at the baseball field. Before him, fathers were tossing baseballs to their sons. Freshly washed uniforms in blazing colors of blue and green. A tall man, presumably the coach, gave infield practice and they heard the smack of a well-thrown baseball hitting a glove. A picturesque scene played out from city to city on any Saturday.

There was plenty of parking, but Manor, instead, turned away and drove past all the open spaces, powering down a side road, leaving the baseball teams and parents long gone in the mirror.

It was time. Manor reached down and pulled out the Beretta 92X and placed the gun on the console, holding it there like it was made of gold. “You don’t want any baseball. I always made sure of that. That’s kid stuff. I’ve got something else in mind for you.”

Gibby Manor reached over to touch the weapon. His father firmed up his grip on the Beretta and Gibby pulled his hand back. The teen was again glued to the cell phone images, yet he kept glancing every so often at the handgun.

Manor was grim faced, like he was ready for something serious to happen. “When we get there, I’ve got a surprise for you. Are you ready?”

“I’m not sure what it is.”

“Oh, you’ll be ready.” Manor kept driving down the dirt road. “How’s the new school?”

“Only been there a month.” Gibby looked bothered by the question.

“And?”

“School’s okay.”

“Just okay?”

Gibby’s voice kicked up a notch. “It’s been a month, okay?”

The road was like a crease in the dense flora. On both sides of them, there were no houses. The road was lined with plants of wild cocoplum, elephant ear and sawgrass. They passed tall groupings of Brazilian peppertree, thicker than crossed fingers. On his right, something zipped across the road and darted back into the maze of greenery. The creature moved so fast, Gibby never got a fix on what kind of animal he saw.

The car came to a stop in front of a rusted old gate with a large NO TRESPASSING sign. Parson Manor, almost six feet tall and twenty pounds over his desired weight, got out of the car and walked to the gate criss-crossed with a heavy chain. He pulled a set of keys from his pocket and held one out to insert into a lock. The lock was the one thing that looked new. Unlocked, he swung the gate open and got back into the car.

They continued down the path, just wide enough for his car, and parked in a small clearing. Gibby Manor got out. His face was marked up with cream in his continuing teen battle to fight acne.

His father pointed to the car. "Leave the cell phone in the seat. We have something to do."

Gibby Manor's body looked like straws holding up a large head. A bit taller than his dad, but he was skinny as a pole. "Where we going? Never been to this spot before."

Parson Manor walked away from the car, holding the gun, keeping it pointed down at the ground. His finger well off the trigger. "I'm taking two or three shots then it's your turn."

"I can go first," Gibby shouted.

"Just two shots. Just hold on."

Twenty yards away, a shooting target was nailed to a live oak tree. Manor spread his feet apart and stared at the target. For Manor, his mind morphed to the past, letting the target represent old ghosts and street fights, hidden secrets of mishandled deals with violent consequences. His one-time enemies and demons that came into his thoughts every so often like daytime nightmares. The memories were created long ago, yet they still made him boil with a certain anger. He raised the gun and calmly fired off two rounds. The report was loud, sound fading into the humid air.

Manor placed the gun on a fallen banyan tree. The tree was probably the victim of a lightning strike. Manor looked at the Beretta. "It's all yours."

Gibby Manor walked up to the weapon with the confidence of a pool shark. The lanky teenager snapped up the weapon and turned it on its side like some hood thug in a movie.

"Not like that! Like I showed you. Hold it right." The elder Manor put his hands on his hips.

Gibby gripped the Beretta with two hands, moved the gun into the proper position and now his aim was directly on the target. He aimed, fired three rounds and pumped his fist.

"Feel good about yourself, Gibby?"

"I got all three in the center. Not bad. I could do this all day."

"Okay, how long you been gettin 'em in the center?"

Without hesitation, “More than a year, straight. Every shot in the sweet spot.”

“Tellya what Gibby. You’ve reached a certain point. Lots of practice shots. I think it’s time for you to go to another level.”

“Another level?” His free hand waved at a mosquito.

“This is my surprise. It’s time to move up in the world with that gun. You’ve had enough training. It’s Graduation Day.” Manor pulled out his cell phone and hit a contact number. “Are you here?” There was a long pause. “Good. The gate is open. Come on up.”

“What’s up dad?”

“Gibby you’ve been firing at targets for a long time. You’re good at it. But that doesn’t mean you’re good enough to protect yourself in the clutch. When your life is in danger. We have to move you to another level.”

“You keep saying that. What level?”

“Gibby, I’ve arranged for you to shoot at a live target.”

“I don’t see any deer out here. A rabbit maybe but that’s about it.”

“Gibby my man, you’re not going to be shooting at deer. No sir, not for you. Today you grow up. I’ve got something else in mind.”

A car drove up and parked next to the Benz. Two men got out. One man Gibby recognized.

Manor grinned at his son. “Naw, no deer today, Gibby. You’ll be shooting at a target alright. But no animals. Time to shoot to impress. Shoot to put down the people who might come after you or me. Today, you’ll be shooting at a man.”

2

Gibby's jaw dropped in surprise at what Manor said, then he quickly regained some composure before his father's gaze turned back on him. Manor's vision was fixed on the two getting out of the car. Manor and Gibby knew the larger man well. Runy Drucker stood a good six-foot-three, square-cut jaw, strong shoulders, with piercing brown eyes that never stayed fixed as though he was always on the lookout for trouble. Manor once asked him who were his people, his heritage and where he came from. Drucker always said, 'everyone and everywhere. An original mutt.' Indeed, with his darker complexion no one could guess where he was born.

The other man was a complete stranger to Gibby. He was much shorter than Drucker, bald with short, calloused fingers and hands. Parson pointed him out to Gibby. "Take a good look. That is our volunteer. I'll tell you about him later."

Manor walked toward them, "Just go in front of the targets." Drucker carried a large equipment bag. Gibby still had the weapon. He placed it back on the tree stump. Gibby could not understand what was happening. "What is this? I don't need to shoot at someone. Whatever you have in mind, we can just use the paper targets."

Manor marched to his son, stopping just an inch from his face, and snarled. "You're a Manor. In order to be a Manor, you've got to fight like one. You will do as I say!"

Drucker pulled vests out of the equipment bag—bullet resistant vests—and handed them to the stranger. Gibby watched the man put on the vests, wrapping himself in the gear. Drucker also had coverings for his legs. The man's head, however, was not covered.

"This man is protected. You see all that stuff he's wearing? You take aim and shoot center mass. Center mass, Gibby."

Gibby protested. "I don't know about this."

Manor was yelling again. "Center mass Gibby, think center mass!" He picked up the weapon and handed it to Gibby. "Remember your training. You've got one of the best guns in the world. You're a great shot. You're ready for this. He's got two vests on. He'll be okay. Just whatever you do, don't let your aim get too high and it's a head shot. You do that and I'll make you dig the grave."

Parson Manor smiled. Gibby did not.

The man stood in front of the targets. Drucker stepped away from him and moved off into the thicket.

Gibby Manor looked like someone who didn't know what to do. He stood there staring at the man clad in protective gear. His target subject was just as anxious. He was nervous and kept dropping his head looking at the ground. Gibby's confidence was gone.

Manor cupped his hands and yelled. "Drucker, tell that fool to keep his ass still, head up. And quit moving!"

Drucker spoke to him in words Manor and Gibby could not hear. The man stood erect and the pinky finger on his left hand kept twitching.

Now Manor was directing his words toward Gibby. "Raise the gun, take aim and shoot."

Gibby brought up the weapon into the shooting position. Both his hands started to shake. He lowered the gun for a few seconds then raised it up again to shoot. The way he moved made the gun look like it weighed fifty pounds. The always-confident Gibby, while holding a weapon, was now just trying to avoid a meltdown in front of his father. The arm shaking was back, the barrel kept moving out of perfect position and Gibby's left leg was bent. Finally, he said, "I can't do it."

Manor was at his side in a millisecond. The words were low and edged in anger. "Listen to me. There are people in my past who would love to clip me one day. I have to rely on the people around me. And that might have to come down to you. Get it together, Gibby. Shoot him now. Shoot him correctly or you'll blow his face off."

Manor stepped away. Gibby bravely aimed the gun again. His hand was steadier. He stood there for almost a full twenty seconds. The Florida early October sun bore down on the four men. A line of sweat rolled down Gibby's forehead, drops landing on his shoes. He lined up the shot, four, five, six times.

Gibby placed the gun on the ground and sidestepped. "I'm done dad. I'm not like you. I can't do it."

Manor was yelling again. "Shoot him, Gibby!"

Gibby picked up the gun, went through all his pre-shoot preps, stood firm and aimed. The barrel wavered in the air. Gibby kept aiming and did not shoot.

"I said shoot him. Now!"

Gibby's voice was almost a whisper. "I can't do it."

Manor rushed over and snatched the gun. "Can't do what? This?" Manor raised the gun and quickly fired two rounds. The bullets appeared to hit the targeted man directly in the chest. The man went down like a tipped-over domino. And he didn't move.

Gibby gasped. Manor lowered the handgun and pushed it snugly behind his back, up against the belt. "Drucker, is he okay?"

Drucker was standing over the man checking on him and gave a thumbs up. "He's fine. Sore maybe, but he's fine." Drucker helped the man to his feet.

Manor was headed back to the car. "C'mon. The man on the ground is Marcus Pendon. He works for me. Will do anything I ask without question. That's loyalty Gibby. Do anything. You still haven't learned that yet. You're not a man yet. Maybe you'll learn it. Maybe never."

Drucker tore off the vests. The man sat and felt around his chest looking for a break in the skin. Nothing.

Manor got back in the car. Gibby was clearly shaken by the whole ordeal. They drove out of the field in silence.

3

Manor parked the car outside his home. "Listen Gibby, I know you got it in you. Next time, be a man. Pull the trigger. I have to go."

Gibby got out of the car and watched his father drive off. The walk into the house was a long one. Home was a two-story building on the edge of the county line. The house itself was in Sun Gold Estates, a gated development of five to seven-million-dollar homes. Once inside, Gibby made it to his room without his mother noticing him. He always kept his door locked and placed the phone near the pillow.

Gibby tossed himself on the bed. On the trip home, he never even touched the cell phone. Outside his window, he had a view of sugar cane fields far off in the distance. The other window in the room faced the Florida Everglades. The house was built miles from a major city and bumped right up against a natural habitat and the cane fields. Only Gibby never used the views. His windows were covered with cardboard and painted black. He kept the outside, outside. In Gibby's room, all the walls were dark gray with a painting of the moon on the ceiling just above his bed. The place was gloomy and foreboding. Just like Gibby Manor wanted it to be.

Hunger took over and Gibby made his way down the stairs to the kitchen.

"What's wrong Gibby?" His mother asked.

He didn't answer. Instead, he sat at the granite counter overlooking the stove and sink, pulled out his cell phone and stared into the tiny rectangle to escape.

Without any direction from Gibby, his mother pulled out a meal from the fridge and pulled back a plastic cover. She was alone at home and was always in full makeup. The off-red nails matched the lipstick. Streaks of gray hair were starting to emerge among the brunette ones. A gold necklace around her neck carried a two-inch, custom-made, 18 carat gold moniker etched in tiny diamonds of double M's for her name. Miranda. Miranda Manor.

"I'm warming up some meatloaf from the restaurant you love. Be ready in a minute." She was overly dressed for lounging around the house, although she didn't mind. Her hips kept the skirt a tight fit and she was better looking than many women her age. She stared at Gibby.

"I wish you would put that cell phone down for two minutes. Now tell me, what did your father do now?"

He kept his fingers busy, texting someone. When he would not answer, she placed the hot plate of meatloaf and mashed potatoes in front of him. Swirls of steam rose from the meal. Gibby finally put down the phone and picked up a fork.

She went over to him. "You know you can talk to me. Whatever you tell me, I won't tell him." Miranda Manor started to hug her son, who shrugged off any attempt to caress him. She stepped back, fingers poised like what she wanted to do was run her fingers through his hair like she did when he was four years old. The hair massage practice went on for years. She continued the habit until a middle school Gibby made her stop.

He was hungry and upset. Pointing a gun at a defenseless man would do that to a person. Right now, Gibby was eating like he wanted to get satiated as soon as possible then head back up to his room. His mother stepped back and left him alone. "Did your father say where he was going?"

"No." The only word he would utter.

"I think I know where he went." She reached down and smoothed down a crumple in her skirt. It was her mission to be ready for whenever her husband came back home. She dressed like she was about to go out, ready to party, ready for his needs. She walked to the large bay window and stared out at the street. The nearest neighbor was seventy yards away, just like Parson liked it. When he was away on business, she was there, like on standby. She grabbed the double M's and held on. If she thought about it long enough maybe the piece of gold could transport her to another place, another situation and away from Parson Manor. She heard the fork drop into the plate nearby.

Gibby finished and pushed away from the table. He slurped down the rest of a soft drink. She tried one more time to ask him the same question from Friday evening.

"How's your first few weeks at the new school?"

When he got near the stairs, she got the same answer.

Silence.

Miranda moved quickly to block his ascent up the stairs, arms out in a second attempt to hug him. "You know the routine." Before he moved away, she wrapped him up tight with her arms, like a mother's beartrap. She finally let him go and he slow-walked up the stairway.

Once she heard Gibby's door was closed, she slipped into some sandals, made her way through the kitchen and out the back door to the one place she always felt secure. Her get-away place. Four southern maple trees set the boundary for her garden. Parson never came back here so she had it all for herself. She moved along the path like she was stealing away, not caring about dirt on the dress. She looked across at *her* spot. Along the back she had rows of milkweed plants to attract butterflies. The palm trees were all laced with attached orchids. Dozens of them. She stopped growing the hibiscus and caladium plants because the iguanas ate all of them. In her late-night dreams Miranda wanted to own and operate her own plant nursery. The details were all planned out. If she was able to convince Parson to back the money, she would pay him back over the span of four to five years. A plan Parson always put down. She headed straight for the chickee hut, a small structure built with wooden poles and a roof made of palm fronds. The tiny place had a concrete floor with an electrical outlet with two chairs, a grill and table. She sat back in the patio chair and waited to see if Parson had returned to the house. After several minutes, she went to a rear pole and removed a large section of wood. From inside the cavity of the hollowed-out space, she pulled a weather protected package. Inside she found what she had stored for many months. Papers on how to file for a divorce.

She examined the paperwork, then kept checking the back door of the house as if Parson might come home at any moment and invade her space. The garden was her sanctuary. A place to hide her most private thoughts. Also inside the pack was a diary and a cell phone. Miranda Manor's private life, her expectations and a way to get away from Parson, were all stashed in that hole. She pulled out a pen and started to write in the diary. Her hand was steady as if she didn't care anymore if Parson discovered her plans or what she was doing just might cost her her life.

She kept writing and when things came to her for the attorney, she wrote more. She looked out again at the dappled shade coming from a collection of crepe myrtle trees and whispered to herself, "I am not afraid."

4

Parson Manor sat at his desk, opening and closing drawers, looking for something. He was a few minutes into his search when Drucker walked into the large office.

Manor stopped what he was doing. "How's our friend?"

"Marcus? He's fine. Sore maybe, but he's fine." Drucker had his own office in the building. The cubicles and glass-walled offices were partially filled during the week. Today, it was just Manor and Drucker. On paper, Parson Manor's business had three hundred employees and a managerial staff of sixteen. On paper. In reality, Manor just wanted seventeen people and two managers. There were just enough people to run Manor's import-export business. Two years ago when an inspector from the city wanted to stop by, Manor hired two dozen more people to work for one day, posed them as employees, their faces fixed on their computers, making it seem like he had a full roster. Inspection over, the need for extra help was ended a day later. Illusion.

"Whatcha need, Parse?" Drucker asked after a moment.

"I keep most things in my head, not on paper or the computer. How we doing with conversions?"

Drucker moved closer to him to make sure everything was heard clearly. For Drucker, a conversion meant laundered money. "We got seventeen new accounts, all safe in the offshore places we set up. I can give you a firm figure on what that means later today."

"Good." Manor let out a sigh. "Thanks for bringing out our shooting guest. Makes for a long day."

"I know. I don't mind. You still thinking about what we talked about?"

"Yeah. That's why I'm here a bit later. More than anything I want to be legit, Runy. Give all this, whatever this is, to someone else. I want to be clean, one hundred percent."

"You're sure?"

"I'm sure. I keep thinking someone is still coming after me. I just want to buy up a bit more land and develop all that property I showed you. That's it. Just oversee that and I'll be happy. Babysit Gibby's kids one day and watch reruns of Maverick."

Drucker laughed. "And you want to give this up?"

"In a heartbeat. I'm tired of this."

For one instant, Drucker thought he saw a new wrinkle form on Manor's face, like he saw him age right there a few yards away. Drucker played with the jade ring on his right ring finger. The ring was a size too large, and the thing always slid around on his finger. Drucker appeared to like it that way, never had the ring sized and kept turning the ring back around to the proper position. Now, the ring adjusting was a mild nervous habit. He spoke directly at Manor. "I have to ask. What do you want to do with our troublemaker? The shop owner who is trying to organize the stores. Let it go?"

Manor rubbed his chin. "Naw. Can't let it go. Send him a nice warning. You're too busy. Let Marcus think of something. Just make sure nothing comes back to us and it's just a warning. Is that clear, a warning?"

"Clear." Drucker thought for a moment. "I'd let it go Parse. If you're serious about this legit stuff, then let it go, man. Move on."

"Can't do it. I want this to go away. Make him change his mind."

"Ok."

Drucker kept a lot of information on his phone, rather than write it down. Probably too much info on his phone, he kept telling himself. He found the information he was seeking, then called Marcus to meet him.

For more than a year, Drucker and Manor hired hackers, black hats, to infiltrate and take over computers of a section of business owners, spreading malware. The takeover required the owners to make a payment in order to free up the computers. Only one smart store owner was fighting back and hired his own people to determine the source of the attack. The owner was organizing other merchants to join him.

"I just want to scare him. Nothing else. Shut this down before it gets too big. I need the money." Manor got up and started for the door.

"Leaving?"

"I gotta make sure my son isn't too pissed at me right now. But he has to learn that when it comes right down to it, he has to be ready. And then take action."

"Is he ready for that? Maybe give it some time."

"He'll be ready." Manor stopped. "You been doing sweeps? No bugs around?"

Manor adjusted the ring on his finger. "I check every day. No, this room is clean."

"Thanks."

On his drive home, Manor saw a graphite gray SUV turn with him and move up in speed. When he made two more turns, the SUV was right there, at times dropping back behind two other cars.

"Following me, huh?" Manor muttered to himself. The handgun was resting on the console from when he'd gotten into the car. His eyes flicked back and forth from the road ahead to the rearview mirror and the car behind him. Manor was convinced he was being followed. He could call Drucker for some backup, then dropped the idea since he was too far away. Manor slowed down to see what the SUV driver would do.

The SUV slowed as well.

Manor picked up the gun and kept it down near his right leg. He was now driving with one hand. The SUV pulled up closer to him.

Manor moved the weapon to his lap, and he was prepared to stop the car. He was ready to shoot, if needed.

The SUV turned left and was gone.

Manor sat there for a few seconds thinking about what happened until a driver in a dirty box truck honked at him to move.

5

Monday morning Gibby Manor pretty much knew his routine at Stander Preparatory High School. Unlike his former school, there was plenty of room here to walk the halls with just twenty-six hundred students. Private high school also meant fewer students in the classroom. He first went to his locker, put away a notebook, then headed to first period English.

The school was a new environment, yet Gibby kept his old habits. Any thought of preparing for the required reading assignment was discarded. Homework, never. When called on to speak, Gibby made up excuses, anything to avoid work.

His main objective for the day was lunch and going home. For lunch period, he would meet up with two people he recently met. When things came to lunchtime meals, private school had advantages. Fresh fruit in small baskets, a smell of cooked burgers scented the air and salad arrangements right out of a magazine.

Gibby was right at home.

Two teens approached him and sat down. One was a healthy six-foot-six. Bayson Clarke, dark-skinned with short black hair, sat his tray on the table, then went back to get a drink. Clarke was once a star on both the football and basketball teams. A year ago, during the basketball regional championship game, a bad call was made on Clarke. The foul allowed the opposing player to shoot two free throws to win the game. Three hours later, the referee who called the play was beaten to a bloody mess in front of his home. Clarke was arrested and kicked off all high school sports. When the ref refused to press charges, Clarke was allowed back into the school. The ban on playing remained.

"You like this place?" Clarke sat down, opening a bottle of juice. His long black fingers made the juice look tiny.

"I can get used to it." Gibby dipped a fry into a pile of ketchup.

"What's up, chumps?" The third member of the group sat down. Solly Ressler sat down with a tray full of desserts and a bag of fries.

Clarke pointed to the arrangement of small cakes. "Dude, you mainlining sugar now?"

"Got to feed the beast."

Clarke sucked down the remainder of the juice and pointed to Ressler's chest. "You eatin' all that stuff, you're startin' to grow tits, man. Have to start calling you Sally."

Clarke and Gibby started laughing.

The laughing stopped when a student entered the lunchroom holding a tray with a few vegetables and a bottle of water. The student found a space far off from everyone else and sat down.

Gibby stared at him. "Who is that puke?"

Clarke shook his head. Ressler took a long look. "Don't know much about him but he gets excused from anything physical."

Now Gibby was even more interested. "Nuthin physical, huh?"

"Nope. Keeps to himself. Always looks like he's gonna be sick. People just stay away from him." Ressler cut into another section of cake.

Gibby was done eating. "Gonna make that kid my mission." Then he turned down the volume of his voice to a notch above a burglar's whisper. "I know y'all just got to know me, but you guys trust me, right?"

Clarke pulled out a second plastic bottle of juice and popped the cap. "Look, I heard about you doin' stuff before you got here. Whatever you got planned, I'm in."

Gibby turned to Ressler. "And you?"

The heavy-set teen had both his cheeks encrusted with sugar powder, never bothering to wipe anything off. Ressler was comfortable being in the background like he was a bystander, not wanting to lead and remaining happiest by being the best example of a follower. "I need to hear more about this big day you keep talking about."

"Good. First, after school, I want to meet that stupid shy kid."

6

Seconds after he got the word on what he was supposed to do, Marcus Pendon started a surveillance on the home in question starting Saturday night. He drove a van close to the mark and sized up the neighborhood—upper middle, which meant one person could afford to stay at home during the day. Pendon needed someone there. Each lot was about the same size, with a few homes on more than an acre. There was foliage everywhere, plenty of places for cover. He didn't see any police patrols. On Sunday, Pendon took note of a man and woman at the house in question. No kids. The man left on Sunday and returned with groceries. Bed around 11 p.m. Pendon had to keep moving his car to different locations to avoid scrutiny.

He rubbed a sore spot in his chest from the bullet shots against his vests.

On Monday morning, Pendon switched to another vehicle, a brown Chevy. His surveillance told him a woman was left in the house. Two hours in, he left the car a full two blocks back. He was standing behind a six-foot-tall hedge of ficus, staring at the back kitchen window. Inside was a woman, moving about, looking like she was preparing something to cook. The husband and his car were gone early. She was alone. Perfect for what Pendon intended to do.

Pendon was a career do-what's-needed man. He remained on Manor's payroll with two payouts. One on the books and one between him and Manor for special jobs. One key for Pendon was always his ability to blend in. The everyman face. His routine was one of looking like he belonged wherever he was trying to infiltrate. Over the years, Pendon carried out burglaries, stole cars and made money drops. He also stalked people, all at the request of one Parson Manor. Pendon was caught just once, years before, holding on too long to stolen merchandise. The case was dropped, yet his fingerprints were now in the system.

He was good at waiting. After twelve minutes behind the hedge, he made his next move. Waiting this long gave him time to look for a dog and check once again for cameras and snoopy neighbors. Pendon stepped toward the rear of the house, reaching the southeast corner. He leaned against the coolness of the stucco and waited some more. The next move would be tricky. He inched toward the large window and looked inside. She was probably mid-thirties. Hair was pulled back and her hands were full of flour. He couldn't see what she was preparing.

Pendon pulled out the knife. The sheath was tucked down on the inside of his pants, not visible under his bland looking gray shirt. The blade was ten inches long, easily. In Pendon's experience, shock value was always good for scaring intended victims. Their eyes always centered only on the weapon which would mean foggy memories of the man who was holding the blade. Pendon eased the wood handled knife up until he placed it on the outside sill. The tip was pointed directly at the window and the woman in the kitchen.

From this spot by the house, Pendon would have his choices on what to do next. He could pull the knife back and move to a door, checking to see if it was open. With his round innocent face, he could pose as a deliveryman, do a quick check on others in the house and force his way inside. Once in, he could control all of the circumstances. A quick death if he wanted or take his time. It was all a matter of what he wanted to do. For now, other plans were in place.

Sunlight glinted off the long blade. Pendon didn't have a lot of time or the woman might see a reflection. He stepped back a yard or so, pulled out his cell phone and snapped eight to ten pictures of the knife, the window and the woman.

After checking to see if he correctly captured the photographs, Pendon carefully grabbed the knife and turned back into the hidden protection of the ficus hedge. Mission accomplished. When he walked back to the car, Pendon kept his profile positive, walking erect, not looking back.

He drove two miles and parked near the expressway. The pictures were sent to Drucker's burner. The next step was up to them.

Once on busy I-95 in south Florida, Pendon kept his speed two miles under the limit. He was hungry and needed a burger.

Once he got the pictures from Pendon, Drucker immediately made a head signal to Manor. A few employees were there, others were at lunch. Drucker went into the office and closed the door. He showed the pics to Parson Manor.

"These are great. You know what to do," Manor said.

"You want the message we talked about?"

"Yeah. As soon as possible."

"Done."

~

THREE HOURS LATER, a curious Parson Manor gave a tilted head signal to Drucker. The big man walked into the office and closed the door. "What's up, Parson?"

"You seen anything? Is he responding?"

"I checked a few minutes ago. Naw, nothing."

Manor rubbed his chin. "Why don't you do a drive-by. See what's going on at the house."

"Not the business?"

"No, go by the house. Be discreet. See what you can find out. What did the message say?"

Drucker pulled out his phone and showed him the email sent by the hackers:

SEE HOW CLOSE WE CAN GET TO YOUR WIFE. STOP THE ORGANIZING. SEND THE MONEY.

The message was under a picture of the knife on the windowsill, blade pointed to the woman in the kitchen.

Drucker put the phone away. "Is that the message you wanted?"
"Yeah. Go see what's going on."

DRUCKER DROVE TO THE NEIGHBORHOOD. There were four police cars in the street near the house in question. Drucker kept driving around until he could see into the back yard. Not easy, but he found an angle. He drove back to the office and pulled Manor aside. "We have a problem."

7

The slender youth backed up, fell and remained on the ground rather than get in a fight. He lay there, as if he didn't know whether to attempt to defend himself or run. Just backing up, the scared teen looked helpless and out of breath.

Gibby Manor made several moves, all fake punches like he was going to swing wildly at the teen, but then each time he pulled back.

"Why you pickin' on this slug?" Ressler stood in front of an angry Gibby Manor. Ressler's midsection jiggled when he moved around. "He ain't a fighter, let it go."

The teen's breathing was labored, and he was clearly in no condition to fight the much stronger Gibby or anyone. More than anything, the teen appeared weaker. His chest was almost concave, his eyes needed rest and his belt secured a small waist.

"What's up with you, man?" Manor was waving his arms, yelling at him. "Why don't you go to gym? What's your problem? Why are you still here?"

The teen was frozen in fear. He just stood there, waiting for the first punch to be launched his way. He didn't even look around for any help. The young man had very short hair, light skin and hazel eyes.

Manor yelled again. "Talk, man! What's your deal?"

This time Clarke with his giant frame, stood in between the two. "We have ways to find out about him. Just let him go. We'll get him later."

"Why you defending him B.C.?" Gibby was still prepared to do harm.

"Just ease up, man. He's too easy."

After four more minutes of humiliation and no responses, Gibby Manor stepped back. The physical threat was over. The weak teen reached for a book bag and walked off toward the street.

Manor stared at him the entire time until the kid disappeared around a corner. "This isn't over with him."

Ressler looked for something to eat in his pocket and came up empty. "Why you got a hard on for him? He couldn't fight you in a hundred years."

Gibby snarled. "He needs to go somewhere else. Another school. Get out of my sight."

The three made their way to a spot they decided to use as a meeting place. They were just out of sight from the outdoor basketball court, a place Clarke knew well. They had pried a bench off its foundation and placed it near another bench, creating a meet-spot. A grouping of palm trees gave them some cover from the sun. Ressler steered the conversation away from the near beat-down. He half expected a police officer to roll around the corner. Ressler, the slowest among the three, figured he would be the one caught if police arrived. No one came.

They talked about girls and the many reasons for not studying. Clarke admitted most of the cheerleaders were texting him, wishing he was still playing b-ball. They rated the lunch food and for a moment plotted what they might do to the kid the next time they saw him away from school.

Gibby Manor pointed to a side of the school where construction had just started on a new soccer field. "See that?" Clarke and Ressler turned in the direction of his pointed finger. "That project, I forget what they will call it. But my father paid for that."

Ressler was mildly shocked. "Your father?"

"Yeah. My dad the money man. Probably why I got into this place 'cause my grades didn't get me here. My old school was lame."

Clarke shook his head. "Think I heard about it. No lockers. What was that all about?"

"Some kid streamed video of himself putting a gun into his locker. After that, they bolted all of them shut. So we had to carry everything, including rain gear from class to class."

"That's messed up." Ressler spit in the direction of a circle of periwinkle plants.

Manor was not finished. "Yeah, but what I need to know is who are the cool teachers?"

"Cool, like how?" Ressler rested his hands on his stomach.

"C'mon, cool. There has to be a teacher here who will order food for you to be delivered. You give them the money, they make the order. Food arrives. We did it all the time at my old school."

"I heard about stuff like that. No, we don't have that here. Wish we did." Clarke stood up and stretched.

During a moment of silence in the conversation, Manor finally mentioned the thing, the reason Ressler wanted to hear. What was Manor's plan for what he called the Big Day?

Although he was a long way from anyone who could hear, Gibby kept his voice low. He stared into the two faces on the benches and the smile spread from ear to ear. Manor asked them bluntly, "Have you two handled a gun before?"

8

Parson Manor, Drucker and Pendon met behind the office building, out of sight from any surveillance cameras from other businesses. Drucker leaned against the building while Pendon appeared anxious. “What you guys want?”

Drucker asked the questions. “So, how did it go?”

Pendon recounted what happened step by step. “I’m sure she didn’t see me.”

“You wear any gloves?” Drucker watched Pendon shift back and forth on his heels.

“I was careful. If I used gloves, I couldn’t take pictures. Believe me, I was really careful about that.”

Drucker said, “I checked up. Police were there and they were dusting for prints on that windowsill.”

“Dusting?” Pendon’s eyes shifted to Manor and back to Drucker.

Drucker kept pushing. “Your prints are on file, aren’t they?”

“No. I mean, maybe. They could be. But that was a long time ago.”

“No maybe about it. If you left prints and they connect this to you, then maybe, as you like to say, maybe they will connect all this to us.”

“Please Parson, I’m pretty sure I didn’t leave any trace. I was more than careful.”

The quiet between them was only mere seconds, yet each second seemed like a year. Pendon looked down at the ground rather than face the scowl of Parson Manor. If there were any words of punishment in the next two minutes, they did not come. After listening to Pendon's explanation, he just said, "Get out of here."

Pendon left fast. When the two of them were left standing, while Drucker waited, he kept rotating his loose ring.

Manor ran his hand across his throat. "I want him gone."

Before Manor had a chance to reenter the building, Drucker sought some clarification. "Gone, like fire him?"

"No Runy. I want him gone. Like dead gone."

Drucker put up his hands, palms facing Manor. "Now wait. I know he messed up."

Manor cut him off. "Not the first time. You want me to go down the list?"

"Parse, let's think about this. We can think of something to be tough on him without that!" Drucker looked around and spoke low. "Again, what happened to going legit?"

"Runy, I'm days away from putting in papers to develop my property. I have a meeting set up with the planning department. If I get their recommendation, I go to the city. It looks very good. I've been very careful to build and keep a sparkling clean reputation. What I don't need right now is for that fool to get himself arrested, mention my name and everything goes away. I've worked too hard."

"Pendon won't talk."

"How do you know that? I can't take that chance. The man probably left his prints at this place. He's vulnerable. And that makes us vulnerable. I don't want him around anymore. I want him dead. Is that clear? Dead."

Drucker was a bit dumbfounded. Whatever he did about Pendon, Manor would want proof.

For the next hour, Drucker planned what he would do next. He came up with a reason for Pendon to meet him, telling him there was another task and this would square him with Manor. Just before 7 p.m, Pendon met Drucker outside a building owned by Manor. Pendon got out of his car and walked toward Drucker. When Pendon was two feet away, Drucker pulled out a Glock40, pointing the weapon directly at Pendon's midsection.

"Get in my car. You're doing the driving."

"C'mon, Runy. I just messed up. You don't have to do this."

"You messed up one too many times. Boss don't like that. Now git in the car!"

Drucker moved in anticipation of Pendon doing a runner. He got in behind the wheel and waited. Drucker eased into the passenger side, never once taking his aim away from Pendon. "Head out to Alligator Alley. Head west till I say stop."

"Please, I'm begging you. Don't do this."

Drucker didn't say another word until they reached a few miles out on the Alley. "Don't even think about crashing this car 'cause you'll be dead before this thing rolls to a stop."

Alligator Alley, or Interstate 75, was the connecting roadway between the east side of Florida to the west side, with a stop first in Naples and other cities. On both sides of the road was the sprawling Florida Everglades, home to thousands of pythons and untold more alligators. Tunnels were built here to allow panthers, bears and other wildlife to cross underneath the road. This was done to protect them after years of animals being killed by cars. There were no lights on the Alley. If one got out of a car, they would see the red eyes of alligators in the water. The entire stretch of road was fenced off.

Pendon's breathing was starting to quicken. He kept wiping his sweating fingers on his pants. "Where are we going?"

"Never mind. Just keep driving." Drucker rested the Glock on his leg, still aimed at Pendon.

Crossing the Alley to the west side would not take long. Halfway across Drucker saw a rest stop. "Pull in here."

Pendon didn't hesitate. He slowed down and parked in one of the many empty spaces. There was no one here. Sometimes truckers would pull over to take a break. Tonight, it was just the two of them.

Drucker opened his car door. "Get out."

"Please no, no. Runy, we go way back."

"Sometimes I regret it. But it's over now."

Pendon moved as slow as he possibly could. He just stood in front of the car. Drucker took out his cell phone and took two pictures of Pendon looking scared with the gun also in the frame. Then, he aimed the gun at Pendon.

"No, please!"

Drucker stood there for a long time, gun aimed, eyes steady on the target. Then, he lowered his weapon. "How badly do you want to live?"

"Please, Runy, I'd do anything."

"Here's the deal. Look over there."

Pendon turned around. Far off from them, perhaps fifty yards, there was another car. "Don't ask any questions, just do as I say." Drucker reached into his pocket, withdrew a set of car keys and tossed the set at Pendon. "The car is yours. I had it brought out here. You drive away and never come back, is that clear?"

"Yes, Runy. Clear. Very clear."

"He wanted you dead. I don't want to see you again. I'm giving you a chance at life. Don't blow it by coming back."

"I'm outta here. Thanks, Runy. I owe you."

"You don't owe me anything. Just keep driving till you hit fifteen-hundred miles from here. Start a new life."

"Will do, Runy. Thank you. Thanks!"

"But you have to do one thing before you go."

THREE HOURS LATER, a very tired Runy Drucker parked in front of his house. He checked his burner phone and the photographs. He sent four to Manor's burner and waited. Seconds later, he got a call.

"Got'm. Thanks. Thank you."

"I did what you said."

"Good. Glad that he's dead. Thanks for doing that for me. And for sending the stuff."

Drucker looked down at his phone. The picture showed Pendon on the ground, covered in blood. A dark black hole was now part of the right side of his head.

"Thanks for doing that."

"Later."

Drucker hung up. He sat in the car for several minutes, then pulled yet another phone from his pocket and dialed a number. "You get all that? I'm worn out." Drucker sat listening to a conversation, then he responded. "Please mark it down, I've been recording this fool for three years now. Tell them I want this investigation to be over. They should have all they need. After tonight, add conspiracy to commit murder."

He listened again. Then, two minutes later, "Just tell them. I did my end of the bargain. Just bring him in."

9

CAIN STOCKER

Cain Stocker moved through the courthouse entrance reserved for prosecutors, judges and staff members. His now all-white hair gave Stocker a reserved, experienced look. One that suited him well in the courtroom. He headed up a unit devoted to potential crimes of RICO, or Racketeering Influenced and Corrupt Organizations. He had all kinds of tools at his disposal and through court orders, he made sure to use pen registers, recording and taking information from phone conversations.

He was wearing one of his old suits since he had just lost twenty pounds. Stocker pressed down the front of his blue blazer before taking it off. The loss of weight made him feel like an accomplished man. A man who was on the verge of bringing down a much sought after target: Parson Manor.

For the past five years, Stocker had amassed an impressive list of wins. He had arrested an organized ring of eight people posing as home-owners who actually stole houses from legitimate owners. Eight arrests and later eight convictions. In the past six months, Stocker got a guilty plea from a woman who ran a prostitution ring out of six massage parlors. Three other cases involved a man selling fake trips around the country, taking in huge deposits and disappearing with the money. Stocker tracked him down in North Spring, Maryland, where he was arrested and extradited back to south Florida. The trial was set for next summer.

All of his cases were sent to the state-wide grand jury. Stocker set aside a full hour to meet with his chief investigator, Sana Bolton. She was a former homicide detective for many years and now readied the case of Parson Manor.

"We ready for the grand jury?" Bolton walked into Stocker's office wearing a business suit and black shoes. She carried a thick file.

"Everything go okay last night?" Stocker wiped lint from his always clean desk.

"About as well as expected. The phone intercepts and the Confidential Informant's recording gear got Manor ordering a hit. We carried it out, with C.I. pretending to do the murder, then letting him go."

"This let him go, is that someone we need?"

"Maybe. I think we can catch up to him one day if we need to but for right now, I still think our main focus is on Manor. Our file is full of what you always called 'the little bricks.'"

"Yes, the bricks. Good." Stocker used the term in court during final arguments. He would always tell the jury each piece of evidence against the defendant represented a tiny brick. As each piece of the case or bricks were stacked up, the prosecution was building a wall around the defendant until finally he or she was closed in all around with evidence. Now the wall was slowly being built around Parson Manor.

Stocker checked his calendar. "I think we can set up the grand jury for two, maybe three weeks away. Gives us plenty of time to line up witnesses, present the case and make an arrest."

"Good." Bolton picked up her file and left the room. The meeting ended much sooner than expected. Just before she closed the door, she had one more question. "No target letter? Give him a chance to explain things."

"I think we can do that. Let me think about it." Stocker wrote something down on a pad. A target letter, if sent, would inform Manor he was the subject of a criminal investigation linking him to a crime. Used mainly by U.S. prosecutors, the practice was applied by some at the county or state.

He walked into a conference room. Bolton sat at the head with three other people. "Cain, what we have is recording 7-4-9-9-6 for identification.

Date, time and location as marked on the recording. Clay, how are we doing on the quality?"

Clay Aferman was the tech supervisor and in charge of the recordings themselves. "If you listen, there are three dropouts, but we should be fine for court evidence purposes."

Bolton looked over some notes. "As you know C.I. has been given the control on a lot of this. If he feels it's too risky and not the right time, the recording team can adjust. Some days we get things right, other days we wait."

Stocker checked his own notes. "We have a lot of audio tapes here. I want to thank the team for doing all the coordinating to get this done."

"No problem. If no one has any questions, let's listen to the last recording brought in by the team."

Cain raised his hand. "C.I. keeping with the rules?"

"You mean staying in contact?" Bolton leaned back in her chair. "In a word no. Since this looks like it's winding down, he's a bit too cocky for me. Takes off for a couple of days at a time. Doesn't check in, that kind of thing."

"Will this be a problem for trial?"

"No. We kinda let him go rogue a bit because his undercover role could get rather messy in a hot second. He has leeway and he has to look and act a certain way in order to stay close to the target."

"Got it."

For the next three hours, Stocker listened to recordings collected by the confidential informant and the recording team. After listening, he was up to speed on all of his little bricks. He made his way home.

Work day over, Stocker drove past the guard, and into his gated community. His house was in a line of seven homes all designed alike. For his entire eleven years there, he'd hardly spoken a word to his neighbors. Stocker kept the life of an elusive solitary man, as if he didn't want the world to know he put people in prison, especially if that person could be a neighbor or a neighbor's relative.

Solitary was not the only way to describe him. He was the father of a son and husband to wife Lace. Stocker allowed himself just one minor fault: a finger deep glass of his favorite whiskey after dinner. Just one.

Lace Stocker arrived home. More than anything, finesse and beauty were among her greatest traits. Standing an inch taller than her husband, Lace Stocker had cornered gorgeous. Even after almost nine hours of work, she appeared like she had never left the house. Caramel-brown skin, red lipstick, blue skirt with matching pumps and the tennis bracelet she received from Stocker as a birthday present. Her forty-seventh.

She looked at the whiskey bottle. "I'll take one."

"Now?"

"Before dinner? Yep. Set me up, Cain. Been a long day."

Lace Stocker headed up a company managing almost three dozen homes being used as rentals. Overseeing the maintenance and upkeep was more than a full-time job. She took the glass, sniffed a bit and took a sip. "Some days," she started. "When it's right, the day goes by like dripping blackstrap molasses. All nice and smooth."

"And today?" Stocker was close to the door, headed for the kitchen.

She took another sip. "Today was terrible. Three broken toilets, had a power outage in one neighborhood affecting two of my properties, had a break-in at another, and a customer took off without making a final payment."

"So, no security deposit for them?"

"You got it." She started to unbutton her white blouse and remove her bra when she listened to the sounds of the house. "Is he home?"

"Ya know I just got here just before you did. I didn't even check yet."

She walked to the other side of the split-plan home, where the other bedrooms were located, away from the master bedroom. She knocked three times. No answer. Lace Stocker looked inside.

She yelled, "He's not here. Did he call you today?"

"No." His response from the front of the house was barely audible.

Now she was worried. Short quick steps took her back to the living room where her husband had just left. She bolted into the kitchen where Cain was pulling out leftovers and stacking them on the counter.

She checked her phone. "Aren't you concerned? I don't see any messages from him."

"I'll call in a minute." The last of the packaged chicken marsala and sauteed vegetables were on the table, ready for the microwave. He checked his phone. "No, no messages. Did he say he had something going on today at school?"

"No." She scrolled through phone contacts and was about to dial a friend when the front door opened. Her son walked in the door and was stopped before he could head to his room.

"Where have you been?" She looked him over, head to shoes.

"Got a late start back."

"And why is that?" Now his father entered the questioning. After ten seconds of no response, he repeated the question, this time with a tiny bit of firmness.

"I missed my ride." The teen looked down at the floor. He coughed a bit, out of breath.

"Missed it? How is that possible?" Now Lace was headed to him, grabbing his face with both hands, looking directly at him.

"I got held up. I mean, not robbed, I mean I got detained a bit. They thought I got home another way. So, I missed it."

"How did you get home?" Her words were comforting. She held his head in a way that he could only look at her. "You know you can't walk too far without losing your breath. You have to be careful."

"I was gonna take public transportation, then I just got an Uber."

She kissed him on the forehead. "Why didn't you call me?"

"You guys are too busy. I can get home. I'm almost eighteen."

She took that as a hint he was no longer four years old anymore and she released her mother-like grip of his face and stepped back. When she did, he coughed again. The same cough he had since he was eight years old, the night he wore a Halloween mask and had to take it off because he couldn't breathe.

"Oh, Camden, you can always call me. Anytime." She stepped to him again, this time wrapping her arms around him in a hug.

He nodded and she let him go. He headed to his room and smiled back at her. He had the same hazel eyes as hers.

10

As usual, Camden Stocker carried his dinner into his bedroom where he watched his computer screen. His was the world of social media platforms and animated films, no video games. He had another twenty minutes of watching before doing homework, then he was free to surf whatever was on the computer again.

Cain Stocker saw his wife eat slowly. “What’s wrong?”

“He never said why he missed his ride, and we didn’t press him. Cam can’t get too excited, or he’ll end up in the ER.”

“I’m sure if he wanted to he’d tell us.”

“Something is wrong. I’ll ask him later.”

“Leave it. He’s got enough going on. This is his senior year. Trust me, just leave it for now.”

Upset face and all, she still looked like the picture from when they first started dating. She was a runner-up in the Miss Florida contest. When Cain, about to graduate law school, attended the contest and protested the second place finish to his friends, Lace heard about his protests and it got her attention. They managed to connect by phone initially. He thought she should have won the thing. She turned down multiple offers to model and, at first, also thought about taking the LSAT. She decided no, then her maze of job stints included acting in two commercials, helping manage a bookstore and bouncing around a lot of go-nowhere positions. Lace went back to school and got a degree in business administration. She ran into Cain again when he gave her a rose with the bloom cut off. Confused, she asked what this meant? He replied, "nothing a flower could offer was more beautiful than her."

She started dating Cain Stocker, the entry-level prosecutor. Back then, his cases dealt with store holdups, purse snatchings and defendants charged with shoplifting. Lower tier crime charges.

"I got another phone call." She took her plate of half-eaten food from the table, moving to the sink.

"Another? What did you tell them?"

"Just like the last five times. I'm not interested in running for office. Of any kind." She washed off the plate and put it in the dishwasher. "The only thing I'm concerned about is Camden. Public office would take up too much of my time. Time away from him."

"You're sure about that?"

"Sure."

"Okay."

A large painting was mounted over a dark wood buffet. Lace, with a ready-for-magazine green dress with a flower-patterned blouse. Cain, with a gray double-breasted suit, white hair all smoothed into place. They were a power mixed couple, their faces full of confidence. She sank into a chair and leaned her head back.

Lace rested for an hour, changed to her workout clothes of yoga pants, a large smiley face T-shirt, and headed to the exercise room. The converted bedroom was where they kept a treadmill and an exercise bike. Tonight, the bike was the choice. She worked up a good sweat, pedaling to the music of the Four Tops, some Marvin Gaye, and a bit of the Doobie Brothers. When she was done, the T-shirt was different colors of dry cloth and sweat drenched.

She reached for a towel and wiped down her face. When she was done, Lace looked up to find Cain staring at her. The tight-fitting gray yoga pants showed off every curve in her body. Cain started to move in her direction. She had wrapped the towel around her neck. Before he could say something in his best bedroom voice, she pulled tight on the towel. "Don't even think about it. You can stop right there. I've got a stack of paperwork ahead of me after I shower."

He turned away and continued down the hallway, then stopped. "You think we should press this missed ride thing?"

"Yes. Just not sure how without making him think I'm spying on him. With his condition, he could get in trouble out there."

"Maybe we should bring him home. Let him homeschool until graduation."

She threw the towel in a basket. "He thinks of himself as grown, not five years old. I'll look into what happened and we'll talk again."

"All right."

11

Lace didn't care about her son's aversion to being driven to school, she was driving anyway. He tried to get out of the car before it stopped until Lace gently grabbed him by the shirt and pulled him toward her. "You will tell me if there's anything wrong, correct?"

"Yeah, I will." He pulled free of her grasp and popped out of the car, then immediately slowed down. Any sudden number of quick steps and he might risk losing his breath.

Before she went to bed Lace had called his ride, another senior, who drives to school. His mother told Lace that Camden never showed and her son forgot to tell anyone. For Lace, there was a gap in the story. She sat in the car and watched her son walk slower than other students, heading into the front entrance. She drove off, switching her mind to the long list of appointments and repairs for all the locations she supervised.

~

"Are you okay?" Her voice made Camden stop. He turned around and smiled for the first time in almost two days.

"I'm fine."

Innocent Chambers was a year younger than Camden, two inches shorter with braces. "Had a doctor's appointment yesterday. You miss me at lunch?"

"Yeah."

"Heard you had some problems after school."

Camden's smile was gone. "You heard about that?"

"It's not all over the place, but yeah, I heard. The new kid? Don't know his name but he's got a reputation already."

"I'll be fine."

They walked down the hallway joined by hundreds of students going in various directions toward classrooms. Off to one side, Gibby Manor and his group were leaning against the wall, waiting for the bell to ring, making sure they would all be late for class. Manor was staring down Camden.

"You promised." Ressler was studying Manor.

"Didn't promise anything." Manor watched the couple all the way until they disappeared into separate classrooms. "Who is the girl?"

Clarke peeled himself away from the wall. "His best friend. I mean his only friend. Innocent Chambers."

"Innocent." Manor laughed. "Doesn't look so innocent to me."

The bell rang and the three were the only students still left in the hallway. Manor thought he heard a noise and turned in that direction. When he looked back at the hallway, he was alone. Clarke and Ressler were gone. Down at the end of the hallway, there was one other person staring at him. Raymond O'Bannon was the school's assistant principal in charge of security and discipline. He was already on Manor's radar as a person to avoid. Right now, he was facing him directly.

"Manor, stay right where you are. Don't move!" The man's voice boomed off the walls. O'Bannon was the right size for the job, well over six feet tall, heavyset with a suit that always looked too small. He kept a walkie-talkie in his right hand and when outside, his golf cart was painted black.

In the hallway Manor was trapped with nowhere to run. All of the teachers were instructed to lock the doors after the second bell.

"Follow me." O'Bannon pointed the walkie toward his office located just off the main entrance. Manor walked stoically into the office. O'Bannon spoke to his secretary, "Tell all teachers that Mr. Gibby Manor will be excused for the day. By me."

"The day?" The secretary was confused.

"The day." O'Bannon pointed to a seat in his office. Manor sat down, not knowing what to expect. O'Bannon took off his suit coat revealing what looked like years of work in the weight room. Custom made shirts expanded in the arms to accommodate big beefy biceps. His shoes were black Nike, the same ones he wore every day, no matter the suit color. He was ready to run, if needed.

O'Bannon poked at a file on his desk. "So look, I'll get to the point. The staff and the teachers at this school expect a lot of things from the students. They expect that because they know the kids who come here, leave and go to some really nice colleges and universities. The best in the country. That means every single second here is precious and valuable because there is no time to waste. Lifetime careers start right here in this very school. Is that clear, Mr. Manor?"

"Yeah, sure. I'm down with that."

"I know your father helped fund a major project and the school really appreciates that, but right now my biggest concern is not the project, it's you, Mr. Manor."

"Me?"

"If you want to waste this extremely valuable time here at this school, we are not, as you put it, down with that."

Gibby heard this exact conversation from previous experiences, and by being called into meetings with the staff. He had sat through all the tough talk from well-meaning teachers, and he'd heard all the expectations put forth to him or there would be consequences. They all had the talk with him and none of them had managed to change Gibby Manor. He knew just what to say and how to respond. "I get your message, Mr. O'Bannon. I do, believe me. I'll do better."

"Well, right now, Gibby, I don't believe you. Your father's influence here will only go so far." He opened the file. "I looked at the paperwork from your last school. You were cited three times for bullying. Suspended four times in a three-month period. Your classwork was poor, but yet your test scores show you're in the top ten percent of all those taking the test. So, my question is, what's holding you back? Are you trying to be like someone?"

"That's two questions."

O'Bannon closed the file. "I think you're trying to be like someone. Maybe someone close to you. What you really should do is be like Gibby Manor, test scores above average. Be yourself and do something with the talents you have. Do you hear me, Mr. Manor?"

"Yeah. I do." Manor gazed down at the floor, then back up at the large figure behind the desk.

"Here's what I'm gonna do. I'm sending you home with a note. You can come back tomorrow. And when you do, I want to see a new attitude. One that shows me you're ready to do the work, ready to be active in class. And stop bullying here at this school."

"Bullying? Who said that?"

"I see and hear things. People tell me stuff. It's time for a change and that change starts right now." He thumped hard on the desk with his forefinger.

There was a silence in the room with no words spoken for almost a minute. O'Bannon gave him time to think about the conversation. "And please know, just like the first day you entered this building, I will be watching you." O'Bannon got up and started to leave. "I'll make sure you get off the property okay. We'll be calling your home to let them know you're coming home early. Please let your parents know if they have any questions, they can come in and we can all sit down. Because if you don't make some changes, that sit-down will be mandatory."

Manor pulled on his bookbag, walked out into the hallway and called his mother to come pick him up. The two of them went outside. O'Bannon sat in his black golf cart waiting until the car arrived.

12

Lace was about to enter her third building location when she got the phone call. "Yes, Lace Stocker."

Her facial expression went from mild concern to near tears. "When did this happen? What hospital?" Then, "I'm on the way right now." She changed direction and drove toward Middle Palms Regional Medical Center. Nervous and scared, Lace stumbled a few times trying to press Cain's name in her phone until she got it right. He didn't answer, so she left a voicemail. "Cain, head to Palms Regional right now. Camden fainted again. At first they thought it was cardiac arrest. Please hurry."

She almost hit another car driving into the parking lot and parked at such a severe angle, another car could not move into the next space. Lace got out of her car without even checking to see if it was locked. The poor woman behind the emergency room desk could not move fast enough for Lace. Her voice was pumped up so loud heads turned in her direction as she called out Camden's name seeking information.

Lace was directed inside the emergency room where she found Camden sitting up in bed. He was connected to a vital signs monitor, showing blood pressure and heart rate. A nurse entered and did another check on his temperature. She smiled at him. Lace calmed down when she saw Camden smile back at the nurse. The nurse put the thermometer away. "He's doing fine. The doctor will talk to you in a bit, he's with another patient." Another smile and she was gone.

Lace was all over Camden, taking his hand, sweeping her fingers across his forehead. She planted two kisses on him before Camden started to protest. "Mom, I'm not a baby."

"Honey, what happened?"

"I don't know. I just remember walking, but it was taking so long for me to get somewhere. And then, I was here."

"You're okay now." She started to kiss him again then stopped herself. His breathing looked even, and Lace finally took a seat near his bed. She could not stop staring at her son. "The school called me, and I drove right over here."

"I know. I'll be fine."

A tall man in a doctor's lab coat walked briskly into the space. "Hello, I'm Doctor Falson. Are you his mother?"

Lace stood up. "Yes."

"He's going to be okay, but we need to keep him just a bit while we run some tests."

"Sure, no problem." Lace was absorbing each of his words.

"I also understand Camden has some history here at the hospital and I have reached out to his cardiology team to let them know he's here."

"Thanks for your help. Can I ask you a question?"

THREE HOURS after getting the voicemail, Cain Stocker parked his car and walked quickly into the ER of Middle Palms Regional. When he gave Camden's name to the front desk, he was directed to the waiting room. He had sent three text messages telling Lace he was on the way.

He hurried down the hallway, joining others rushing inside with worried faces, calm medical staff, and others with family members consoling someone who just got word of a loved one. With each step he didn't know what to expect, moving his own level of concern upward. Stocker didn't see Lace at first, then he searched a grouping of big chairs.

Stocker found her sitting, both hands clasped to her head while pressing back her long black hair. Stocker started his questions. "How is he doing?"

"He's fine. For now."

"Who found him? What happened?" Stocker sat down next to her.

"The security guy, Mr. what's his name?" She snapped her finger as if that would help bring up a name."

"O'Bannon." Stocker helped her.

"Yeah, O'Bannon. He found Cam on the floor by a stairwell. Apparently he got behind in getting to class and just dropped down right there."

"He was by himself? No one else around?"

Lace took in a deep breath. "Just him. I'm just glad O'Bannon was there. He could have been lying there until the next class started. But O'Bannon called for help. They also got out the equipment because they didn't know if he went into cardiac arrest or not, but they felt a pulse."

"Can I see him?"

"Not just yet. That's why I'm down here waiting for you. They took him in for some more tests. They might keep him a day."

"Okay." Cain Stocker leaned back into the soft cushion of the big lobby chair. "Anything I should know?"

Lace leaned back as well. "They think his heart wasn't pumping enough blood and his pressure dropped until he lost consciousness."

"This again?" Stocker stacked his arms on his chest.

"Yes. This again. We might as well face it, this will only get worse."

Stocker turned to his wife. "Is it too early to ask? Do they think it's connected to what we fear?"

"Well, his cardiologist is in the mix. They're not saying anything just yet, but I think we both know where we're headed."

Stocker reached out and pulled Lace into a tight hug. He whispered into her ear. "We both love him too much. We'll work through this. I don't care what it takes or how many doctors, but we will make sure he gets healthy. That I promise you. No matter what."

They didn't see her at first since she was standing near them not saying a word, just staring and waiting for a chance to speak.

Lace looked over at her. "Innocent?"

"How's Cam?" She stood there, book bag down at her feet, one cheek marked with dried tears, hands moving from her face to her side, left knee slightly bent.

Lace got up and embraced the teen. “He’s going to be all right. He’s with the doctors right now.” Lace gave her one of those health lies one tells others to make them feel comfortable, knowing the situation is much more dire than she can reveal. “You just left school?”

“They gave me a release. I had to come and see how he was doing. Got an Uber.”

“Thanks, honey. This is Camden’s father, Cain.”

Cain Stocker gave a mild wave from his chair then checked his cell phone for any messages from the office.

The teenager’s eyes darted from the entry into the ER rooms back to Lace’s face. “I suppose I should go home. Could you please tell him I hope he’s okay?”

“No problem.”

Chambers pulled the bookbag to her shoulder. “This happened second period but I didn’t know right away. I came as soon as I heard. I just hate to think of him on the floor with no one around.”

Lace tried to reassure her. “Mr. O’Bannon got to him pretty quick. Thanks for coming. I’ll make sure he gets the message.”

“Thanks.” She turned toward the exit door.

“You want my husband to drive you home?”

“Naw, I’ll be fine. If it’s okay, I’d like to come over and see him when he gets home.”

“That’s perfectly fine. Take care.”

13

The long rambling explanation started as soon as Gibby got into the car with his mother. "There was a misunderstanding. Maybe he thought I was wrong, but I was headed to class." He was pleading with her since the first thing she did was take his cell phone. His usual practice was to stay off his home laptop and only use the cell, so now he was cut off from the world.

"Your father's not going to like this." The SUV powered down the street. The sun glistened off the double M's of gold bouncing off her chest. "What happened? They're saying you've been missing classes, not doing the work."

"I can do the work. It's not that hard. I just need some time to get it done."

"Then do it." The car turned into their development. Their house was a minute away. She parked near the Benz, making sure there was plenty of space between the SUV and the red car. Didn't want to come even close to scratching the 450.

"Go ahead," she said. "I'll meet you inside."

He went into the house.

~

Gibby sat in the living room, forced to be there, trapped really, while his mother walked in and, part of her routine, blocked his path to the stairs. She read over the note that she and Manor were both supposed to sign.

"I read his version, what's yours?" She placed the note on the table.

"I can do better."

"This says you've been late for numerous classes, you don't turn in work and when you do it's half finished. What's going on with you?"

"I just have to find my space."

"Do you like this school?"

"Sure. It's fine. I'm still learning how to fit in."

"Talk to me, Gibby. I'm doing all I can to show you all that time spent in school will help you do whatever you want. This is important." Her hard stare made Gibby look away from her. "You're nothing without some education."

"Dad never finished high school. He's doing fine now."

She was caught. Either put her husband down directly to her son or defend the actions of a man who routinely bulldozed common sense. "Your father was lucky. He knew a few people, they gave him a break. You, Gibby, you can't count on that."

"My dad knows people."

"Sure, he knows a lot of people. He gets you in the door at some company and then what? If you don't know anything, if you never studied hard enough, you won't be there very long. Please, Gibby, you've got to study."

There was a long pause before she nodded in the direction of the other side of the house. Miranda studied him like she was trying to find more words to say, something to better describe the value of classroom work. "C'mon Gibby, you know the routine." She held on to him until he started to protest, then released him. "Go ahead, he's inside."

For Gibby, inside meant the office and library. He put down the book bag in the hallway and stood before the mahogany desk. Manor put down a set of glasses, connecting eye to eye with his son. "Sit down, Gibby."

The teen sauntered to a tall backed Naugahyde chair. He squirmed, trying to get comfortable and could not. Manor noticed. "Not liking that chair? That's exactly why I wanted you to sit there." Manor swiveled around in his three-thousand-dollar, back-supported office chair with vibration feature. "Gibby, I want you to feel as uncomfortable as possible because that's the way I feel." Now Manor was standing. "Do you have any idea what I went through to get you into that school? The money I spent?"

"I know it was a lot."

"That was the only thing I could do because you messed up so much at your old school, no one was going to take you. You were facing alternative school. I did all that, spent all that so you could get a decent, let me change that, excellent education." Manor was talking and waving his hands to emphasize each word. "What's going on with you?"

"School wasn't important for you dad. And look at you now? You're doing great. Besides, I know all that stuff."

"Gibby, I didn't have the brains you have. I was a street tough kid. Some say a thug. And I got by with that. You don't need that. You can do anything and you're throwing it all away. Now, get off your ass, go upstairs, do your homework and think about doing better."

Gibby didn't want to give in on the argument. "What's wrong with me doing what you did? I can tuff my way through things. I want to be like you."

"Please, look at me. I've changed. This is the Parson Manor I want you to copy. No more tough guy. Use your brains."

Manor put the glasses back on and stared into a computer. There was nothing more said and Gibby picked up his bag, walked out into the hallway and trudged up to his room. Any texting or calls to Clarke would have to wait. Walking up to his room, he saw his mother push the much-desired cell phone into her purse and head to the back yard garden.

Inside his room, Gibby walked to the calendar on the wall and circled the upcoming Saturday. Then he pulled out a sheet of paper and started writing the same three words over and over. For the first time today Gibby Manor smiled. There was a small bloom of euphoria building up in his gut and spreading over him. The feeling was so great, he started to head for the black coverings over the windows and rip them down, stopping and opting to let it all stay covered up. He was writing with a purpose, a very real goal was right there in front of him and he was going to do this deed. He kept writing until the same three words filled up the page and he turned it over and kept writing the same thing. When he ran out of room again, Gibby put the pen down, smiled and looked at the calendar one more time. The paper was put in a drawer, then he stopped one more time to read the valued line.

THE BIG DAY

14

Parson Manor walked into the office loaded down with two briefcases and four map containers. He waved off any attempt to help him and dropped off everything in his office himself. Minutes later, he popped out of the office and headed directly to Runy Drucker. "Are we gonna be ready for next week? Can't wait for the city to take a look at this."

"We're ready. You're gonna like this. Follow me."

Drucker led him into another conference room. There, two members of the staff were standing by, ready to pull away a large sheet. "Take a look."

The two yanked back on the sheet to reveal large models on a giant flat board. Drucker was ecstatic. "Here you go, Parse. Your dream."

"Oh my. It's here! I thought this was coming next week."

"They delivered it early. I told them to put in a rush."

The model included several buildings representing the stores Manor wanted to build on his site. There was a strip mall, a theater and two restaurants. On the other side of the model, there was a five-story office building. In the far righthand corner was a development with forty tiny houses inside a development. There were fake trees and roads and a retention pond for storm water runoff.

The whole model project was sped up to make sure it was completed.

Manor had instructed Drucker to cut all corners, yet do things legally. No one bribed.

Manor's eyes grew big. "This is fantastic. Exactly what I pictured in my mind. My little development. This is great."

Drucker motioned for the two employees to leave and when they did, he closed the door. "Everything you wanted. Mixed use development with retail space, restaurants, offices and the large development of homes."

"I just hope they approve all this. I really want this to move forward." Manor looked over the model like a man sitting before a nine-course meal and not knowing where to start eating. "I love it. Just love it."

Drucker got into his *just the two of us* voice. "Between us, we don't need any more money from those biz owners, do we?"

Manor grabbed his chin. "That's a touchy one. You check on what's his name's place? Police come looking for him yet?"

"Far as I know, Pendon's place has been quiet. No police, no nuthin. I managed to put in a note with the post office, saying he moved. I gotcha covered there."

Manor looked serious. "We're just about there with the money. Mixed in with our other transactions we still have to clear more than six mil. Trust me, I'll turn it into a clean six million. Every dollar that goes into this place has to be clean."

"I think we got that. All clean. But at some point, we have to turn off the spigot, don't you think?"

Manor looked down into the tiny fake window of a restaurant. "I know. I sound greedy. You're right, Runy. What's over is over. From this moment on, I'm all legit. Stop everything. No more hacking. We're done. I'm a businessman, right?"

"You're a businessman." Drucker took out his phone. "Mind if I take a pic of you and the model?"

"Go right ahead. We can put it on our website. I want the world to know. Manor Mall is coming." He was shouting now. "Everyone come on down. Manor Mall!"

All while he moved, Drucker was careful not to do anything that might reveal he was wired. Months before, Drucker let authorities in to install cameras and microphones. He also had a mic built into his big belt buckle.

Drucker would then walk around the office pretending to look for bugs and claiming he found nothing, when in fact, investigators were always looking in and listening. Early every morning in the office, Drucker checked to make sure the camera equipment was untouched. He got in before anyone else to make sure. If he discovered they were moved, Drucker planned to leave and not come back. Movement of the cameras meant Manor found out and would be hunting for a snitch. Drucker would make another call to his handlers later in the day and plead to end the charade and make an arrest.

The model makers even labeled the streets after the man himself. Manor Parkway intersecting with Manor Road.

Drucker took up to ten photographs. Manor standing and smiling, pics of him pointing to the buildings. He had plenty. Once Drucker put away his camera, Manor turned serious again. He started pounding his right fist into his left open palm. Soft at first, then harder and harder. “Reason I ask about our missing guy is because I want all this to be perfect. No screwups. And if they had caught him and he talked, it would mess up all of this. This whole plan could just disappear in a second. I can’t risk it.” He again pointed to the table of miniatures and moved with his right as if to punch a hole into the brand-new model, then stopped abruptly. “One guy talking would just destroy all my dreams right now. Any person like that has to be destroyed, even if I have to do it myself.”

A monotone sound served as the ringtone for Manor’s cell phone. He pushed the phone to his ear. “Yeah.”

Drucker watched his face contort into a mashup of angry eyes and crushed brow lines. Three times Manor tried to interrupt only to be talked over by someone on the other end. About two minutes later Manor put his phone away. The look on his face now was one Drucker had not seen in years, a tough, ready to fight expression. Manor’s words were flat, coming through gritted teeth. “Tell everyone to leave and go home.”

“You sure about that?”

“Runy tell everyone to get out of here. I won’t say it again. We’ve got a big problem.”

For the next few minutes Drucker went through the office telling all they were done for the day. Once everyone left, Drucker approached Manor. “What’s up, Parse?”

“That was my lawyer. My criminal lawyer. He just got word that they want to give me a chance to appear before the statewide grand jury.”

“Appear? What does that mean?”

Manor reared back and kicked a large hole in the once perfect model of shops and restaurants. Tiny buildings went flying like something out of a sci-fi movie. He had to pry his foot out of the board. Manor’s words were more like grunts than actual phrases. “Someone’s been talking. Has to be. Maybe it was Pendon. But he’s dead, right?”

Manor looked at Drucker hard. “Sure, Parse. I took care of it myself.”

“Maybe he was talking before you did him. This is not good. I could lose everything.”

“We haven’t seen anything official yet. They haven’t done a search warrant so maybe we have time to clean things up. Ya git me? Did they say when this might happen?”

“No, no word yet.”

Drucker sounded like he was calculating. “I can get into Pendon’s apartment and check things out. Is there anyone else you can think of who might be talking?”

Parson Manor shook his head. His eyes were fixed on nothing in particular as he walked around the office deep in thought. “No one has contacted you, right?”

“Me? No one. I’m upfront about that kind of stuff. Let me get over to that apartment. Let’s not talk on the phone anymore. I’ll just meet you at our usual place. Until then, don’t trust the phones or texts.”

“You trained me well, Runy. I haven’t talked to anyone or sent any texts. And you check the office for bugs. We should be good.”

Runy tried to hide the line of sweat running down his forehead. He slid the jade ring on his finger until the fit was just right. “Okay. I’ll see you in two hours. Trust me, we’ll get through this.”

15

Runy Drucker managed to pry open a sliding glass door to the apartment of Marcus Pendon. Inside, Drucker found a sink full of dirty dishes. Drucker snapped on gloves and went through the process of pretending to look for Pendon's connection to the statewide grand jury, even though there wasn't one. He checked books, a few, dirty socks, plenty. In the bathroom Drucker discovered a brush. Carefully, Drucker pulled out a fingerprint kit and brushed down the handle. He found two very clear fingerprints. Then Drucker came out with a tape, cut off a piece and lifted a good print from the brush. Next, Drucker produced a letter from the statewide grand jury. In the letter, which had Pendon's name and address, Drucker deftly applied the print to the paper. Once that was done, he took out a second letter and repeated the process, lifting another print and applying it to the official looking paper. When he was done, Drucker left one copy inside a book on the coffee table. The other letter was stashed inside an envelope that was slid inside Drucker's pants.

He cleaned up and continued to look around. A pile of what looked like unpaid bills was on the kitchen table. If anyone checked Pendon's mailbox, there would probably be a lot more.

Finished, Drucker quietly opened the back sliding glass door, looked around and walked off toward his car.

One minute before the appropriate time, Drucker parked his car at a remote warehouse. The warehouse contained individual work units paid by the month. Manor had Drucker rent several around the county. There was no one here, and at this location there were no surveillance cameras. Three minutes later, Manor drove up in the gray SUV. He got out, looked around and walked up to Drucker. "Anything?"

Drucker pointed to the warehouse. "Let's go inside."

Both men stopped at the metal rollup. Drucker opened the lock, raised the rollup door and made his way into the shade. Drucker kept the lights off. He pulled out the envelope. "Here, put on some gloves." He gave Manor a pair of plastic gloves.

Manor put them on then took the envelope from Drucker. "What am I looking at?"

Drucker was blunt. "Man was setting you up. Take a look. It's a letter from the statewide grand jury I dusted for prints. He must have been cooperating with them. Don't know for how long but he was a rat."

"Unbelievable. I've known this guy longer than you." Manor was studying the letter. "You found this in his apartment?"

"Yeah. Now we can do a quick check." Drucker, wearing gloves, did a similar trick he did in the apartment. He dusted and found another fingerprint on the letter. "Now, with my directions I had a few of our employees file their fingerprints with us, me included. Take a look at the print found on this letter and the one we have on file for Marcus Pendon."

Drucker handed Manor a magnifying glass. He moved from one piece of paper to the other, moving the glass up and down to increase the size. He looked at the print on the letter, then studied the print on file. Manor did this several times, going from letter to file fingerprint. "Son-of-a-bitch. They match."

"I was afraid of that. He must have been leaking stuff but again, we don't know for how long. It was good to let him go."

Manor stepped back, showing surprise in his face. "I thought I knew him, but I guess I didn't. How can we check on what he told anyone?"

Drucker tucked the letter back into the envelope. "Look for a target letter. Your attorney or you might get one at home. If you get one, that letter might give some hint. The main thing is we need to clean up all connections as soon as possible. So you know, I already cancelled the planning board meeting. We need to figure this out first."

"Good move." Manor looked around as if looking to see if someone was near the entrance to the warehouse unit.

"There's no one here. I made sure about this place." Drucker wanted to leave, then had one more thing to say. "I hate to say you should listen to me more, but we shouldn't have hacked the store owners. They just cause trouble. We have to shut down everything now. All money transactions need to cease starting today because we don't know what they're monitoring."

Manor shook his head. "I really need that money. I'm so close to what I need."

"Your need is about to put you in jail unless we clean up on our end. Shut this down. Cut yourself loose. Keep making yourself look as legit as possible. Maybe your attorney can find out a few things."

Manor gave in. "Okay. You win. Shut everything down. Release the computers of the store owners, no more laundering. I'll work with what I have. Maybe I can even get some investors."

"Now you're talking."

Parson Manor almost grinned for the first time since he got that phone call. "If the leak was Pendon and now he's dead, and with everything closed down, maybe we'll be in the clear with nothing to fear." Manor got into his car and drove off.

Runy Drucker just looked at him leaving as though he were watching a man about to slam his head into a meat cutter.

16

When Miranda Manor felt something was wrong, she paced. Just minutes after Gibby left for school, with Parson out of the house, and breakfast eaten, she got a strong urge to walk. She put on her jogging outfit, a floppy hat and walked a half-mile in the Florida sun. When she turned around and got home, the will to walk stayed with her. After downing half of her bottled water, she moved with short quick steps from the back door patio area to her garden. Once there, she turned around and walked to the patio and then back again. Miranda did this a few times then moved toward the Chickee. She leaned back in her favorite chair and pulled a phone from her pants. This was the phone she kept hidden from Parson.

She dialed and waited. “It’s me.”

The person on the other end spoke in hushed tones. “I told you, you can’t just call me like this.”

“I know, I know. But I had to hear your voice.”

“What’s wrong? You sound upset.” The man’s voice was louder now.

“I miss you. Maybe if you can find some time—”

“It’s not a great time right now. There’s a lot going on.”

She tapped her right foot like she once did when Parson first started dating her. A movement that showed she was really excited about something. Once, she told Parson the quick tapping was the same as her heartbeat when he was around. Miranda Manor lost all of that strong sense years ago when her love for Parson ebbed then was gone forever. Usually, her words for the voice on the phone were warm and genuine like she used to feel. Now she was a bit nervous. "It wasn't that long ago you made some time for me. I can hear your heart through the phone. You want to be right here with me. I know it."

"I just can't come right now. Things are really tight."

Miranda's next few words sounded tense. "He keeps me here like some kind of locked up toy. He won't let me have any friends. Yells at me if anyone even looks at me. I know he keeps track of where I go. Last week, I caught him checking the mileage on my car to see if I went somewhere. I need you! Right now. I know you feel the same way."

"I do. I just can't right now. Maybe." He stopped as if he was working something out in his head. "Maybe in a couple of days. We can do like we did before. You can leave through the back of your garden and I can pick you up. I have to stay away from your cameras. He's got them all over the place. We will get together and I will really make it up to you."

"You promise?" Her foot was tapping so much she could hear the loud cadence.

"I promise. You and I. We'll get together and I'll make you forget all about him."

"I would like that."

"I have to go." He was gone.

She waited for a few minutes to see if he would call back, then pushed the phone back in its hiding place. The phone was once given to her by the voice on the other end.

In the warehouse, Runy Drucker put away his own phone. The hookup with Miranda Manor started out without any fanfare, a chance meeting when she was allowed to go to the garden shop to buy plants. She ran into Drucker and they started a conversation. The talk led to more talks on the burner phone he provided. He didn't want to take things in the direction they went, yet he yielded to her aggressive movements toward him. It was impossible for him to ignore a passionate woman. Drucker stood and dug his fingers into his forehead in small circular motions as if his actions were plunging him into an extremely dangerous area.

He was already working with authorities to secretly tape Manor, he faked a death, placed blame on someone else to be the leak to the grand jury and he was involved with the wife of the subject of the investigation. He eased up and stopped the rubs then opened the drawer and stared at the weapon that was stored there.

For the past month Drucker was quietly scouting places to move once Parson Manor was arrested. The tactic involved finding a hiding place known only to prosecutors so they could reach him, a place where the subpoenas would come when he would be called on to testify. In the last twelve months Drucker had moved twice, positioning himself a moving target, not wanting to stay in one place too long. His doors were triple locked, surveillance cameras installed by himself. He always kept a low profile and didn't mix with any of the neighbors. Even now, there was no desire on his part to meet up with MM. It was something she insisted on. Drucker pulled hard on the rollup door until it snapped down into place. The task of recording Manor was not something he wanted to do. This was something he had to do. They insisted, or he would go to prison.

He got into his car with a game plan in place. He would go back into the office, pretend to close up the loose ends like Parson wanted, and make like he was a dutiful employee. Then when the day moved into evening, he planned on seeing the other woman in his life, his real public girlfriend, and have dinner with her.

17

Again, Cain Stocker met his wife at the hospital. He saw the trauma in her face. The once almond skin tones looked drained pale. She was without makeup and her always perfect hair was somewhat unkempt. "What's wrong," Stocker took her right hand and held it in his palm. He could feel Lace trembling, her bottom lip quivered.

"Camden went into cardiac arrest hours before they were going to release him. I didn't want to say that in a voicemail."

"What? Is he okay now?"

A single tear made its way down her left eyelash and dropped on her cheek. "They think so, for the moment."

"What does that mean?"

"It's what we've been talking about for years now, but Camden always managed to move forward. It's his heart. They got it beating again and he's stable."

Stocker took her left hand as well. "Stable. I hate that word. It doesn't mean anything."

"Stable just means it's under control. At least for the moment. We can't see him just yet. Maybe in an hour or so. Cain, if he wasn't in the hospital, where he got help right away. If he was out on the street and away from a defibrillator, I just don't know what would have happened."

"The schools have them. I always thought he was safe there."

Lace wiped down her cheek. "Once we get in to see him, I'm not leaving until he leaves. Not gonna let my boy out of my sight. They warned me it could happen again. No telling when he will get out of here."

"He's so young."

Lace smoothed a lock back into place. "We've done the research. We can't ignore it, this thing has been with him since he was a kid. It was my mistake to think it would simply go away one day. We have to look at ways to get him healthy."

For the next several minutes, they just sat there together, Stocker moving his arm around her shoulder, pulling her into him, saying nothing, just offering comfort. He looked at her until he got her attention. "Don't be mad at me but I went into his room last night and there was a letter on his desk. I shouldn't have read it, but I picked it up. It seems he was writing to his friend, what's her name, Innocent, and he was explaining what was wrong with him. All of it. Looks like he wanted her to know specific details of his condition."

"You sure?"

"Positive." Stocker drew his arm back. "Sometimes people don't want their medical condition to be some sort of family secret. Looks like he wanted her to know. If that's the case, I can do that for him."

"If you're sure that's what he wants, then I can explain it to her."

"Lace, you sure?"

"I can do that. I have her phone number and we've been texting. She's coming over after school. I'll do it then." Lace's phone rang and she promptly ignored the call. She laughed. "That's my office. They've been calling me since I got here. Seems I have two locations without a working toilet and five missed appointments to show property for rent. I just can't think about that now. My mind is just on Camden."

"You have someone who can run things when you're not there?"

"She quit. Got a job in Pensacola. I was looking at resumes when this all happened." Lace got up and looked at the front door. When the automatic doors opened, she saw a common South Florida phenomenon. Out west was a divided sky. On one side, there were almost no clouds against a seamless blue horizon. Just to the right, dark clouds were stacked up like tight fists. It was raining on one side of the parking lot while the other side was dry. "Seems like we've been in this place a thousand times."

Stocker lamented, "For a while, I thought the cardiologist's office was going to be our second home. Then he got better. When he got to high school, I just got my hopes up too high. And now this."

The office for the cardiologist was on the other side of the building. Whenever Camden arrived, he was clearly the youngest in the office. Lace turned to Stocker. "I remember the shocked look on people's faces when we walked in the door. They were so much older, and he was a child."

Camden had built up a long history of E.K.G.'s, echo cardiograms, blood tests, heart x-rays, stress tests, with a full range of treatments.

"This isn't going away. The medicines he's taking, the precautions. If this is going to be his near future, we have to rethink things."

Just feet away, the scurrying around the waiting room continued. Nurses called out names, people rushed about and the lone figure who did not move one inch was the security guard. Stocker ignored calls to his phone. His chief investigator was trying to reach him. Sixteen minutes later, a nurse approached them. "You can see Camden now."

When Drucker went into the office, the last of the employees were heading out the door. "Watch out, he's tearing people's heads off," one person said.

Before Drucker got three feet inside the door, he heard Manor's voice shouting at someone. Before he had a chance to sit down, Manor called him into his office.

"Runy, I'm counting on you to make sure everything is shut down tight. And starting now, no text messages, new burners, and this is our last conversation of any meaning in the office."

"Got it, Parse. I'll make sure. Anything else?"

"I've got to do a few things. I got to refile the site plans, cancel a few more meetings and do a talk-over with my attorney. I'm hoping he knows what is going on. I'll be away from the house for a few hours. I told the wife to call you if there's any problems. You okay with that?"

"Sure, Parse. Don't worry about it. We'll get through this."

Parson Manor stuffed a few papers into a briefcase and marched toward the door. Drucker was the only one still in the office. There was a decision to make: drop dinner plans or see Miranda.

18

Camden Stocker's eyes were open. The teen looked exhausted. He was hooked up to a number of lines to check his vitals. His parents were sitting in chairs close to the bed.

"I want to go home." Camden's words were soft, almost inaudible.

"How do you feel, honey? Doctors say you need to stay for some more tests."

He looked at her with eyelids almost closed. "I feel weak. But I still want to go home."

"Not yet. Soon, I promise." As Stocker spoke, he kept looking at the numbers on the vitals monitor.

"Have you spoken to Innocent?" His eyes were wide now, voice a tad stronger.

"She's been here," Lace said. "She's very nice. Been texting me, asking how you're doing."

"Tell her, mom."

"What?"

"Tell her everything. I want her to know."

"You sure honey, all your medical history—"

"Everything. If they would allow her in here, I'd do it myself. She's the best—" He ran out of breath and never finished the sentence.

Stocker studied his son. He watched his chest rise and fall like he was laboring to make the effort. His weight looked the same, yet his height growth was stagnant.

The teen had grown into his almost-six-foot height, yet in the hospital bed, for Lace, he looked like a child. She could see her own features in his face, the same color eyes, cheekbone placement, the forehead. She was looking at a copy of herself in child form. The moment was hard for her, like seeing herself in a male form growing weaker.

Stocker tried to come up with words of encouragement and nothing came forward. He just sat there unable to do much, his whole body felt like he was sinking into his chair, being pulled down into a bottomless pit. His cell phone hummed again. This time he had to take the call and he stood up to go out into the hallway.

"What is it?"

"We're getting a lot of movement from T-1. I don't want to get into it on the phone. Are you headed to the office at any time soon?" The question was coming from his lead investigator.

"I can't right now. I'm in the hospital with my son. Can you handle it?" For Stocker, T-1 was Manor. The other voice on the phone sounded apologetic. "Sorry, I know you have a lot going on right now. I just, we just needed to update you on a few things."

"Let me get back to you." Stocker put away the cell phone. Lace gave him that look like his job was more important than anything and she couldn't do anything about it. "Cain, go take care of that. We're fine."

Stocker looked at his son. Camden gave a weak nod. "Okay, I'll be back as soon as I can." He got up and hugged Camden. "See ya soon."

He was gone. Just the two of them in the hospital room, Lace ignored dozens of text messages regarding the properties she managed.

A nurse came in, fixed on Camden. "How we doing?" The nurse logged on to a computer and started reading a medical file on him. Four minutes into her check, she updated him. "Camden, we've got you set for some more tests. You up for that?"

"Whatever you need."

"Good. I'll be back in a few minutes, get some more blood from you, okay?"

Lace liked the nurse. She seemed knowledgeable about Camden's case. Cam had the look like someone who wanted to ask a dozen questions and gave in to making sure he was reassured.

"Cam, let us know if something is wrong, okay?"

"I'm feeling better."

Lace fiddled with her phone. Another text. This one she did not want to ignore. "Innocent is downstairs. Okay if I leave you for a few minutes and speak with her?"

"Sure mom. And, like I said, tell her."

"I will."

Lace made her way down from the third floor, and through the maze of hallways until she was by the hospital entrance. Innocent was there, anxious and jamming her fingers to her face, biting a fingernail, then she stopped. Before she said anything, Lace motioned to the outside. "Not here."

They walked to a group of trees several yards away and found an empty bench.

Lace didn't know where to start. And she didn't want to just say the obvious. "Camden is a very sick young man. And he's been that way since he was eight years old. We didn't know what was going on with him."

Innocent stopped her. "Is Cam okay with you telling me all this? I don't need to know everything."

"Cam is the one who told me to tell you." Lace's eyes were flashed with a hazel brilliance, her voice was calm and the words right on point. "You've probably noticed Cam losing his breath, sometimes fainting. That's how it all started. We didn't know what was going on until the doctors and the tests showed us exactly what he was going through."

Innocent interrupted again, "Please tell him I'm thinking about him. I never asked him what was wrong, but I knew he wasn't well."

"He's in a very bad way. You're a good friend."

Innocent said, "Some of the kids call him sick boy. I hate that. They pick on him when they could show him some patience."

"I taught him to be strong. Kids can be cruel. That's why it's great that you're there for him."

"Anything I can do to help."

Lace took a deep breath. “The exact nature of what’s wrong with him is a long phrase but to put it plainly his heart is not right. And it hasn’t been right for a long time and from what we’re being told, it’s not going to get any better.”

“I’m sorry to hear that.”

“It’s not anyone’s fault. This came to him by birth. It’s something that is extremely rare, from what we’re told one case in five thousand. Cam’s heart muscle has been replaced by scarring or fibrosis and fat. Stop me if this is too much for you.”

“No, please. If Cam wants me to know, I have to be strong like you said.”

“All this replacement of normal heart muscle by fibrosis is causing Cam to have heart electrical disorders, arrhythmias. And they can be direct threats to his life, a lowering of cardiac function and the increased chance of heart failure.”

“I knew something was really wrong 'cause he was never in gym class. He always walked slow and stopped a few times. I never, never complained. I just walked with him at his speed.”

“I thank you for that. Cam thanks you. That’s why he trusts you.”

“I know.” She turned her brown eyes toward the bench, blinking a few times.

“We have done, let me change that. What Camden has done is he’s been through a lot of treatments. We’re doing everything we can to try and give him a normal life.”

“I try to do that, too. We laugh, we share stuff online. I—” A tear started to form and her eyes filled.

“Ah, none of that.” Lace reached over and handed her a Kleenex. “You said you were strong, right? Well, we can’t show that in front of Cam. What he needs to see is you actually showing him your support. And that means no tears when you finally get to see him.”

She wiped down her eyes. “I can do that. I’m strong. Anything for him.”

Lace still had more information to give Innocent when Camden’s nurse approached. “You’re still here. I was hoping you didn’t leave yet.”

“No, I’m here. What do you need?”

“His cardiologist is here, and he says he needs to see you.”

“Innocent, I have to go. I’ll contact you.”

19

Late afternoon driving, Drucker struggled with a person on the phone. "Sorry about tonight. You know I always make it up to you."

The female voice was pleading. "Three times you do this. Three! Just 'bout to git dressed."

Drucker turned the corner and parked outside a development in the shade of a banyan tree. "I know, I know. I'm bad."

She softened up, her tone taking on a bedroom tease. "I know you're bad. Bad all night. I'd like some of yo bad right now."

"I have this thing I have to do. And you know I can't talk about things. Just chalk me down for owing you a lot when I see you."

"You better."

Drucker tossed the cell phone on the passenger seat and then drove his car down a dirt road. The road took him along the outside wall of the development. On his right, a few homes were far enough away, no one seemed to mind him. Drucker parked again, this time near a canal. The small body of water ran through the development and was supposed to be a feature for the residents. The result was an entry for critters to invade the neighborhood when the canal emptied out to the Everglades. The opening also gave Drucker a path to the back of the house. Before he had a chance to stop, he saw her standing near the rear exit gate of the garden.

Miranda Manor could not contain her excitement. "Didn't think you would come." She opened the door to Drucker's car, placed his cell phone on the dashboard and leaned into him, arms open, enveloping him. Her kiss was passionate, one that was once reserved for just Parson. He had to finally, gently, push her away. "Aren't you afraid one of your neighbors might see us?"

"I don't care. What I care about is you."

She started to lean into him again. Drucker stopped her. "You talk to him?"

"Parson? No. And I don't care."

"He might be in a pissed off mood when you see him. He's in some trouble. Law trouble. Told me today."

"He's always been one step ahead of anybody. They will never get him. He's Parson Manor."

Drucker checked her, toes to hair. She wore the black stockings he liked, hair combed long, tight charcoal skirt and a light gray blouse, collar spread open, showing cleavage. The one thing missing was the double M necklace Parson gave her. He glanced at his watch.

"Got somewhere to go?" Her hand moved toward his pants, then she moved in close again, this time pressing her lips up into the crook of his neck, and whispered, "Right here."

"What?"

Her wry smile matched the invitation from her eyes. "Right now."

"Right here in the car? We can't do that." Drucker's gaze scanned the two gates near them.

"No one's coming out here. My neighbors are way over there. They won't see anything." She pulled on his belt.

"I can't right here." Drucker stopped her pursuit by giving her a long kiss. "I only have a short amount of time. I have to get back, besides he might show up."

"You're always running off. What we need is a special time like we had seven months, four days, and six hours ago."

"You remember it that close?"

"Down to the minute. We could use that same motel. Very discreet."

"I'm thinking of something bigger than that. A chance for us to have a lot more time together. We just have to wait a bit."

"Wait for what?"

"I can't say right now. Just keep being the good wife. I'll let you know."

Her mild frustration turned to ecstasy. She peppered his face with kisses, finally putting both hands on his face and holding him there.

A bolt of panic moved through Drucker. "Where's your son?"

"Don't worry. He's staying with a friend."

"I've got to go. Just keep checking that other phone I got you. When the time is just right, we're taking off, you and me. We'll get you out of here, I promise."

She kissed him one last time before sliding over to the door and exiting. Miranda kept looking back at him as she walked down the dirt path to her gate. Once in her garden she sat in the patio chair and just stared at her collection of plants. The grin on her face was planted there for the few minutes she had to herself. She had to prepare a dinner, something Parson would like if he was going to be in a bad way. She picked up the double M necklace and put it on. "Can't wait for the day when I can pawn this thing." She moved toward the house and, once inside, closed every single button on her blouse.

20

It was almost 8:30 p.m. when Drucker walked into the office. Manor was there, with half the lights in the place turned off, sorting through papers.

"Where ya been? Been trying to reach you all afternoon." Manor pulled out a small stack of documents and put them in front of him.

"Doin' what you wanted. Got all the employees working out of their homes for now. They are buttoned down. Reminded them they have non-disclosure agreements, and not to speak with anyone. If they are contacted by authorities, they all have a business card for your attorney."

"Good. Can they keep things going staying at home?"

"We'll see." Drucker packed up his own stack of papers. "Don't want to leave anything behind if they come in here."

"I'm almost done. We can take some of this stuff out to your warehouse." Manor stopped what he was doing. "Been talking to my attorney. He thinks they wouldn't be so bold about this investigation unless they had someone to rely on."

"A mole."

"Exactly." Manor grabbed a sharp letter opener. "Someone, let's say, on the inside. Someone who could pass on things. Maybe even record a few things. I thought about who that could be. And I want you to scour our employee list. We already know Pendon was a possibility. We have the letter. But they can't rely on him anymore since he's dead."

"They would have to rely on other stuff."

Manor turned the opener in his hand like he was holding a knife. "If I find out just who is the rat, I'll cut out his eyes myself." He stabbed down hard, thrusting the opener into the soft dirt of a desk plant.

"I can help you with that search if you want." Drucker looked across the room at the ceiling to wall black and white photographs of the port. Giant pictures depicting the work going on at the port with large cranes moving containers, stevedores working the equipment. The photos were Manor's idea to show the aspects and the strength of the import-export business. Drucker used the moment to change the subject. "Gonna miss this place. I'm assuming you're going to shut down this place. Eventually move somewhere else?"

"That was the original plan. When the development got going, I would build a new office location. All the site plans have been submitted. We're so close, Runy. So close." He pulled the now dirty letter opener up to his face. "And I'm not gonna let some MF'er ruin this for me. Not when I'm this close to closing this deal. I can't let that happen."

"I'm with you, Parse."

Manor took out a box and put all the documents from the desk into the container. He also carefully placed photographs of Miranda and Gibby into the box. "My whole life is them." His words were barely audible. "Bought her a new ring. She doesn't know it yet, but I plan to give it to her tonight."

"She'll like that."

Manor pointed to the box and five others in his office. "Help me carry all this out to my car. I want this place clean, clean, clean. Nothing left behind."

"No problem."

"Everything good on the other end? We gotta shut down all operations, turn all of it green and slowly close down the offshore stuff."

"I'm on it, Parse. One hundred percent." Drucker reached into his pocket and handed Manor a thumb drive. "Everything we just talked about is on there. All the files. Everything. Open it where you think it's safe and check it all out. We're leaving nothing behind."

"Good. Don't know where I'd be without you." Manor looked around like he was making sure he did not leave anything behind. "One more thing, Runy. Been talking to my attorney. He says that all this grief is coming from a statewide prosecutor named Cain Stocker. You ever heard of him?"

Runy Drucker was never an actor, nor wanted to be one. For one moment he had to act as if he was hearing the name for the first time. "Naw, Parse. Never heard of him. He's the mug coming after you?"

"Yeah. This Cain Stocker guy I want to know better. I want to get into his life, find out everything I can about him and his family. I want our black hats on this. Dig into it. If you ain't got the time I'll find somebody, but I want to know the face of my enemy. And I mean everything."

"Parse, you can't touch this guy. We just gotta tighten up, remember?"

"I know, I know. That's all I've been doin' is tighten up. But still I want to know what this Stocker guy is like really up close, all the facts about him. Everything. Got it?"

"Got it."

Manor locked eyes with Drucker. "I started looking this guy up. Got a picture of him. I know what he looks like. Googled his ass up and down. I want to know more."

The two men carried boxes down to a gray SUV. After the last trip down, Drucker turned out the lights and looked around like this was the last time he would be there. Outside, he waited until Manor was gone, then walked to his car, and used the designated phone number to check in.

"Yeah, I know, you been looking for me. You get that last part?" He waited for an answer. After a few seconds, "All I want is for you to arrest this idiot. I want this cloud removed from me. Let me testify, and I can get on with my life." He put away the phone and drove home.

~

WHEN DRUCKER GOT to his place, he grimaced. A woman was sitting by his door. She was not smiling. Drucker got out and held up his hands as a way of explaining where he was.

"Was at your office. The place was almost closed. They told me you were out. You said you were there working."

Drucker started turning the jade ring on his finger. Before he took another step, she sized him up. "I see ya messn' with your ring. You always do that when you're anxious about something. You anxious, Runy?"

"Not at all."

"Then where were you?" Renla Parker was petite. The smallish-sized black woman had a voice that did not fit her body. The words were strong, and even speaking in soft tones her voice had a tendency to cut the air. She wore a dark blue skirt, blue heeled shoes and a matching purse. Two bracelets dangled from her left arm.

"Well?" she said.

"You know I don't do everything at the office. I was out doing what I have to do. You're not always going to find me there, you know that."

She didn't wait for him to come to her. Parker got up and walked to Drucker, taking him in with a hug and squeezing. Her arms barely reached around the much larger Drucker. She leaned into him then drew back. The half-smile she showed Drucker turned to flat angry lines on her face. Her arms whipped back down to her side. "I can smell her on you. Who is she?"

"Smell what Ren? I've been all over the place. Come in contact with all kinds of people and places."

"I know what I know." She pointed her right finger toward him like an accuser. "I've known you too long. Know when you're up to something. Come out with it, Runy. Who is she and how long have you been seeing her?"

"There is no one. I promise. Just you."

"I could tell it in your voice on the phone. Something was up. Came on over here. Been waiting ever since. Don't do this to me, Runy. Don't do this." Her words were like thrown knives all coming at his direction. He looked around to see if the neighbors were coming to the window.

She snapped at him. "Don't look around. Look at me. I'm the one who bonded you out the first time you got busted. I've always been there. I'm not gonna let some hustler get her hands on you without a fight. You belong to me, Runy, is that clear?" Her pointed finger curled back up into a tiny, balled fist.

Drucker pleaded. "I hear you. I hear you."

"I don't think you do." She pulled out a Glock 19 handgun from her purse then pushed the weapon back down.

"Why you flashin' Ren? No need for a gun in the conversation. I'm your man. No need to go extreme."

"I have to make a point. If there is a she, I'll get very extreme." She pulled the purse strap up on her shoulder and walked past him toward her car. "You go get your head right. And like you said on the phone, you better make this up to me. I got to be up in the morning, but I'll call you tomorrow and you will answer the phone."

"Good night, Ren."

"Good night yourself." She tossed her purse inside the black and red 2005 Ford Thunderbird. The car was polished and spotless. She got inside and stared at Drucker the entire time she drove off.

THE FIGURE in the old van with blacked out windows was also staring at Drucker. When Parker drove past, the figure leaned back to remain out of sight. Once she was gone, the surveillance of Runy Drucker continued. There was a case on the floor of the van. Inside the long case was a killer's collection of weapons. There was a Sig Sauer, three combat ready knives, night vision goggles, two long rifles, several pairs of gloves, and three more handguns.

The figure held up a pair of binoculars and focused on the front of Drucker's house. Lights came on inside the place. A notepad sitting next to the figure had times and locations written down, a complete list of where Drucker visited in the past twelve hours. The mission for the figure was simple: stay in place for most of the night and be gone by morning. This was not the kill date, this was all still in the surveillance mode.

Lucky for the figure the moon was just a sliver of light, nothing to expose the van covered in dents and gray body filler.

21

2:45 a.m. The three sat in a car watching the front of the convenience store. The place was almost empty, just the store clerk and one customer were inside. The street outside was quiet, no one else in the parking lot except for the car belonging to the customer. What existed of the moon was covered in dark clouds. Two of the three sat in front, one in back.

"How long we got to sit here?" The question came from Ressler.

"We have just a few more minutes." Gibby kept his watch on the front doors rather than turning toward the teen.

Ressler had another question. "So, this is your idea of the Big Day?"

"There is a door next to you. All you have to do is get out and go home."

"I'm ready." Clarke's head almost touched the inside of the car.

"I don't know if I want to do this." Ressler squirmed in the back seat.

"This is the deal. I scoped this all out. We put on the masks, go in, demand what we want and make sure he does what we say. We leave, count the money, then I put the car away."

"Why now? This exact moment?" Clarke said.

The always confident Gibby had all the answers. "This guy gets off at 3:30 a.m. He's tired and at the end of the shift. He'll be rubbing his eyes any moment now. We want him tired and not able to describe us later. We just go in and take over the place. If we swarm him, get in quick, get out quick, then we'll have nothing to worry about."

The three could see everything going on inside the store. The customer paid for a six pack, grabbed his beer and left. He got into a large pickup truck, fired up the engine and drove away, peeling tires.

Ressler continued to look around. "What about cameras? Got to be cameras."

Gibby was calm and still like pond water in the early morning. "Got cameras. They don't work. Dummies. Like I said, I checked this out."

Clarke turned to Gibby. "What if this guy is strapped?"

Gibby pulled a bag from under his seat. "This guy doesn't have the guts to use anything even if he has a weapon. Besides, we'll be armed."

"We're what?" Ressler sounded scared. "Damn Gibby. I thought you were just kidding about one day handling a gun."

"I got stuff for each of you." Gibby reached into the bag and gave Clarke a handgun. He kept the Beretta for himself. When he pushed a gun in Ressler's direction he froze. "I'm not taking that. You never said anything about an armed robbery."

Gibby gave a soft laugh. "We're not going to use them, fool. These are just to scare him, that's all. Scare him."

"The one who is scared is me. I'm sorry, Gibby, but I can't do this."

"In life you have to prove yourself. This is your day Solly. This is my day. Gibby's Big Day. The same for B.C. Prove you are as tough as you claim. Take the gun."

"I thought we were gonna run in, scare him, take some stuff and run out."

Gibby moved the gun closer to him. "Not today, Solly."

Solly Ressler looked at the handle of the gun being shoved his way. His eyes bulged and he leaned back while grabbing the door handle at the same time. He left in such a hurry, the door was left open. Ressler ran with a speed he had never shown before. The round-figured teen was gone and around the corner before Gibby could say another word.

Clarke rested the gun on his lap. "You think he'll talk?"

"If ole Sol knows how cray I can get, he won't even think about saying anything."

"So what next?"

Gibby reached into the glove box and withdrew a small black device with tiny prongs sticking up.

Clarke stared at the thing. "What is that?"

He held it up like the find of a generation. "Well, first I have to wipe it down. This, B.C. is a cell phone jammer. Once this is turned on, this area, including the store, will become a dead zone for cell phones."

"Where'd you get that?"

"When we're done, I'll tell you where." Gibby nodded in the direction of the store. "This is an old building and I suspect an older WiFi. This thing should also disable the alarm system. So even if he tried, no one will come."

"Very nice, man."

"It's time to go."

Both of them dabbed eye black around their eyes and wrists to cover up skin color. Gibby wiped down the jammer until it looked clean of fingerprints. They each put on a balaclava and donned gloves. They were wearing long sleeved shirts and dark running shoes. Clarke pressed his weapon into his pants. Gibby led the way, armed with the Beretta and the jammer. They moved quickly to the front of the store, making sure to keep low. Gibby waited until the store clerk was preoccupied going over items. They leaned hard against the large glass windows, checking the inside and staring out at the parking lot, making sure there were no new customers. If anyone came, they could easily run back to the car. Gibby turned on the device and placed it on the ground. They had to wait a minute for the jammer to work. Both continued to look around the parking lot for anyone coming. The only noise was from a gathering of cicadas. Gibby pulled hard on his mask and whispered to Clarke. "You ready?"

He nodded yes.

Gibby entered the store first and waited until Clarke was also inside. He raised his gun and shouted. "All the money or you die!"

The clerk, face covered in acne, did not move at first, apparently from shock. It would take another directive to get him moving. "Give up the money! Now!" Gibby moved closer so that the gun was just a few feet from the clerk's face.

Clarke moved to the clerk's left, gun pointed, looking like he intended to shoot. The clerk's head jerked back and forth between the two gunmen, nervous and not sure where to find a bag. Finally, he produced a store plastic bag, opened up the drawer and started pushing bills into the opening.

"Faster! Move faster!" Gibby maintained his watch over the clerk. Clarke kept his head on a swivel, guarding the door and watching the clerk. No one was coming. They had the store to themselves. There were six aisles in the store and two large mirrors. Clarke positioned himself in the exact spot Gibby told him to go when they were in the car discussing their plan. This was a spot for Clarke where he might not be so easily identified and to avoid eye contact with anyone who might be in the store. The clerk was finished packing the bag with money and just when he was handing it to Gibby, the bag dropped to the floor. The clerk was clearly flustered, tried to pick up the bag twice and dropped it twice. "Pick it up!" Gibby's voice thundered in the caverns of the store. The clerk gave Gibby the bag. There was one last instruction. "Get down on the floor and don't get up, you hear me? Don't get up!"

Just when the clerk was about to get on the floor, Gibby backed up into the aisle and knocked over a can of beans. The loud noise when the cans hit the floor caused Gibby to jump. He panicked and accidentally shot off a round with the gun. In his quick movement, the gun pointed upwards and the bullet shattered a ceiling tile and bits of the busted up ceiling came shattering down in a rain of white powder. The clerk dropped to the floor and pushed both hands around his head. Gibby and Clarke ran to the door, swung it open and ran fast to the car. Inside, Gibby threw the bag of money in the back seat. Both of them pulled off their masks. He had kept the car running. Once he got the car in drive, Gibby sped off in a predetermined path away from the scene.

"Keep going! Go, man!" Clarke was screaming at Gibby. Then, "You gonna leave that jammer?"

"It's clean. Let them find it."

Gibby used a car with a V-6 engine. They heard the roar of the pistons pumping when Gibby stepped hard on the gas. When he looked in the mirror, Gibby saw what he thought were blue police lights. "One thing I did not count on."

A worried Clarke turned and looked back. "Is that?"

"Yeah. I think it's a cop on routine patrol. We gotta move." Gibby pushed his foot almost to the floor. The speedometer showed the car was doing seventy, now eighty. Gibby pressed harder.

"I don't think they're following us."

"I want to make sure." Gibby was all big eyes focused on the road ahead. They were driving past a park and houses on the left. Gibby blew through two stop signs. The speed was now reaching one hundred miles an hour.

"Gibby, slow down, man. It's just us out here."

"Can't slow down. Gotta go." Gibby almost hit a parked car. The V-6 churned at a loud hum. The power of the engine, a galvanizing mix of pumping pistons and a flow of gas, pushed Clarke back into his seat. Houses, cars, signs, trees, everything moved past them faster with each block. Gibby drove like someone possessed. He was now full of an adrenaline rush, a natural high that kept him laser tracked on the street and nothing else.

"Toss the guns!" Gibby's eyes were still centered on the way forward.

"You sure?"

"Toss them."

Clarke lowered the window, poked his head out a bit and wrestled with the hard breeze contorting his face. He aimed twice and threw the guns out his window. Two plopped into a body of water. The third gun rattled on the sidewalk and slid into some bushes.

Clarke looked back again and all he could see behind him was a blur of dark shadow and objects getting smaller at a rapid rate. "We can slow down, Gibby. Slow down!"

"Not yet. Gotta get safe."

Gibby's right hand momentarily slipped off the steering wheel, causing the car to drift too much to the side. The car careened into a parked car, sending off a spray of white sparks like the tips of lightning. He tried to get the car steady and instead smashed into the side of another parked vehicle. The sideswipe slowed down the V-6 like an out-of-control pinball. Gibby mashed the pedal again and the car kicked into higher speeds.

"Slow down!" Clarke was no longer looking back and just stayed looking at the street ahead.

Gibby's body language was in an agitated mess of a full meltdown, his senses in overdrive, taken over by the hysteria of getting away. He drove off like he didn't want to slow down.

Clarke kept yelling over the high-pitched growl of the engine. "Why did you shoot?"

Gibby gave a one-word response. "Accident."

"You coulda killed him, Gibby."

Several yards ahead, a manhole cover had been reset improperly so the cover was raised up an inch or so. Gibby's gloved hands were locked on the wheel. The front right tire hit the manhole cover and the car jumped up in the air just slightly. The upward movement was just enough for the V-6 to redirect the front of the car toward a parked pickup truck. In an effort to avoid hitting the truck, Gibby turned the wheel hard to the left. The maneuver pushed the car into an oversteer and Gibby was now fighting with the steering wheel to get the vehicle moving in a straight direction. The effort did not work, and the car was now moving full speed in the direction of a concrete power pole. Gibby yanked the wheel right and jammed his foot on the brake pedal, only to find nothing was going to change the direction of their path. The pole ahead was becoming larger, and both boys raised their arms in a last-second attempt to protect themselves. The car jumped the sidewalk and, for a second, went airborne.

The deafening impact of the car with the concrete pole was a horrendous crash. There was a loud cataclysmic slam of metal on concrete. The pole did not move, and the entire front of the car bent around the solid tall object. The hard sudden stop had a catastrophic effect on the occupants inside the car. Clarke's body was a human projectile, and he was thrust through the front windshield and kept going until his body landed face-first on the sidewalk. Gibby's form cascaded up and above the airbag, sending him through the jagged glass, and he was dumped on the hot hood of the V-6. The only sounds came from the hissing of radiator fluid dripping on the street, car parts falling off and the desperate gasps of Clarke's body seeking air. Now on the pavement, head turned to one side, Clarke tried to say something. His lips moved a bit in a last effort to cry out and then he was quiet. Blood seeped from his ear and mouth. His eyes stayed open, frozen in the final moments of his life.

A guttural ache ebbed from the lips of Gibby Manor like a plea for help. The loud ache made him sound like one massive collection of broken and shattered bones wrapped in skin.

22

BOOKER JOHNSON

All of the high school students in the room were there one hour before the start of classes for a Career Day guest, Booker Johnson, reporter for Channel 27 news in south Florida. Johnson only had twenty minutes for comments, then he took a few questions.

Stan Gibson, English teacher, stood. "I want to thank Booker Johnson for taking a few minutes from his busy day to speak to our future journalists. Mr. Johnson recently received his fourth Emmy Award, and we want to congratulate him on that achievement."

The group of fourteen students clapped. Booker gestured to them to stop their applause. "Just one last thing before I go. Remember I started out by doing a simple test. We'll find out now how that went. I gave three students a name for the exercise. The task for three others was to ask the name of the person like it was an interview and write down the name." He looked over the class. "One by one, for the interviewers, please tell us the name you wrote down?"

The male student stood up and spoke so low Booker had to get him to repeat it. "I interviewed Jason Stock."

"Okay," Booker started. "And how did you spell his first name?"

"Jason. J.A.S.O.N."

"Thank you. Someone else. What name did you get?"

A girl stood up and spoke in a strong voice, "Amy Gyson. First name spelled A.M.Y."

Booker thanked her. "And finally the third person."

A tall kid in the back stood up. "I asked the name of Emily Crocker, first name spelled E.M.I.L.Y."

"Thank you all for helping us out with the experiment. You might remember I gave these names to three students in your make-believe short interview." Booker turned to the three students who received the names from Booker. "Okay, did these students get the first names spelled right?"

The three students all shook their heads no. The class then heard each student spell the temporary name each was given. "Amy, spelled A.I.M.E.E." The second student stood, "I was given the name Emily, spelled E.M.E.L.Y." And the third, "My temporary name was Jason. The first name spelled, J.A.Y.S.O.N."

"Thanks again for doing this. I was not trying to embarrass anyone, but my point is you simply have to get your facts right starting with the name. Some names are spelled differently. So if you pursue a career in news, and I hope you do, take the time to get it right. Again, I'm Booker Johnson and thanks for inviting me."

The class applauded until the first bell sounded. They all filed out into the hallway, headed to their first class of the day. Booker's phone started buzzing. "I'm here. What's up?"

On the phone was Claire Stanley, assignment editor for Channel 27. "We need you to head right to a scene. It's been working since five this morning. You in a position to move?"

"Yep. Just text me the address. Email me any information and I'm on my way."

"Good. The morning team has been there. We need you to take over the story for the noon."

"Got it." By the time Booker got to his car, he had the address and he was moving. Fourteen minutes later, Booker parked near the On-The-Way Convenience store. The layout was like dozens he had seen in his twelve years in television. Police had control of the location, yellow crime tape was up all around the store. An evidence marker was placed near the front entrance, with several more inside the store. Booker saw a very distraught thin man talking to police. A gathering of people stood by the crime tape, gawking.

Booker walked up to Merilee Yang, morning reporter for Channel 27, and stopped. She was moving around the small crowd of people looking for any witnesses. When she was finished, Booker again approached. "Any luck?"

"Not yet." She was looking over her notes. "You ready?"

"Go." Booker had out his writing pad.

"The Public Information Officer will be out here soon to confirm all this, but this is what I got. Two men with guns came in the store and demanded money. Not quite sure of the time but police will confirm later."

"Okay."

"The men got cash, got into a car and drove off. There are at least two scenes, maybe three. Just over a mile from here there is a second scene. Bad crash. They ran into a utility pole. The pole is concrete. One dead on scene, the second was taken to the hospital in what I am told is very critical condition."

"Where are you getting this information?"

"The officers who got here first were kind enough to give me some information to use for the early morning newscasts."

"The two people and the smashed car, do police think those are the robbers?"

"For now, a strong maybe. They keep saying they will know more in a bit and update us."

Booker walked away and stood in front of the store, his chest pressed up against the crime scene tape. He studied the store, the parking lot, everything, including the road leading away from the lot. Yang moved next to him and pointed to evidence marker 7.

"See that thing next to the evidence marker? We're not sure what that is."

"It's a cell phone jammer."

"To jam the clerk's cell phone?"

"Yep. And maybe the security system. They are easy to get, and the bad guys are using these more now. But you didn't get that from me."

"I know. I'll confirm it with police. Thanks, Book."

"What exactly does the desk want us to do?"

"For the noon, I'll be live at this location. You will be live where the car was found. By stopping here, at least you have a sense of where this all started."

"No problem." Booker knew certain things said on the street were a given. By the desk, Booker was referring to the assignment desk. In the field, all things were shortened up, like P.I.O, the person responsible for giving out information about any event involving police. Booker called into the desk and asked for Claire Stanley. For Booker, Stanley was the heart of the newsroom. She was in contact with every reporter, got updates from them and also provided new information to reporters. Her duties would shift to the producers who write all of the stories in a newscast. More than anything, the key word in a newsroom was communication. All sides of the operation had to be constantly speaking with each other: photographers, reporters, producers, and those on the assignment desk.

"Yeah, Booker."

"I'm doing a second part on this for the noon, correct?"

"Yes. After the noon, you'll take over the story for the five and six. For noon, there will be four in the box. You, Yang, a reporter at the hospital and the helicopter. All four of you will do reports, starting with Yang at the scene, then you, the hospital, and finally our guy in the helicopter. There will be an umbrella lead. When you get to the car scene, you'll find the license plate has been covered up. We have no idea who these guys are. That will be your responsibility going forward. Get out of there as soon as you can and get over to the car. Call me if you need me."

"Got it." He ended the call. For Booker, the instructions were documented into his thinking. Four in the box meant the public would briefly see four different angles of the story on their TV at once. That would be up for just the one-minute lead-in done by the anchors in the studio. Umbrella was a general talk-over by the anchors depicting the four aspects and to show Channel 27 had the story covered four different ways.

Booker walked back to his car while he continued to survey the store scene. If police released the clerk, maybe he would be willing to speak. Yang was ready. Booker drove out and had to take a long way around as police had blocked off a few streets leading to where the car was located. When he got to the damaged car, Booker got out.

He immediately noticed the yellow tarp, a covering put over a body. A crime tech was taking a series of photographs. For cases like this, police would also put up their own helicopter to take aerial photographs of the path the car took and the car itself.

Booker examined the car. The vehicle was an older model with mismatched rims. The windshield was gone, and glass was all over the street like scattered diamonds. The front of the car was a dented mess of metal shaped like a giant U and wrapped around the pole. The smell of spent radiator fluid was everywhere.

"Glad you could make it." Junice Coffee stood behind a camera mounted on a tripod. She was easily the most sought-after photographer in the newsroom since her video work was beyond impressive and she always got the money shot.

"Sorry I'm late. Had a speaking engagement. Any sign of the P.I.O?"

Coffee said, "Someone is coming out soon."

Booker again looked over the demolished car and one person on the ground. "People always wonder why sometimes the body is there so long. They just don't understand police want to get things right. For the victim and for the family. Getting it right means it takes time."

"I think the medical examiner is on the way. Won't be long now."

Booker looked down the street and saw the dented cars. He looked over to Coffee.

"Yep. I got video of them."

An unmarked police car pulled up and the woman who got out was a familiar face for Booker Johnson. Brielle Jensen who worked homicide cases for the past four years decided to move over to P.I.O. The information would be coming from her. She wore her hair pulled back, and even though she was P.I.O. and not on the street, she always had what Booker called *cop's eyes*. Her vision was always moving, always taking in her surroundings and always ready.

She stepped up to a semi-circle of cameras on tripods. Coffee was already recording.

"Hello, my name is Brielle Jensen. I'll be giving a short briefing on what we have as this is still an ongoing investigation." She checked her notes before continuing. "At approximately 3 a.m. two men walked into the On-the-Way convenience store, armed, and they demanded cash. The two men got an undisclosed amount of money and drove off in an older model Chevy, heading west on Spolluck Road. Their car collided with a utility pole in a single car crash. One male is deceased on scene, a second male was transported to the hospital in very critical condition. A sum of money was recovered from the car, along with masks. We will have more when we are able to release any new information."

Booker spoke up. "Was the clerk hurt? And did they use a phone jamming device at the convenience store?"

"The clerk was unharmed and is cooperating with police. As to any evidence we found at the scene, that is part of the ongoing investigation."

Another reporter jumped in. "Any word on the identification of the men in the car?"

"Not at this time."

Booker Johnson looked up from the notes he was writing. "We're hearing they left the scene driving fast."

Before he could finish the question, Jensen answered, "An officer on routine patrol found the situation of the robbery in progress. I want to be clear, at no time did our officers give chase. The suspects took off at a high rate of speed without any intervention from our officers. The two men were not wearing seatbelts, and both were ejected from the car."

Hands were busy writing notes. Jensen angled her body away from the microphone and put her notes down at her side like she was done talking. Questions brought her back to the microphones.

"Did you recover any weapons in the search of the car?" Booker waited for an answer.

"We are conducting an active search. That's why the roadway is still closed. We have officers out there right now. We will send out an email blast as soon as we clear the roads." And with that, Jensen was finished. She walked back to her car, placed the notes on the passenger seat, closed the door and walked over to Booker.

"Book you puttin' on some weight?"

"Naw, just a bit. You like P.I.O?"

She was already turning away from him like the conversation was going to be very short. "P.I.O. is temporary. I have some family stuff soon, so I didn't want to be tied to another homicide case. I'll be back there. Later, Booker." For a moment Booker kept thinking that, in his experience in south Florida, there was always a good relationship between law enforcement and local TV journalists. No one talked about it, but it was there.

Jensen was in her car and driving. He'd have to keep checking his phone for new email updates. Booker called Yang and found out she also did a short news conference at the convenience store. So now everyone was updated.

Coffee stepped back, taking her face from the eyepiece of the camera. "For a moment, I saw the person on the ground."

"And?"

"He looked young, Book. He was no man. Black kid, I'd say he was in his teens. Looked real young."

"How did you see him?"

"A detective removed the tarp for a few minutes to get a better look at him. I couldn't shoot any video anyway." All local TV stations had a policy of not showing video of deceased victims.

"Thanks, Coffee."

"And that kid, he was wearing some really nice kicks."

Booker was listening and looking elsewhere. "Expensive?"

"Real expensive shoes. Either they were robbing to buy more stuff or why was this kid, with possibly money already in his pocket, why would this guy do this?"

"Pressure from someone else maybe. I'd really like to hear about the I.D. on this teen. Talk to his parents. Get a fix on why."

Junice Coffee stood about five-five. She had a slender build but could haul equipment with the best of them. Quiet most of the time, afraid of nothing. If other photographers got in her way, she moved them out like an offensive line. Her hair was kept back in a ponytail to stay out of her face.

What the public was never told was a TV crew's inner thoughts on what happened, why it happened or who was the perpetrator. Crews always talked out a story, especially if it was a murder mystery. Booker and Coffee were keen on weighing facts and statements, along with police accounts.

One reason for doing this was to keep ahead, figuring out what direction the story should go, who should be interviewed. What bothered Booker was why just so-called kids needed to hold up a store.

Booker sat in the news van writing his portion of the story. He stayed away from mentioning the hospital or the original scene since others would be covering those angles. Later in the day, he would have to cover all of that himself. He made one more check with the desk to see if there was anything new or a fact he needed to include in his report.

Just seconds after noon, Booker stood before Coffee's camera and listened in his earpiece as Yang started her report. She stated all the facts mentioned by Jensen, and added local flavor like what a neighbor told her. When she was done, Yang tossed it to Booker.

"Channel 27's Booker Johnson is at the location where the car crashed."

"Thanks, Merilee. I'm going to step out of the way to show you where this car ran into a concrete utility pole. As you mentioned, there were two people inside. One person is deceased. Police had this to say about what happened."

Booker's video story was fed into the station twenty minutes earlier. His one-minute-ten second video included his voice describing the car scene and two sound clips of Brielle Jensen and her comments. He waited for what was called an outcue, or the last thing mentioned in the report. When he heard the outcue, Booker started talking in a twenty-second wrap-up. Done talking, he waited for the producer to say the two words letting him know he was off the air. "You're clear."

Still youthful looking for being in his mid-thirties, Booker was tall, black, and with all the TV courses in college, the trained, smooth on-air voice was always there.

The noon newscast moved on to other stories and topics. The responsibility for covering the story now belonged to Booker and the assignment desk. The medical examiner's van drove up and once they got the okay from detectives, they removed the person on the ground. A tow truck, engine humming in the distance, was on standby to remove the car.

For Booker, there was a lot to process and a long list of questions to be answered. Who were the people in the car? Was this robbery one of many during the night or just the single incident? Sometimes robbers will go on a spree, hitting several places in a short span of time. Most of the time those suspects were heavy into drugs and needed the money to feed a habit. Booker wasn't so sure in this case.

The car was removed. The vehicle would be transported to the police garage where the crime techs could really go over it. All of that was out of view of the public. Booker got a call.

"What's up?"

Claire Stanley ran down things from her own list. "I got a backup photographer coming your way to get video of the search for the gun. Once the car is gone and the scene is clear, go back to the store, see what you can get there. Yang will stay at the store until you get there so we don't miss anything. Anything I should know?"

"Coffee says the person here was young. Maybe a student somewhere. Once we get a name your folks can check it out?"

"You know we're ready. Once next-of-kin is contacted, I expect an I.D."

"This was the only overnight robbery?"

"So far, yes."

Conversation over, Jorge Dominguez arrived to get more video of police searching the streets for the weapons. Booker arrived at the convenience store, got a bit more information from Yang and watched her leave. Thirty minutes later, while there was a change of news crews, Booker kept his voice down and got Coffee's attention. "Let's take a walk around to the back. Some of the police tape is down."

Without saying anything, Coffee unsnapped her camera from the tripod and followed Booker around to the back of the store. Another ten minutes later, the rear door opened. A tall young man with acne emerged and started walking to his car.

"Are you the clerk?"

He nodded reluctantly.

"I'm Booker Johnson from Channel 27. You have a second?"

23

Booker waited to see if the clerk wanted to talk. If not, the conversation was over, Coffee would shoot a short bit of video, then a walk back to the front of the store.

He was talking. “I was scared.”

Coffee was already camera up on her shoulder and recording. Booker moved the microphone closer to him. “You see much?”

“I just remember they had guns, I know that much. I can’t say a lot. Company won’t like it.”

“Okay. Did they say anything?”

“Just to hand over the money. I did what they asked. I just kept staring at those guns.”

Booker said, “Any surveillance video?”

The clerk shook his head.

“What’s your name?”

“No name.” He turned to his car, got in and started the engine. Ten seconds later he was driving around to the front parking lot. Booker and Coffee were walking to their van when two other news crews arrived, running. Booker didn’t say anything. No need to antagonize other reporters. If he did, he always thought Karma could work against him one day, so he stayed humble.

"You get anything?" One reporter asked.

"Just a bit." Once the clerk was gone there was a good chance no one would be able to find him later in the day. The interview was short and gave Booker just a slight edge of information the others did not have at the moment.

Before Booker checked in with the desk, he wanted to do a few more things. He mapped things out with Coffee.

"Doesn't look like we'd miss anything if we take a short trip from here."

She gave that wry Coffee smile and bent eyebrows. "Whatcha got in mind?"

"There are several houses leading to and from this store. What we're missing is surveillance video. Let's try a few homeowners."

"Let's go."

One tricky part was always trying to find new elements while two other TV crews are parked just yards away. Booker decided to leave the van and just go on foot. They both slipped away and found themselves walking down the street without others tagging along. The first two homeowners did not want to talk, nor did they have any surveillance cameras. The third homeowner almost said yes then changed his mind. They moved on. They crossed the street and started to check there. When Booker looked over his shoulder, one other crew was now following his lead and knocking on doors. The fifth homeowner had a direct view of the convenience store across the street.

"Yeah, I got a door cam and two backyard cams directed at my back door. I haven't checked for any video." The man was in his early 60's, looked retired, and his wife kept showing a facial disapproval to any conversation with Booker. He checked the feed from his cell phone. The man shook hands with Booker. "Craig Monroe."

"Thanks, Craig. Got anything?"

"Maybe. We were asleep when this all happened, but we did hear something. I wasn't sure what it was, then I kinda heard a shot fired." He kept checking his video. "Around 3 a.m. you say?"

"Yes. In that area."

"Okay. Here you go. See what you think."

Booker checked the nighttime video. The three of them, Booker,

Monroe and Coffee watched. They saw the car parked for a long time, then one person got out of the car, ran off and never came back. A few minutes later, two people stepped from the car. They saw them put something on the ground, presumably the jamming device, then they went into the store. The video ended there. They kept checking and there was only black.

"Lost the feed," Monroe shrugged his shoulders.

"But you got them going inside the store. Okay if we get a copy of that?"

"No problem." With some help from Coffee, the man emailed the video to Booker. After studying the tape, they recognized the car as the same one in the crash. The three, then two people inside could not be identified. Still, they had the robbery going down on video.

"Now, I don't want to say anything on camera."

"That's okay, Craig. The police might be knocking, looking for this video."

"I think I'll call them first. Let them know I have it."

Booker prepared to leave. "That would be good. They would like that." They walked back to the van so he could call Stanley. After a ten-minute conversation, she told him he would be the lead on both the 5 p.m. and 6 p.m. newscasts. "We got your surveillance video of them going in. Looks like you've been working the story hard. See you on TV."

She hung up. Now came the writing of two versions of the story and feeding them into the station to get ready for the two newscasts, unless something really new happened.

In twenty minutes, the *new* arrived in the form of Dominguez. The photographer opened the door to the van. "Got you some video you might like."

Booker stopped writing. "What's up?"

Dominguez used the news van to send the video. "I went knocking on doors like you did and I got the car moving really fast down the street. No crash but I got the car."

"Nice work." Booker checked the video. The home surveillance video clearly showed the car driving at a high speed and then the vehicle went out of frame. The actual crash was not visible; however, Booker and Coffee saw a flash of light indicating when the car hit the utility pole.

Booker added the new element to his story. "It's probably best we don't see the crash itself anyway."

Dominguez said, "One other thing. I got video of police recovering a weapon."

Booker kept his eyes on the monitor. "Excellent."

In the video Dominguez had captured video of a crime tech photographing an evidence marker with a gun next to it. After several photographs were taken and measurements recorded of the proximity of the weapon to other objects, the gun was placed into an evidence bag to be marked. The video showed the tech walking the bag all the way to the crime van.

Booker called Stanley on the new elements. She was pleased.

When all the writing was finished, he recorded his voice, Coffee edited the two stories and they were fed into the station.

Just past 5 p.m. Booker was live in front of the store, explaining what happened. The report included the surveillance videos, the short sound clip of the clerk, the scene and the gun that was found. When Booker finished the live report, he sat down and wrote a lengthy story for the Channel 27 website. He then wrote a note for the late shift reporters and assignment desk so they could follow up on the story for the 11 p.m. newscast.

With word from Dominguez, Booker and Coffee decided to move their live location to where the car crashed. Dominguez told them high school students were showing up and placing flowers by the tree.

And there was another new element. Booker got the email just as Claire Stanley called. Police sent out the news release. They identified and put out the name of the deceased teen.

24

When Booker and Coffee parked the van, a few cars were already there. Within minutes, six more cars pulled up, all of them packed with students. Booker was now looking at perhaps fifty teens, many of them carried flowers and placed them near the utility pole. One portion of the sidewalk had a long scrape where the tow truck dragged the damaged car. One teen even had a photograph and placed the picture near five lit candles.

For any other person there, even with a long look, there probably wasn't much to take away from seeing such a scene. For Booker Johnson or any reporter, the look was vastly different. Booker was a paid observer, a person sent anywhere to specifically take things in and then turn to a camera and verbally tell the world what was witnessed. One time Booker was sent to a house fire, with just seconds to set up and start talking to a live camera. After just taking mere moments to observe, Booker reported exact details on what floor the fire was engulfed, how many fire trucks were there, an estimate on the number of fire fighters, the two people being treated by paramedics, how bad was the traffic tie-up, and the desperation of people running out of the building. He gathered all his information from just one long stare. A casual person on the street might not be able to pull that off. For Booker, the reporting was something routine. Now, he was there, on scene with the dead and remembering the faces of those who knew the deceased.

One teen, a girl, with brilliant brown eyes and long hair took stock of Booker Johnson.

"Did you know them?" Booker thought his question was lame, yet he had to start somewhere.

"Yeah, I, or we all knew one of them. The one who died." She placed her flowers on the sidewalk. The makeshift memorial was growing in flower arrangements. "We all heard about this at home and organized some cars."

Booker's information from police was the dead teen was a student named Bayson Clarke. "Everyone called him B.C." the student said. Her eyes were fixed on the photograph of Clarke in uniform. "The whole school liked him. He was on the basketball team for a while. He was good."

Coffee stood back at a distance and got video of the teens gathering at the pole. Booker kept the microphone aimed down and didn't press anyone just yet on speaking on camera. "And did you know the other person in the car?"

"No. I heard he's a new student. I didn't know him, but we all knew B.C."

Two other TV stations were also holding back, giving the students a chance to grieve and process what happened. A male student approached Booker. "B.C. could have been a special basketball player. He was already special to the people you see here."

Booker stepped back to read an email from Claire Stanley. He called her. "We're at the utility pole. A growing scene here. If you have a second crew available, send them to the convenience store and sit on it."

"No problem. Done. Listen Book, we have a mug shot of this kid Clarke. Seems he tracked down and beat up a ref at his home. The ref didn't want to press charges and it was all dropped. Trouble is, the kid was eighteen. That's why he's in the system."

"Got it. I'll use the photo in the six o'clock piece. And we have all this video of the students. Maybe some interviews. I don't know yet, we'll see."

"Okay."

Booker turned to the group of students. No one was talking as they walked around staring at the street and the black mark on the pole left by the car. Across the street, homeowners stood outside and watched. Even the usual rush of cars headed home was gone. The moments were almost reserved for the gathering of grievers. When the time seemed right, Booker approached the girl he had spoken to before. "My name is Booker Johnson. We're going to stand back over there. If anyone wants to speak for the group to let us know why Bayson was so liked, we'd like to hear it."

She nodded and joined the group. There was a light discussion between a few of them. When they stopped, three students approached the reporters. Microphones were pointed in their direction. "We're here to say everyone liked Bayson. We know this is a terrible situation but whatever they are saying about him, we knew Bayson to be caring. We will miss him."

A male student stepped forward. "Bayson was one of a kind. Funny. This could have been avoided. He needed to get back on the basketball court. The school misses him. We miss him."

The third student changed her mind and decided not to talk. There were no follow-up questions. The three went back to the group and, en masse, they started walking back to their cars. Six minutes later, they were all gone. Reporters were left with the flowers and a marked-up pole.

25

His reports wrapped up for the day, Booker stopped by the assignment desk and spoke with the nighttime assignment editor Bruce Newhall. A former reporter, Newhall still had the voice that TV coveted—deep, commanded attention and was trusted. Four years before, Newhall had a scare from skin cancer. The doctor recommended he stay out of the sun and he complied, ending his TV career on his own and moving to the assignment desk. The crews respected his work since he could speak on all aspects of news gathering from in front of and behind the camera.

Booker sat up on the assignment desk and listened to the cacophony of police scanner voices. Newhall had memorized all the codes used by first responders, police, school bus drivers and others. Like other stations, the desk used several scanners, both from devices positioned on the desk and also websites devoted to police scanner traffic. Listening to them was an art. Anyone sitting in front of them deciphered what was a definite news item and what was routine conversation. Fire units would say a code 1 fire and that meant the building might be fully engulfed. Code 3, nothing or false alarm. Newhall had the option of sending a crew, the helicopter or both. He also, Booker liked to recall, had the ability of thinking in five directions all at the same time. If something major happened, beside the original location, a crew might have to be sent to the hospital, the police station, the jail or other options. So, when Newhall sat on the desk, he had to know where all of the crews were precisely during any given moment. He had to figure what crew was closest to a scene.

"Any suggestions for the night crews?" Newhall's voice had the clarity and depth of a booth announcer.

"You might check on the makeshift memorial. I don't know, maybe a swing by the school, although I doubt anyone will be there."

Newhall was taking notes. "I'll let the morning crews go by the school."

Booker rubbed tired eyes. "Any word on the other teen in the car?"

"Not yet. Police let us know there won't be any more updates today." Newhall tapped his keyboard. "Okay, Book, check this out." He brought up YouTube and hit a few more keys and hit play. On the computer monitor they both watched a thin black teen drive the length of the court and dunk a basketball. They watched another play with the same teen weaving through two defenders and driving to the basket for a nice layup.

Booker pointed to the screen. "Is this Bayson Clarke?"

"Yep. Been checking out his game highlights. This kid had a great future." They watched a compilation of up to ten plays, all with Clarke making shots from inside and at the three-point line. Newhall looked up at Booker. "Two coaches, who did not want to go on camera, said this kid didn't know it but two college teams were ready to give him a workout. They didn't care about his scrape with the law, they just wanted the kid to play. And now this."

Booker shook his head. "What a shame. I didn't know all that earlier."

Newhall cleared his screen. "Sorry, didn't know myself until the 6 p.m hit. We started getting phone calls. This kid Clarke could have been the real deal. He just didn't get a chance with the right people. Any new word from police?"

"Well, it's kinda wrapped up." Booker got up to go. "They have the money, don't have to look for suspects. All they have to do is an autopsy, see if this other person survives and get a statement or charge him." Booker started to walk away and stopped. "I just have a feeling there's something more to this. The kid, Clarke, was not in need of money from what the kids say. What was he doing there? What made them walk into a store and demand cash they didn't need? They weren't part of a gang. No initiation as far as I know. I don't get it."

Booker quickened his steps, moving toward Claire Stanley. "Before you go, I have a request."

"I'll try." Stanley put down her briefcase.

"I'd like to stay on this story tomorrow. Depending on what the morning crews find, I know I can pull something together for the pitch meeting."

"Send me—"

They both said it together, "An email. I know."

Stanley left the newsroom. Booker was also about to leave. His mission for the evening was talked of for months: a sitdown with his girlfriend Misha. After much conversation back and forth, she was ready to move into Booker's apartment. Tonight was the time to make final preparations over dinner. Booker was four feet from the door when the power-charged voice of Newhall boomed over the newsroom. "Booker, stop."

He turned around. Newhall was waving him back to the assignment desk. "That kid, Clarke? His father wants to speak on camera tonight. And he won't speak to any other reporter. Booker, he just wants to talk to you."

26

Miranda Manor's hands were drenched in tears. She wiped the tears with her hands when the Kleenex got too wet. Next to her, Gibby Manor was hooked up to various tubes, all intended to keep him alive.

When she got the call around 7 a.m. about her son, she didn't believe the police officer. She swore Gibby was in his room and when she went to check and found he was not there, the panic started to set in. She called his cell phone, left messages and tried to figure out where he could be because there was no way in creation she'd thought her son would be involved in a car crash. She told the officer Gibby didn't own a car. When she went to the garage and checked the Parson fleet, then yes, an old Chevy was missing. The keys for most of the cars were on a board. She got Parson up and both of them drove to the hospital. They'd stayed by Gibby's bedside since they were allowed to see him.

Another meeting with doctors was set for 8 p.m. They also had an earlier meeting with detectives. She pulled Parson out into the hallway outside room 214.

"The police say he was involved in a robbery?" Her words were full of disbelief. "A robbery?" She stopped to pull out more things to dry her cheeks and eyes. "He didn't want for anything. We gave him anything he needed. Got him into that school. If he needed money, I'd give him everything." She moved into Parson, leaning her head against his shoulder.

He lightly rubbed her back, an effort to give her comfort. "We talked about a lot of things, but I didn't see anything in him about wanting to rob a store. Nothing."

"But they said they recovered a gun. That has to be your Beretta." She stood back from him.

"I know. Looks like he got it from my office. He knew where I kept all that stuff."

She looked back at her son, his eyes closed, intubated, the sounds of a life support machine doing the work Gibby's body used to perform. Miranda Manor was overwhelmed by the sight of him almost without life. She stood there and wailed. The loud scream and cry caught the attention of the nursing station. Two of them came to her assistance, guiding her back into the room and away from other families.

Miranda Manor took her son's left hand in her own and started whispering to him. "They say we're supposed to talk to you when this happens. Well, I'm talking, and I'll keep talking until you get better. I promise, Gibby. I promise." She looked down at his hand. "I remember your hand when you were a baby. You grabbed my finger with your tiny hand. Your entire hand around one of my fingers. And you wouldn't let go." A tear fell on the bed sheet. "You wouldn't let go and I'll be right here holding on to you." She started to rock back and forth humming to him. All she could do was hum and talk to him softly. There were just the sounds of her voice and the soft beeping of the machine.

When Parson entered the room, Miranda turned on him. "This is all your fault." She stood and was using both hands to pound on Parson's chest. Tears, balled fists, shouting, all directed at her husband. "My son did this to prove something to you. Be a big man like his father. You kept pushing him, pushing him. And now look what happened."

"I don't know what he was doing."

"He wanted to be like the tough-guy Parson Manor. You pushed him to use that gun, didn't you? You mocked him, made him feel like he had to do something to be..." She never finished, backing up until she flopped into the chair and put her head in her hands.

Miranda pointed to her son, hands together like a plea, desperately asking for help. “Make him wake up, Parson. Please, you have the power to do so many things. Do something for your son. Make him wake up. Please, I’m asking you. I’ll do anything you ask. Just do this one thing. Make my son wake up.”

“Miranda. We have to face it. They say he’s clinically dead. At some point soon, we’re gonna have to let him go.”

“Never. I can’t do that. I can’t do that to our son. I’ll never let him go.”

“We have to do that. He died in that crash. We have to accept what happened.”

The quiet cadence of the machine was now the prominent noise in the room. She was done talking for now. Done complaining.

Manor gave his wife some space alone without him. He walked out and leaned against the door. He noticed the busy nurses, all of them listening, waiting for any warning signals coming from Gibby’s bed. While Manor was standing there, he saw a person walking down at the far end of the hallway. This was the person Manor was told was determined to put him in prison. He could not believe or understand why Cain Stocker was in the hospital.

27

When Booker Johnson arrived outside the home, the front door of the place was closed with several business cards stuck in the jamb. A news van from another station had just left. Booker was working with night photographer James Collier, nine years' worth of experience with two Emmy Awards of his own. Collier was known for getting himself into tough places like getting video of a carjacking with a child left inside the car. Collier just happened to be unloading his camera for an entirely different story and saw the assailant and got a notion to start recording. Collier's video was put on the Internet and shared with police. The video clarity was so good, police got a good look at the suspect's face and actions. Three hours later, after the car and child were abandoned, the man was taken into custody trying to board a public transportation bus. The child was unharmed. Collier's specialty was winning Emmys for spot news coverage.

"I usually work by myself. Howya doin' Booker?"

"Okay." Booker checked the front of the house one more time. "A sad one."

"No problem. I understand he wants to see us but if that changes, I'll move back."

"Understood." They got out of the van, Collier got his camera and tripod, what photographers called sticks. While they walked to the door,

Collier kept his camera pointed down. Before they reached the porch area, a man opened the door. He was tall, much taller than Booker. His chin was etched in gray hair, and he was almost bald on top. The man looked around as if he didn't want any others to follow Booker into the house.

"You can go into the family room." He didn't shake any hands and Booker decided not to offer. "My name is Raymond Clarke. I don't go by Ray, I use the full name Raymond."

"Sure, Mr. Clarke. I'm—"

"I know who you are or you wouldn't be here. My wife won't be talking. She's in the back still crying."

He led Booker and Collier into a room with a cabinet full of trophies. "Two of those are mine, the rest belong." He stopped for a moment. "They belonged to my son. Bayson was a great kid." The older Clarke looked to be at least six-four, straight shoulders and long fingers. He was a shade darker in skin tone than his son with brown eyes.

"I'm sorry for your loss. And thank you for speaking with us."

"All the other stations were here. I turned them all away. The first thing I want to ask if you could please take that stupid mug shot off the air and toss it." He handed Booker a nice color photograph of his son, smiling and looking like the world was his to take.

"Will do. I'll make sure to change things as soon as possible. He's just going to set up over there, if that's okay?"

"No problem."

Collier held up his hand. "I just need a minute. Have to go back and get my lights." They both waited until they got a nod from Clarke. Collier went back to the van.

"Are the trophies all for basketball?"

"It's almost a split, half for basketball and the rest for football. He loved both sports."

"Did you play yourself?"

"Me, yeah, a bit. But I didn't have half the talent of Bayson. He was the one." His face and voice took a downturn. "Now I have to pick out a suit for his funeral. Don't know when they'll release his body."

Collier knocked softly then reentered the house. He opened up a long thin black box and set up two sets of lights. One light directly aimed at

Clarke, another from the side. The tripod was next with Collier snapping the sticks into an upright position, and then he placed the camera on the mount, did a few more adjustments and handed Booker a lavalier microphone for Clarke. Once clipped to his shirt, he sat down. Booker had his own hand-held microphone. Once he got the nod from Collier he was recording, Booker posed his first question.

"We, who didn't get a chance to meet your son, tell us about him?"

"Bayson? Well, he was a great son. He did well in school, worked hard. Loved sports." Clarke stopped just briefly when all of them heard whimpering growing louder coming from a back bedroom. Clarke kept going. "Like any teenager, he had a few problems, but he worked them out. He was, we thought, headed in the right direction. I guess we were wrong."

"How did you hear about what happened?"

"I have some neighbors in that area, and they were all talking about this car crash. About how loud it was and so I kinda knew somethin' about it. Then the police showed up at the door. My wife was also here at the time. I'm retired from working at the airport. We're in shock. There's no doubt about it. This is a real disaster."

"I saw some of the videos. Your son was a talented basketball player. Was it his intention to go to college?"

"We were hearing things like that. We were not sure if that business with the referee was going to stop things, but I want everybody out there to understand Bayson was a good person. And not just because he was my son. Trust me, I admit he was not an angel, but he was a good man. His temper gets a bit too much sometimes but trust me, we lost a good one."

Booker went down his own checklist of what he wanted to cover. "Again, thank you for speaking with us but you had a reason for calling Channel 27."

"You were the only one who just stayed with the crash information. The others tended to dwell too much on his arrest, which was put to the side. I know you had the mug shot, but you also used a photo of Bayson in his uniform. I just wanted to speak with you."

"Any idea, if what we're being told is correct and confirmed by police, any idea what he was doing at a convenience store? And possibly with a gun?"

"Bayson knew about guns and how to handle them. I taught him. But this store thing. I don't know where that started or where it came from. That is not like Bayson. Not at all. Someone put him up to this and I'm going to follow up on this. I have my own thoughts, but I'll just wait until I know more."

Booker looked around the room and parts of the house. The home appeared well kept. Just a side view of the kitchen looked clean, dining table dust free. From what Booker was able to determine, Bayson Clarke came from a stable environment. Just a fraction of a face peeked out from the bedroom. The woman was thin, just a touch more than five-one. Her eyes were swollen, one hand grasping the other, nervous. She looked tired and needed rest that might never come again.

"Before I go, what one last thing would you want to say about Bayson Clarke?"

"That he was headed right and something went wrong. I put it on myself that I didn't see it. I don't know what happened, but Bayson had goodness in his heart."

Interview over, Collier got a few two-shots, or video of both Booker and Raymond Clarke, then he removed the microphone and started to photograph the trophies in the cabinet. Clarke motioned to Booker to come out into the hallway.

"Yes?" Booker took out his notebook.

"I couldn't say this on camera, but did you find out anything more on the kid who was driving the car?"

"No, police haven't released much so far."

"The kid's name is Manor. Gibby Manor. I did some digging on my own, but the kid's father is a bit notorious. Parson Manor. Maybe you've heard of him. I can share a bit of what the detectives told me. Rather they were asking me, did I know anything about this Gibby Manor kid. I don't but maybe you can find out a lot more. They're gonna limit me but please go after the truth. Find out why those two were in that store. I know my son. He wouldn't plan something like this. Go along maybe, but he wouldn't set this up. And one other thing."

Booker was quickly writing notes. "Yes."

"My son was hanging out with Manor. I saw him just once. He was apparently new to the school. But his other friend has been around Bayson since fourth grade. A kid named Solly Ressler. You need to talk to him. Find out what he knows. Believe me, he knows something. Ressler, first name Solly."

"Thanks. I'll look into it."

They packed up everything and Booker carried the light kit back to the van. Once inside, he called Newhall. "Okay, Booker, unless something breaks, they got you set up for the lead story at eleven. They want to know if you want to be live at the makeshift memorial?"

When Booker and Collier got to the utility pole location, the area was full of flowers and candles, all dedicated to Clarke. When Booker spoke to a live south Florida TV audience, he pointed to the massive array of flowers. There were large self-made cards, all with messages of loss. Booker went on to speak about a father's love for his son. His edited package ran almost two minutes, long for TV standards. The insert included most of the comments made by the father, along with video of the trophies, and all the information and sound clips gathered during the day. Booker wrapped everything up with a live comment about waiting for more information from police. When he was finished, he called into the station and Newhall.

"Good day of work, Book. Sad stuff. Listen can you update the web on your way in?"

"Yes, that will work. I have something for you as well."

"Sure, Book. Whatcha need?"

"Okay, I'm going to send you an email. I'm giving you a few names to check out. The first name is a guy named Manor. Parson Manor. His son is Gibby. I can't confirm it yet, but the father here says Gibby Manor was the one driving the car. The one who was taken to the hospital. What I'm looking for is info on Parson Manor. I need a full background check. Everything you can give me. The father says he's quite notorious. I want to know what that means. Run a check on all the names but I really want to know as much as I can about Manor the father."

"Got it, Book. I'm on it."

28

Drucker was on the phone with Manor for twenty minutes. All the time pretending he didn't know much about Cain Stocker was draining on him.

"Would you believe it, he was right there. Down the hallway from my son's room. I gotta know why he was there. I already called the hackers. I need you to do what you can, Runy. Do this for Gibby. Find out what that man was doing in the hospital. He was not there for himself. Gotta be a reason. Find out what it is."

"Sure, Parse. I'll see what I can find out."

"There is no *see* what I can find out. You find out, got me? Find out exactly and get back to me tonight if you have to, cause I'll be right here. I ain't movin'."

"Sure." When Drucker put away the phone, there was a puzzled look on his face as if he did not know how to proceed. He had only worked with handlers from investigators of the statewide grand jury and only met Cain Stocker twice. He was so close to ending his undercover C.I. stint he wanted things done and over.

Something caught Drucker's attention. A flash of something outside the house and down the street. He dropped into protection mode and turned out all the lights in the house and pulled his Sig Sauer from the holster strapped on his right side. He looked out the window and didn't see anything. Drucker looked for any kind of movement. The time was a few minutes before midnight and the street was clear of most traffic. He moved quickly through the rooms and made his way out the back door, holding the Sig upward. Drucker hugged the side of the building, walking fast to the front, stopping near the front door and staying in the shadows.

He leaned outward just a bit to get a view of the street. Nothing stood out as a problem. Drucker was very tired, and he didn't need another worry to keep him up. After moving all his belongings one more time, the rental house he found was situated so Drucker could look out for any oncoming cars. He was positive there was a flash and maybe a noise.

There was movement on his right. The Sig came up quickly and his hands moved the weapon into the shooter's position.

"Gracious, Runy. Don't kill me." Renla Parker emerged from between two cars. "Put the gun down, darlin, I ain't gonna hurt you." She was wearing an ultra-skin-tight, graphite gray skirt with a purple blouse and standing on four-inch heels. Her steps clopped loudly in the too-quiet night air.

"Whatcha doing here? I coulda popped you."

"Honey, you look like you ain't poppin' nuthin." She walked up to his face, stared directly into his eyes and leaned on his chest.

"You sniffin' me again? That smell is just me."

She drew back. "Yeah, that's just you alright. I just wanted to surprise you. But baby, you look po' tired." She fell into a smooth voice, taking hold of one of Drucker's cheeks. "Po boy, what got you so upset, huh? My Runy need some of momma's good love?"

"Tempting. C'mon inside." The gun was already down. He took her by the hand and together they walked up to the door and made their way inside.

"I left early. Let my staff close up." Parker was the owner of a bar and nightclub, where wanna-be singers crooned covers on popular songs every Friday and the dance floor was hot.

Drucker did a quick look-around and found nothing.

"Baby, your power go out?

"Just checking on something. You see anything strange when you drove up?"

All the half-smiles turned serious. “You really are bothered by something.” Parker also looked out the window and down the street. “This thing you’ve been working on, how bad is it?”

“The office is shut down, the owner’s son is just barely clinging to life and I’m not sure what tomorrow is gonna look like.”

“Say what? His son died?”

“I didn’t say died. He’s on life support. Doesn’t look good.”

Parker sat down on the couch and kicked off the tall heels. “What happened?” Just as soon as she asked the question, Parker snapped her fingers. “Wait, is this the kid I heard about on the news? Robbery? Crunched his car?”

“The same. My boss is at the hospital.” Drucker got back into his big chair, the one overlooking the street.

“That’s really awful.” Without hesitation, Parker got up and stood behind Drucker and started a back rub.

“Thanks. I need that.”

She looked over the house and her eyes fixed on a large wooden box sitting next to the dining room table.

“Baby, I never saw that before.” She left him and walked fast toward the box, hands out like she was eager to see what was inside.

“Hey, where you going? Don’t touch that.”

She stopped a foot from the carved outside of the wooden container. “What’s in there, important stuff?”

“Never you mind, just come back here and continue with that back rub.”

Parker ignored him and reached down to lift the lid.

“I told you, Ren, leave that thing alone. Just leave it.”

“Okay. Okay.” She looked at the box like the thing might contain a lost heirloom. She moved back to him and placed her hands back on the tender sore parts. For the next several minutes, Renla Parker gave Drucker her special collection of long strokes, smoothing out cable-tight muscles. His head got wobbly from the warm hands, until his eyes would blink open and closed from the sure pleasure of Parker’s love hands.

Another seven minutes later, Drucker turned out the lights and led the petite one down the middle of the house into the back hallway leading to the master bedroom.

Seventy yards down the street, the beat-up van moved back into position, rolling slowly and with purpose until the van was parked in a desired viewing spot. The van was cloaked in the hues of the night. Even the bumpers were coated in gray splotches. The figure inside the van slapped at the worn console as if letting the binoculars reflect directly into Drucker's face might have been a monumental mistake, yet it was momentarily turning on the headlights by accident that was the cause of the flash of white beamed down the street. The figure waited to be discovered, only nothing happened. Disaster was avoided. A quick move of backing up and out of sight was needed to make sure there was no detection from Runy Drucker.

The conversation on the satellite phone was short and to the point. The figure listened and did not talk. A person on the other end voiced directions on what to do about Drucker: Not yet.

29

When Booker Johnson opened the door to his apartment, he smelled the cut-up sausage and green peppers coming from the kitchen.

"Yes, I stayed up. And yes, I cooked one of your favorites." Misha Falone turned to him, and he was caught by the Misha smile. Her cheeks always seemed to be in the position of a grin. Nearly matching Booker in height, she was a pure Midwesterner who said pop instead of soda, desired deep-dish over thin, and though almost risking immediate death, had mastered the skill of skitching—the extremely risky art of hanging on to the back bumper of a car or bus and riding down an icy street, shoe soles grinding down with every block.

"You stayed up?" Booker put down his phone and started changing into something comfortable. "It's midnight. You didn't have to wait up."

"I wanted to be up when you got in. I saw the six, missed the eleven but I read stuff on your station website. Let me guess, you missed dinner again."

"Yeah, I did." He walked in the direction of the aroma.

"Tossed in some garlic like you like, it's all part of the snap and crackle."

The cut green and red peppers had cooked down to a nice bed for the sausage. She moved the skillet to a row of potholders and pulled a roasted bun from the toaster. "I know it's the wrong time to eat but you don't have to sample much, just take in a nibble."

Booker leaned in and kissed her on the already grinning cheek. "Thank you." He sat down to a smaller cut-down version of a full sandwich and took a bite. Through the chews, "Wow, I could get used to this."

Booker looked at the two suitcases near the door. "When is the rest of your stuff coming?"

"In two days. My brother is bringing it in and no, you don't have to help him. He'll be here and gone. Trust me you won't know he was even here. I don't have that much."

The *that much* was the culmination of a year of dating, a breakup, and two reunions. "Are you sure you want me here?"

Booker wiped his mouth. "I want you and everything you got to bring with you. Please stay, Misha Falone."

"Okay. I'm staying." Briefly, the smile went away. "How bad is this one?"

"The two teens? I'm not sure. There is a lot we don't know. I have some unconfirmed information but there's not a lot to go on. If they don't move me on to something else, I have to find out what and why they were at the store, robbing the place."

"Could it be something simple like money to buy some expensive shoes?"

"I really don't think so." Booker started to recount all the things he had seen during the day. He told her all the facts he had gathered and she listened. The listening part was one factor that drove them apart in the past. She did not, in the slightest, care one bit about what he did. That was before. Misha Falone, the executive assistant to a manufacturing firm, was always absorbed in her work and not Booker's.

"I'm trying to be good. I watched two other newscasts and compared."

"And?"

"You had way more information and interviews. Does that count?"

"That does but that's not what counts for me. If I miss something I catch up to my competition, but I really want to get at the truth." He took another bite. "Thanks for the meal. I haven't stopped since I spoke to that high school class."

"I won't mess with you tonight." Again, the smile was back. "You need your sleep. But tomorrow, you're all mine."

"A promise."

Booker put away the rest of the food, storing the sausage and peppers. He had just mere hours to rest and get ready for a pitch meeting in the a.m. Newhall sent him an email with the information he requested. Booker went to bed dreaming about the details gathered during the day and how to proceed. The questions had him thinking in many directions. He would wait until morning to sort it all out.

30

By the time Booker walked into the newsroom, he had received four emails from Merilee Yang, the early morning reporter. Her first news hit was just after 6 a.m. going live like Booker at the utility pole. She also traveled to the school to see if any more students wanted to comment. The results were described in her email, however, she moved on from the school since the school district was not happy she was there. Booker made a few calls when he arrived, checking in with the police public information office. One of the stations went live from the hospital where the surviving student was in I.C.U. They had no new interviews there.

Booker walked into the pitch meeting with a clear set of goals for the day, not knowing if circumstances would let him reach them all. The pitch meeting was the closest thing a newsroom had to a thinktank. This morning, six reporters were in the meeting along with Booker. Led by Claire Stanley, she went down her list of ideas and follow-ups, then reporters got a chance to pitch their own stories to cover. Some stories came with an added element to push them forward for consideration, like surveillance video. Many times, police agencies sent in video, with the hope and chance the public might be able to identify the suspects. There were videos of bank robberies, home burglaries, smash and grab thefts. All of them came with a directive to a tip line.

Booker looked over his notes and pitched. "We already know about the background of the student who is dead, Bayson Clarke. We spoke with his father. We don't know much about the teen still in the hospital. I have a name, but police won't confirm it just yet. I think in a day-two follow-up I could try to firm up the name. Also Merilee Yang this morning got a bit of information on a kid I heard about last night. Solly Ressler. He supposedly is associated with Clarke and the driver of the car. Yang also got new interviews this morning. Clarke was very popular."

Two producers were paying close attention to Booker, along with the news director. Booker kept going. "They found one gun but did not find any others. I'm going to check something right away and I'll let you know what I find. The last thing is the father of the injured teen. Newhall sent me some information on a guy named Parson Manor."

Another reporter jumped in. "I think I heard of that guy. He's got some big project about to kick off and break ground."

"Good to know. I'm being told it's his son who is in the hospital. Manor has been the subject of two investigations, both for money laundering but nothing developed. He's got three arrests, two in one year, followed by one the year after that. All of them involved fighting after an argument. One fight was over a parking space. All three arrests ended up being nolle pros cases, or dropped by the state. No reason given on why. Technically, he's clean and no more arrests since then. There was a small article about him three years ago on the money laundering, but again, it's been quiet since then."

In the meeting, Booker was given the go-ahead. The two producers told him and Claire Stanley that unless he had something new and solid, they would keep him out of the noon newscast.

When Booker got the word on what to do, he left the meeting. When he checked, Coffee was already outside, waiting in the van.

"Morning, sunshine." Coffee looked fresh and ready to go. "Had my espresso. I'm wide awake. Where are we going?"

"Later on, we might go to the hospital. For now, I want to go to the convenience store."

"Sure." Coffee started driving.

Two miles into the trip, she pressed Booker. "What do you think we'll get? The clerk already talked."

"Thinking about it, I'm going down a checklist of what the police might be looking for with the daylight. What's still missing from the investigation?"

"The second gun."

"Exactly. I just want to make a stop at the store and go from there."

When they pulled up, the store was still closed. Inside, Booker saw a crime tech taking pictures of the ceiling. Coffee parked, set up the sticks and started recording. Booker stayed quiet so he would not get his voice recorded by the camera. Inside, they saw the tech looking up at the empty space where a ceiling tile was once located. After a series of more photographs, a ladder was brought in, and the tech went up and poked around.

Coffee worked the camera controls, panning and focusing until she was satisfied. Booker saw some cans were on the floor. He had no firm idea on the series of events that took place in the store. And it was no good to speculate on camera.

Booker looked around. There were no other TV stations there. The tech kept digging until she came down with something in her hand and placed the object into a bag. When she walked out and placed the bag in the crime van, Coffee took a moment and stopped recording.

"We got lucky, Book. We shoulda been here hours ago. But we got it."

"Had to be a bullet. We can check later with P.I.O." For the next sixteen minutes, Booker watched the tech act as if she was finished.

Booker pointed to the road. "We're done here. I want to go on the same route the car took."

"And?"

"I just want to follow that route."

Coffee packed up the gear and they drove off in the same direction the car would have taken. They drove slowly and let other cars pass them on the road. The task was simple: look for anything dropped along the route. They were halfway to where the car ended up and Coffee stopped abruptly. "Look up ahead."

Before them, they saw the van of the police dive team. Out on the small lake they saw bubbles. Coffee parked close while not getting in their way and started recording. She carried the camera on her shoulder. Booker brought the tripod, and he would wait until she got some video first then she would snap the camera on the sticks.

There was a police officer on the bank with a long rifle pointed down, yet ready. This was Florida. Dive teams routinely placed an officer nearby looking for curious alligators. The officer was there to protect the team. Booker walked down closer to the divers. When he got within a few yards, he saw a table and there he observed a weapon. Booker could not make out the gun maker, but he called Coffee over to take a look. She got there and the recording continued. Another news van drove up and the photographer looked like he was on steroids, moving fast to get his gear out and record. He ran up and stood next to Coffee. Both of them got video of the gun.

Booker looked out on the water and there was a lot of movement. He tapped Coffee on the shoulder and she moved her angle to the water.

In the midst of a large swirl of bubbles a diver's hand protruded up and out of the water holding a second weapon. He came up and walked up to the bank, carefully placing the second gun on the table. A crime tech did a long series of photographs before the gun was bagged up and placed in the van.

A third reporter-photographer crew drove up and the process was repeated, with a photog moving fast out of the van in an attempt to get into place. The problem was the weapons were already put away and the van was closed up. He got nothing except the divers packing up.

Booker got on the phone to Claire Stanley. After a short conversation with her, he turned to Coffee. "We're in the noon newscast."

MINUTES AFTER BOOKER finished his report and Coffee was packing up the gear, breaking down the tripod, he noticed she was staring at him.

"Whatcha thinking, Book?"

"We saw a blurry somebody leaving that car the morning of the robbery. And now police have recovered three weapons. Two of them and three guns were used."

"Yes, and all three were probably tossed out a car window."

"I wasn't sure before but I'm positive now. The third weapon was for the person in the car, the one who took off. Whoever that is they know or should know what was about to go down."

Coffee slid the camera into a metal box to protect against theft. "Okay. Third person who got cold feet. So where is that person now?"

"Exactly. Clarke's father gave us the name of Solly Ressler. I asked Yang to ask around this morning. No one has seen Ressler. That maybe he wasn't in school yesterday and he's still gone."

Coffee got behind the wheel. "We are going to take a lunch break, right?"

"No problem. But we have to find the parents of that kid."

31

Parson Manor stood outside the hospital room and reached for his phone. After two rings, Drucker answered. "Runy, you got anything on this guy Stocker?"

"I'm working on it. You can't just reach out and get that kind of info. Not for a guy like this, it's too dangerous. I mean what if somebody in authority finds out you're seeking information on the guy who is prosecuting the case?"

"I've got a lot on the line here." Manor lowered his voice to just above a whisper. "We've got a lot on the line. Both of us. Think about what we've been doing. We're talking years for us both."

"I thought about that. I think about it every day. I got somebody who was supposed to give me straight up info that we can use."

"How soon?"

"Soon. I promise."

"Well, I'm in here and I can't go anywhere so I need people to do things for me. Call me."

The conversation ended and Manor walked back into the room. Miranda was talking to her son like he was two years old. The talk was constant and did not let up. The constant cadence of the machine was in the background. She turned to Manor. "I don't care what anybody says we're not turning that machine off."

"Miranda, at some point we're gonna have to face it."

"Look at me, Parson. I'll take on anybody. Doctors, lawyers. I don't care. My son's machine stays on, is that clear?"

Manor's jaw dropped slightly like he didn't know what to say to her. There were so many things on his plate and the trick was not to show any concern for those other issues, just focus on the one son, the only child in his life. "We'll do what we can."

Miranda Manor's eyes were blazing with anger. Her words for Parson were controlled and calm. "What I really want, and I mean this with all my heart. What I want Parson is for you to be in this bed. For some way to make a switch and have you almost gone and give me back my son." Her face shifted from hot contempt to reason. The change jolted Manor, like he was facing another person. He didn't recognize the woman who was his wife.

She let go of her son's hand and stood, facing Manor. "I've been thinking about this. We could set this same equipment in the living room. Make the calls, move in the life support, hire staff to help watch him and Gibby can be right there with us in his own home."

Parson almost shook his head, then let out the deepest sigh. "You know what the doctors say. He can't breathe or circulate his blood. Neither one. Without that machine, he's just not there."

Her words were sharp and angry. "Stop saying that. He's not whatever the doctor says. Not my Gibby." She returned to her post of sitting next to him and holding his hand, gently stroking his skin.

Manor opened his mouth like he was going to back up his comments then stopped when he saw she was singing to Gibby again. The soft melody was something she sang to him as a baby. The machine was doing all the essential life tasks for the body. Gibby was helpless and too far gone. All Manor wanted to do was prepare a funeral.

He got an email from his attorney. Manor took a seat and read the message to himself. One thing was evident, the attorney was making things clear there must be a very solid case against Manor. And solid meant years behind bars. Maybe a lot. Manor felt a headache coming on. His last meal was sometime yesterday, the last good thing that happened to him was several days ago. He plodded around like the entire world was coming down on him and nothing could change his fate. Manor looked like a man riddled with guilt, as though Miranda's words were correct, Gibby was here because of him. All the hurtful, challenging things Manor threw toward his son were coming back to him like barbed darts.

"Okay," Manor said. "I'll look into what you say. Maybe do some renovations. I don't know if everyone will sign off on this, but I can try."

"That's all I ask. Just try Parson." She actually gave him a full hug, something left out of their relationship for a long time. "Thank you."

Manor left the room and leaned against the hospital room number, a spot he'd visited often. He looked down at the end of the hall and a different face came out of the room. Manor made some gentle inquiries about the patient there and was told they were gone. No more sightings of Cain Stocker. With hospital information rules solidly in place, there wouldn't be much coming from the nurses.

More than anything, Manor needed space. The confined room with a near-dead son and a grieving wife left him almost choking for relief. The only relief now were the moments in the hallway and just about as far as he could go while staying close to Miranda. He moved around like a caged tornado, ready to unleash and tear down everything in his wake. The investigation, an upset wife, now Gibby, all of it was coming on like the storm was much bigger than his pent-up presence in a hospital room.

Manor excused himself and went downstairs to the lobby and outside. He wanted to talk with his attorney again and plan strategy. The last thing he heard was an indictment could be coming soon and he wanted to be ready.

32

Booker Johnson got the call. The one he was expecting from Claire Stanley. He really wanted to stay on the story, yet he knew he had to grasp the reality of time limits on a news story. There was something Booker called the three-day rule. No matter how big the story, its true life for the newscasts mainly lasted just those three days. Three. First the initial story, usually spot news, then the second-day follow-up. If enough good facts were developed, there would be a third day for the story. Booker was told a crash involving the teens where the money was collected, the guns found, was fast on the way to a two-day story. The whole future of the story depended on whether Booker would generate enough new facts to make the story relevant.

"They want to move you on?" Coffee stopped outside a fast-food spot.

"Yep. They want me back checking the court docket and other stuff."

"We pretty much tackled the story. We got the clerk interview, surveillance video, the guns and the father of a kid in the car. The hospital says the other kid's parents don't want to talk and the correct decision was made to make sure the family had privacy. Even though the dad might have a bad history, there's never been an arrest that stuck. There's nothing to put on television. The one angle that's left is finding whoever ran from the car that morning. That's it. And police are probably tracking him down as we speak."

"You have to be right."

Coffee disappeared inside for burgers and bottled water to go. Booker and Coffee liked to eat in the van, and they were always prepared to leave and go anywhere, for anything. She munched on the burger, Booker sat scrolling through his phone. "There's one thing we haven't done," he said.

Coffee's mouth was full of food. When she didn't answer, he kept talking. "We should ask for the 911 calls from the clerk or neighbors."

She swallowed. "What will the tapes give us that we didn't know before?"

Booker knew she had a point. After a public records request, a police department could release the calls made by the neighbors to the 911 call center.

"You better eat something, Book. Remember what happened to you last Thanksgiving."

"Like it was yesterday." While the world was set to eat a well-prepared meal, Booker, like first responders and police, found himself working the day. He passed on a quick meal somewhere and got the call to answer a large warehouse fire. The place took up a city block, was filled with rusty cars and a tall mountain of tires. When the fire reached the cars, there were small explosions. And the burning tires put out a black cloud thick enough to block out the sun in the area. Channel 27 wanted what the news business called wall-to-wall coverage. Since the station did not have a football game, those in charge called for a stop in regular programming and put Booker on TV for a straight two hours. The helicopter pilot was called away from a full house of guests and got up in the air for live video.

Someone was kind enough to offer Booker one Chicken McNugget from their bag. That, for the day, became his entire Thanksgiving meal. Since then, Coffee always reminded him of making sure he didn't miss a meal.

Coffee finished the burger and sipped on the water. Booker finally took a bite from his sandwich. "Been looking but I can't find this kid Solly Ressler. Name won't come up anywhere."

"I'm guessing you don't want to go by the school."

"No way. They'd like us to stay away." He took another bite. "He might be too young to show up in our search sites. I've got to think of something else."

"Why you pushin' so hard on this one?"

He crushed up his bag. "I think there's something more to this. A lot more. But I might be at a stopping point for the moment. We'll do our live hit and I'll go back to checking courts."

When he wasn't on spot news coverage, Booker was the main reporter for Channel 27 to cover court cases. In doing so, the beat meant he would check the morning bond court document for news leads. Booker prepared for what the producers wanted: just one live hit for the 5 p.m. and he would be done for the day.

Solly Ressler started biting his nails when he first heard of the crash on the news. The teen videotaped all three local TV stations, especially Channel 27. They had the interview of B.C.'s father. He had somehow convinced his mother to let him stay home for two days, claiming he did not feel well. There would be no excuse for missing another day of school. He sat on the bed then got up and walked around. After a few minutes, he sat on the bed again. Ressler was a mass of tangled emotions with no one to confide in. His best friend, Bayson Clarke, was dead. There was no word on Gibby, but it could not be good.

More nail biting. He always had someone there to tell him where he should be, the friends he should be associated with and just about everything he did was dictated by others. On his desk was a book with all of the class photographs since elementary school. Bayson Clarke was in almost all of them.

He went to the window and looked out for the fiftieth time, waiting for police to show up at the door any moment. He went over what he might tell them, writing things down on paper to get everything right. He never touched the gun when Gibby shoved the weapon in his direction. He never went into the store. He did what Solly Ressler should do, and he refused to be a part of the so-called Big Day. He was a big kid now, no longer tied so tightly to his mother's wishes and commands. Even the big kids had a limit. Going to school was close to the top of the list. He flopped on the bed and looked up at the ceiling in the room and the large photograph of a large pepperoni pizza firmly taped in place.

He punched his pillow three times and pulled out his cell phone. His right thumb scrolled down to the cell phone number to Bayson. A number he would never call again.

"Make things like before," he whispered to himself. The pillow took another punch to the middle. Then he hit the pillow again. Then again. For Ressler, before meant before the arrival of Gibby Manor, before there was any talk of the damn Big Day. He gave up eating too much, a sure sign to his mother he was not well. "Before," he said louder. "Before!" Now he was yelling into the pillow and kept up the punches until his fingers were starting to chafe.

33

"All this time and I've never been here before." Runy Drucker walked inside the small apartment. "Thanks for letting me stay here so sudden-like."

Renla Parker let a warm smile stretch smoothly across her face. "Now I've got you all to myself." She went over to a console of video equipment and a large screen TV. She hit a button and soft, placid jazz pumped through three speakers in the corners of the room.

Drucker went from one window to the other and looked out onto the parking lot.

"Baby, you still skittish about something. What is it?"

Drucker shrugged like nothing was bothering him. His actions gave him away. "Just that we're all being careful. There's some big investigation going on and my boss might get caught up in it."

"Caught up? Does that mean you, too?" Parker went over to the console and turned the music down just a bit. "I want to hear this. What investigation?"

"C'mon Ren. I can't talk about it. I don't know much myself. Just that the firm might be getting a hard look by some authorities. I don't even know who."

A look of care and concern moved into Parker's face. "Well, if you want, you can stay here as long as you want. I know you, and I don't think you'd be involved in anything."

"Me? Naw. Not since I helped you at the bar."

Renla Parker rushed to Drucker, pushing into him and wrapping her arms around him, bracelets clanging on her wrist. "I know. You were the best bouncer I ever had. Even went to jail protecting me."

Drucker gave her forehead a light kiss. "That guy deserved it, grabbing you like that."

"Well, the police didn't see it that way. But it's all cleared up."

Parker checked her shoes. "I wear these heels specifically so I can lift up and try to reach your chin. You're too tall, Runy."

Drucker looked at her purse. She noticed. "I know you don't care about my bag." She went over to the handbag, opened it and looked inside. "You want to know where I keep my gun."

"I just want to know where everything is in case I need it."

"It's there. But now that you're here do you need to go back to your place? Bring some clothes?"

"No. Just thank you for taking me in."

"I've never seen you so off. Makes me wonder if I'm okay with you being here."

This time Drucker moved to her, pulling her close to him and landing a few soft kisses. "No one scares you. Nothing and no one. Besides, I'm here."

She reached back and tapped the purse. "Yes, I keep the gun in there, ready to go." Parker looked into Drucker's eyes. "I don't want to scare you or anything but just don't go messing around. No side woman. Is that clear?"

"Clear."

Parker reached down and picked up a remote to pump up the music. They danced and swayed with the beat. Drucker was so caught up in the moment he didn't notice his phone going off.

PARSON MANOR TRIED TWICE and could not reach Drucker. "C'mon, man." The attempt yielded no response. He put away the phone and looked up at the tall walls of Middle Palms Regional Memorial Hospital. He leaned up against the outside wall, looking like a man who wanted to change his past, change his very existence. For now, he was faced with a problem. Even with his son just barely there, an investigation moved forward.

34

This time, it was Booker who provided the meal. Sandy Shoes restaurant was right on the water. Located near the Intracoastal Waterway, the place was positioned so diners had clear sightlines of the Atlantic. Facing east, there was no sunset, so the restaurant built a fireplace just off to the right. The tall bricks reached up and through to the ceiling. While the manager kept the fireplace off during the hot Florida summer, the cool fall temps gave way to some brilliant flames, especially at night.

"I like this place." Falone looked over the menu, then the view and back to the menu. "Not sure where to look, the water or what to order."

"Take your time." Booker had already selected his favorite: shrimp scampi with broccoli, tiny potatoes on the side with a bowl of conch chowder as an appetizer. The waitress dropped off two glasses of water with sliced limes. "You both need more time?"

"I do." Falone was still checking.

"No problem. I'll be back."

Booker leaned back in his chair and shared the view she was enjoying. "So many great restaurants."

"I know. Your friend ever going to start that club again?"

"The restaurant club? Two couples in it moved away. And we..." Booker stopped talking.

"That's okay, Book. We broke up. You can say it. But we're back together again. We can do anything we want."

"I liked what we did, each month picking out a restaurant, a place we never visited before."

Falone put her menu down. "I liked it 'cause we spent all month, texting each other on where we should eat. Then four couples meeting, eating a great meal and the conversations."

"Maybe we can but with a smaller group."

The waitress returned. Falone handed her the menu. "I'll have the salmon, grilled, with garlic potatoes and asparagus. No appetizer for me."

After the waitress took Booker's order, she thanked them and left.

Booker looked at Falone's hands. "Can't believe you're not on the phone swiping away."

"I did it again. Left the phone at the apartment."

"We're better off tonight without it."

"Listen, Book, you can talk about it."

"About what?"

"Your story. I know you're just itching to tell me. Go ahead, I'm all elephant ears."

"I don't want to bore you."

"You won't. This is the new Misha. The one who will listen this time. If you want to talk about what you're covering, that's perfectly fine with me. And if you want to hear about my job and the world of manufacturing, we can do that. I'm not ready to let Booker Johnson get away from me this time."

"There's not much to say now. I think the story is wrapped up."

"But?"

"You know how I get with my hunches. I just feel this crash, the death, there's something else. I'm not sure why but police are not releasing anything on the kid in the hospital."

"The parents put out a no information on him?"

"That's what the hospital says."

"Then that's it. Unfortunately, one of them is deceased. The other we don't know about. No one to prosecute, money returned. You can let it go if you want."

"I know. That's what everyone keeps telling me."

"Don't worry. If you want to kick it around, I'm here to listen."

"You're right. I have to move on." Booker moved on to other subjects. They talked about places they'd like to visit in Florida. There was always the planned trip to see a space launch. Booker wanted a return trip to Key West and the Florida Keys. The west coast was added to the conversation with mention of Naples, where the sunsets were golden. They detailed possible trips to Estero Island or Fort Myers Beach.

The arrival of the food did not stop the chatter of destinations. They laughed until the decision was needed on a dessert.

Check paid, tip added, Booker looked toward the pier. "Want to take a walk?"

They walked down the worn gray wooden planks and leaned up against the railing. Several people fishing took up most of the space along the end of the pier. Out in front of them, the waves of the blue-black Atlantic rolled to shore then disappeared into the sand. A breeze kicked up Misha's hair and her attempts to pull the locks back into place were impossible. Finally, she just let the wind take over, sorting her hair the way it wanted.

He stared at her. "You know I'm guilty, too."

"Really? Of what?"

"I had my part in why we split. Complained too much, missed too many meals, put you to sleep talking about my work."

"Remember, that's over. That was the old us. The new us shares everything. Is that clear, Mr. Booker Johnson?"

"Clear."

"Book?" Her voice was soft and almost absorbed by a fresh gust.

"Yeah."

"I'd like to ask you a very important question. This just might be the most important one I'll ask in our relationship. It's the one question I ask at the right time. I've been preparing to ask you this for a long time." She leveled her brown eyes at him and waited.

"Okay. What is it?"

She placed her hand over his and murmured. "This is really important, Booker."

"Okay. Believe me, you have my attention."

She leaned up close. "Can I bring my dog to the apartment?"

"Your what? Of course." Both of them laughed in the moonlight. "That was your big question? I thought you were gonna ask me..." he stopped.

"Ask what?" The cute smile persisted. She let go of his hand. "Bet you thought I was gonna really get serious on you."

"Ah, yes."

"I was messing with you. My dog can't come right now. I move around so much, she's with my mother in Chicago. And besides, my mom doesn't want to give her up."

"Why up there?"

"Because my company had me on the road traveling, in and out of airports in the past fourteen months. I haven't seen my dog in like forever. May not recognize me."

"We'll have to go to Chicago."

"Really?"

"Sure."

They walked back to the restaurant, then back to the car.

35

Cain Stocker didn't want to leave the room. "Dad, stop staring at me. I'm all right." Camden was sitting up in his bed. Lace fluffed up a pillow and let him settle back until he was comfortable.

"You two can leave. I'm not gonna faint."

"We just want to make sure you're fine." Lace took micro steps toward the door. Stocker was already out into the hallway. They both left but kept the door open.

When they reached the family room, Lace started first. "He says he's fine, but I don't know."

"He's not fine. We're just waiting for the next thing to happen."

They kept their voices low. Lace went to the bedroom and returned in her tight yoga pants. "I'm gonna get on the bike for a bit with my headphones on. If you need me, just come on in." She walked off toward the exercise room.

Stocker didn't want a drink or any television. He opened the door and walked out into the front yard. He was there perhaps six minutes when a voice came at him from his left.

"You like to stack bricks. Isn't that what they say about you, Mr. Stocker?"

A shocked look ripped across Stocker's face. He was standing just a few yards from Parson Manor. "What the fuck are you doing here?"

"I'm just out taking a walk, like you, Mr. Stocker."

"Stop calling me Mr. Stocker. Get away from my house."

Parson did not move. "I came to see you."

"You go right now or I'm calling the police. I can't be anywhere near you without your attorney, you know that."

A sneer marked up Manor's face. "Did you know our sons went to the same high school?" He watched and saw a surprised expression on Stocker's face. "Oh, so you didn't know that. Yep, my boy Gibby went to the same place as your son."

"Just get your ass away from my door. Now!"

"I have to tell you something. Some things I don't want my attorney to hear."

"The only thing I want to hear is you walking away, right now." Stocker started walking back toward his front door.

"I wouldn't do that, Mr. Stocker. This has to do with the health of your son."

"My what?" Stocker looked around. None of his neighbors were out or near a window. The puzzled look was still on Stocker's face. He saw no car for Manor, and he was in the middle of a gated community. "You can forget about talking about my family. Go now or I promise you the police will be on the way."

"Your son, what's his name? Camden? Yes, I read all about his medical condition. It's sad."

Stocker stopped. "What do you know about it?"

"I know about a lot of things. Three years ago, an unknown someone hacked into two hospitals including Middle Palms Regional Memorial Hospital. Thousands of patient records were stolen, sucked into the dark web. And what do you know, a certain Camden Stocker was included in that patient information theft."

"Manor, be aware that what you're saying and about to say could be grounds for charges."

"Oh, Mr. Stocker I'm not saying I took those records. What I am saying is that if a certain person saw those records, they'd know your son suffers from an extremely rare heart problem going back to when he was eight years old, am I correct?"

"You don't get to know anything about what is correct or false. I need you off my property right now."

"I'm not going till you hear me out. The records say your son's condition is such that if he does not receive a heart in the not-too-distant future he will die."

Hearing the words about Camden made Stocker stop and listen. "Please don't do anything with that information. We've kept all that part from him as much as possible."

"Surely your son knows he needs a heart, which is sad because he's so young."

Stocker was silent like he was weighing all that he was hearing. "Manor, you're a man under investigation standing in front of my house talking about stolen or hacked medical records. This is the last time I'm going to tell you. Leave now or face the police."

"My son is dead, Mr. Stocker. He's hooked up right now to devices and machines to keep him with us. All that is fine with his mother but to me, I lost him. You could say I lost him a long time ago." Manor looked up at the night sky. "There is absolutely nothing you could do to me right now because the one thing that mattered to me in my life is gone."

"Why are you here?"

"There is something I can do for you. Something for you to think about. But the thing is you don't have much time."

Stocker searched the front of his house. No Lace coming outside to hear anything. "I have time."

"I don't think so. I checked on the thing your son has and there is a time stamp. Young people with his condition die from this and, yes, it's rare and, yes, he's very young, but unless something happens, you will lose him like I'm losing my son."

"I'm sorry about your son Manor, but you should go home."

"And lose the chance to save your son Camden?"

"What are you saying?"

"It's simple. The doctors have approached us about organ donation. I can make a directed donation. Give my boy's heart to your son. Save his life.

We keep this talk to ourselves and no one will know. Now what kind of price can you put on that? A heart. Your son would live. You can see him go to college, have a family, be a grandparent."

"I know you, Parson. I know about your dealings. This is about the worst thing that's ever been put to me. It's vile."

"You get my son's heart if you do away with the investigation. Drop everything. Shut down the grand jury stuff and my son Gibby's heart will be yours for Camden."

"I can't believe you're proposing this. Shameful, just like you."

"You say you know me. If you know me, then you know somehow I always manage to avoid the jail door. That's not for me."

"I would be breaking the law. I'm probably already doing that now just by talking with you. It would mean prosecutorial misconduct at the highest level. Obstruction of justice. Jail for me and you. You really want to do that?"

"Mr. Stocker, what is your son's life worth to you? If he's worth everything in this world, the choice is simple."

Stocker stood frozen by Manor's words. He should have been in the house already, calling police, checking surveillance video, door cam vid, doing everything possible to get rid of the vermin still standing in the front yard.

Manor played his last card. "I know all the facts. With my special people, I can learn anything about you. Your son has been on the transplant list for a couple of years now. I checked. Your son and my boy have the same blood type. All you need to do is the testing to see if they're compatible and that's it. My lawyer can oversee the donation, we keep it quiet, and we insist the doctors make this happen. You want this. I need it."

Stocker rubbed down his face with his hands. Standing frozen was now several minutes too long.

"I see, Mr. Stocker, I got your attention. You're thinking about it. That's good. That's very good. The more you think about it, the more you can see a way to make this work."

"I can't say anything."

Manor said, "Don't say anything right now. I get it. This is a big decision. For all of us. But I'll tell ya what. I'll give you until tomorrow night. Same time tomorrow. You think about it and trust me, I'll find a way to see what you decide. If you don't make a move by then, my son's heart is headed to some hospital on the western part of the United States. I won't say where, but the deal is you cooperate or my son's heart goes somewhere else. Like I said, it's that simple. Good night, Mr. Stocker."

Parson Manor walked off into the stillness of Bay Court, into the middle of what one website described as the safest in south Florida, past the front security post and the guard who was secretly paid to take a break for an hour. Manor walked a long trek down the road with wide grassy swales, where morning ground fog swelled up in the predawn hours, leaving the open undeveloped land covered in wispy clouds until a fresh hot sun burned everything away and the promise of a new day was evident everywhere one looked.

36

Runy Drucker put the burner phone down with authority, smacking the thing on the desk. Working at Parker's apartment, he tried for the fourth time to reach Parson Manor. On the fifth attempt, against his better judgement, he left a voicemail message. "Parse, call me right away. I talked with our friends. I don't advise what you're thinking. They gave you hospital stuff. I think I figured it out. Don't do it. Call me." He slid the phone across the desk until it careened against the wall. Friends was the word Drucker and Manor used for their small network of hackers. He couldn't wait any more and locked up and got into his car.

Not sure on where he was going first, Drucker drove toward Manor's house. During the thirty-minute drive, he kept looking at his phone expecting a callback. A call that never came. He drove into the complex and did something he had never done before. Drucker parked in front of the house. All the other times, he approached the massive eight-foot doors with Manor. For Drucker, the clandestine meetings in the back did not count. He rang the doorbell.

Miranda opened the door. Her hair looked a bit matted down like she was combing the strands with her hands and nothing else. Her eyes were puffy and she was carrying a bag. "Oh Runy. I don't know if you heard about my son." She leaned into him, and Drucker quickly moved back to avoid any contact with her. Miranda ignored his hesitancy and grabbed him anyway, holding him close to her. "They say my Gibby is dead. But I'm not going to let him go."

"That's what the doctors are saying?"

"The only one fighting for him is me. I miss you, Runy."

He managed to again move backward and step away. "I'm looking for Parson. Is he here?"

"Right now, I don't know where he is. I'm only here for a quick minute to get some more clothes and get back to the hospital."

"This is urgent and I'm trying to stop him before he does something." Drucker broke off what he was going to say.

"Something urgent?"

"I just need to find him right away. I've been calling and he doesn't pick up."

Miranda locked the door behind her and checked her watch. "I've got to get back. Please call me. I wish I had you with me in the hospital."

"You know I can't do that."

He walked her down to the car and waved to her when she drove off. Drucker looked at all the surveillance cameras by the front door and the ones aimed toward the lawn. He walked like a man who didn't care if the boss saw him hugging the wife. Drucker got into the car and sat down. The burner rang.

"Parse?"

"Runy, I'm busy. What's up?"

"Our friends have been talking to me. You hashing something up with the man who is targeting you?"

"I don't know what you're talking about."

"It would be better if we could meet up somewhere."

"Can't happen right now, Runy. I'm bouncing between the hospital and a couple other places."

"I know what info you got. Please, before you do anything, talk to me first."

"Maybe it's too late. Maybe it's just time for you to stand aside and let me work this out." The phone went dead.

Drucker tossed the phone on the passenger seat. In Drucker's world he knew both men, and the information from the hackers about the son of Cain Stocker had him lining up all the angles, connecting the dots.

"Can't trust either one of them," he yelled at the dashboard. Drucker wasn't looking at many options. The business was shut down publicly with employees working from home. Drucker drove with a confused look, not wanting to trust Stocker and Manor seemingly in the midst of a deal without him involved. He kept going until he reached his own home. Paranoia was sweeping through Drucker and all of his self-protection tactics were taking over. All of his senses were on heightened alert. This was the time to close ranks. He picked up the phone and had most of the numbers dialed for his contact with the statewide grand jury. Distrust seeped in again and he put the phone down. His new set of plans now included Renla Parker's place or somewhere to hide.

"Don't trust them," he repeated.

37

Booker spent a scant twenty minutes on the phone, checking on past stories, updating information when he got new facts. He was also looking for news stories, items to pitch for the morning meeting. More than anyone, he liked to be the first one into the office. The morning routine included reading the newspaper online and watching the stories from all stations in the area. He left the building alone, headed for his designated morning assignment, the courthouse.

For Booker, this was his realm. He knew most of the attorneys, judges, and most of all, the court bailiffs. If there was an important hearing and he needed to get his camera inside, the bailiff was the one who was in charge.

The first stop was bond court. Each day, a list was placed outside for anyone to read. The list included the names of all those arrested late afternoon or overnight. Every news station sent a rep to go over the list, mark down any interesting cases and send information to the call desk. Booker found two D.U.I. cases where the defendant's names sounded familiar. There were dozens of loitering, trespassing cases, all of which were bypassed by Booker. Three cases were the names of people who were arrested on a V.O.P., a violation of probation. The defendants in those cases were denied bond until a judge determined if they violated the terms of any sentencing agreements and the bond in their case. In Booker's experience, judges had a dim view on probation violators. He wrote down the names of the three for a background check. For any one of the cases, if the original charge was covered heavily in the news, a follow-up could be done.

For the moment, Booker was working without a photographer. If something major developed, a phone call would yield one or more photogs, depending on the story. Sometimes he heard of a pending arrest. The main jail was nearby, and Channel 27 would dispatch a photog to watch the jail door.

One name stood out on the V.O.P. group. Mitchell Kurber. Booker remembered the story. The guy liked to climb up to the second floor of apartments and look for sliding glass doors left unlocked. The weird thing was he never went inside a place, he just stood there. In the first two arrests, the judge assigned a psychological evaluation and time served, meaning the short time he was in the jail would serve as his punishment. Only Kurber kept showing up on balconies. Booker called the story in, and Claire Stanley said the producers would use the information on the noon newscast as a short update, but no live report.

Once Kurber's name was called, he was held without bond. More tests were ordered, and a report date was listed—the report date on when he would come back to court and all sides would update the judge. Booker checked the website of a competing station and noticed they spelled Kurber's name wrong.

By noon, Booker's fate on a possible assignment was unknown. He was assigned to breaking news. He hooked up again with Coffee and the task meant he would wait somewhere in the middle of the city and wait for an event to happen.

In the early afternoon, Booker got a call from the desk. There was a disturbance at a sandwich shop, a popular spot for high school students. Channel 27 only wanted him to check it out, nothing more. The whole situation seemed like a twenty-second mention on a newscast.

When Booker and Coffee arrived, police had the entire situation under control. Coffee got out and started photographing. They were joined by one other TV station. Booker tried but could not get any firm information at first. The place had a history of being a place for students to come and fight, usually over a girl. Two teens were on the ground and not in handcuffs.

Since they were juveniles, Coffee only shot video of their legs and feet, no faces. Over Booker's right shoulder, he saw Detective Brielle Jensen arrive. Acting as P.I.O., she gathered some information, relayed facts to Booker and he was free to move on to another story. After twenty minutes, she walked to the two reporters.

"Simple misunderstanding," Jensen explained. "Words between a few students, one student was pushed, a fight started and the owner called police. I think these kids will get off with a warning and a promise to play nice-nice."

Booker did not ask for a sound clip from Jensen. Her information was enough. Jensen got in her car and drove off. The crowd of teen students were urged to go home and started moving away as the two in custody were about to be released.

Booker said, "I think the police here are waiting for parents to come and get them."

When the crowd dispersed, one or two students walked in Booker's direction. "Everyone going to be okay?" he asked.

"Oh, yeah," a boy told them. "One kid got upset 'cause he lost his friends. Somebody said the wrong thing and they got into a fight."

"Thanks." Booker jotted down a few notes. He asked the boy one follow-up question. "The one who lost friends, you know him?"

"Yep. The whole school does. He was friends with those kids who died in the car crash. That kid over there, his name is Solly Ressler."

38

The other reporter was not close enough to Booker, so the name Ressler probably was not heard by him. The name wouldn't matter anyway since it was not made public or put in his reports. Booker knew immediately who Ressler was but never saw his face before. He pulled Coffee to the side and gave her the new information.

She answered back, "This kid?"

Booker nodded.

Solly Ressler was heavyset, loose matted hair, a pair of aged gym shoes, and what appeared to be a food stain on his shirt. His jaw was reddened from the skirmish. He leaned up against a police car and shared words with an officer.

The other TV crew got into their van and left.

Booker called the station again. He explained all the facts to Stanley. After listening, she said the information would be passed on to the producers. The story was being taken out of the newscasts since a teen fight was not enough to pass on to the public. However, Booker was told he could stay there and find out if Ressler or his parents wanted to speak. Booker Johnson was officially out of the newscasts, for now.

He waited outside the sandwich place. One parent had already arrived and picked up a male student. Ressler was still there. He looked downcast, and for a few times, looked over at Booker. Coffee's camera was on the ground.

A few minutes later, a man drove up in a Toyota. He was wearing glasses, wore a business suit and black shoes. When he approached the officer, the man showed some identification. There was a short conversation and the younger Ressler was released into the custody of his father. The officer got into his car and backed out of the lot.

The talk with the father lasted several minutes. Booker was gauging when or if he should approach them. He raised his hand, showing a sign of hello from a distance and waited. More conversation between father and son. Then, both of them walked toward Booker.

"Hello. I'm Gus Ressler. My son and I recognize you from TV. You spent some time with Bayson's father. I saw the interview." The elder Ressler looked over at his son then back to Booker. "I don't want Solly to speak to you on camera and I won't either, but I can tell you a few things."

Coffee put her camera away and waited in the van.

Booker said, "I understand Bayson was very popular."

"Mr. Johnson, Bayson and my son were friends going back to elementary school as I'm sure Mr. Clarke told you. This has really been hard on my son. Things were great at the school, sure they got into a few minor problems but nothing like robbing a store. I can tell you off camera and you can quote me, when Solly was confronted with this whole robbery idea, he backed down and got away. He wanted no part of what was planned. None of it." His voice intensity carried to another level.

Booker told him, "What we might do is use the surveillance video and use your quotes. Have police already spoken to you?"

"Oh, yeah. They spoke to both of us. Once they realized Solly wanted no part of this, they moved on. But again, this has been very hard on him."

The younger Ressler couldn't wait any longer and started talking. "I watched the news. I miss Bayson every day. Wish I had the power to change that night. I shoulda stopped them from going in there."

Booker asked, "You okay? Looks like you caught one in the face."

"I'm okay. Some idiot tried to make it like Bayson was the one who set up the robbery. It wasn't Bayson, it was Gibby. Gibby Manor."

"The new kid in school?"

"Yeah. Gibby is okay once you get to know him. I just think he was trying to follow something his father did."

The older Ressler pulled at his son's arm. "We've got to go. Get him home to his mother."

"I understand. Take care."

The two Resslers made the walk back to the car. Just in case, Coffee recorded a few seconds of the sandwich spot. They got into the van. Booker had enough information to update the newscast and the website. They waited for breaking news the rest of the afternoon only to find things would stay quiet. For now.

39

For the next five days Booker put everything behind him on the crash with the two teens and his attention was on getting Misha Falone moved into his apartment. Luckily, she didn't have much and the move was done in less than a day. They had just a few minor issues to work out. Now they had two coffee tables and needed one. She had knickknacks to place on the kitchen counter, while Booker was a neat freak and liked to keep the counter clean. This time around in the relationship, there was a promise of compromise. Some knickknacks were added to the kitchen.

Booker welcomed the fact Misha liked to cook. For a person whose time was constantly swallowed up by the job of TV reporter who missed a lot of meals, this was a nice change. Their days together were pleasant and without discord. There was a renewed deep respect for each other's jobs and the time and energy needed to succeed. Booker's life was a long stream of court hearings on defendants in the news, minor breaking news and the constant devotion to making sure the Channel 27 website was always updated.

He made a few calls on the robbery and crash, along with his list of other story updates. These were calls he made in the early morning hour before the throng of producers and reporters walked in the door. Everything on the crash was quiet. Police released the 911 calls made by neighbors. All the calls were virtually the same. No one witnessed the crash itself and all accounts were about the aftermath. They described the loud collision. One person checked for a pulse and then moved back. A few snippets of the calls made it to one of the newscasts.

MIRANDA MANOR NESTLED into the patio chair in the shade of the chickee hut, wearing all black. She sat there motionless, staring down at the ground, eyes looking dazed. Manor approached her.

"You coming inside?"

"I hate you, Parson. I hate you with everything I have. You didn't give Gibby a chance. I told you to keep that machine on."

"He was gone, Miranda. Everyone told you that. Our son was gone the moment he entered that hospital. There was nothing anyone could do."

In her hand was a picture of Gibby when he was a baby, not more than six months old. She kissed the photograph and held it with trembling fingers. There were things to remember, things to never forget. Miranda was alone with him when he took his first steps. In the early years she was the only thing in his life. All that changed when Gibby turned twelve. She, at times, stared off toward the back of the garden and her one escape, Runy. The rendezvous with him was a lift. She looked at the door as though she wanted Runy to walk in, right up to her and take her away. Then she again fixed her gaze on the concrete patio floor. "I'm dead inside. Everything ripped out. I begged you. You didn't move."

"I had no choice. I couldn't let him stay hooked up to that machine forever. This was the only choice we had. We got him the best casket they had. You liked the choice, you said so."

"I didn't know what I was saying. The only thing I know, Parson, is Gibby would do anything you said. He looked up to you. Wanted to be like you in every way. Look what that got him. It got him killed."

He started to move toward her, arms outstretched, but she repulsed the movement in her direction. Manor stood there standing near her in silence. He looked back at the empty house. Manor had not invited anyone to the service.

She finally looked up at him. "You didn't even invite Runy. You could have at least let him come. He's always stood by you, and I thought he would be here."

"You're close to Runy?"

"I'm close to all your employees. All of them. And not a single person from your company was there. Like you've been trying to hide us away all these years." She kicked at a trail of ants. "Well, it doesn't matter anymore. The one thing I loved in this world is gone."

"You still got me Miranda. I'm here."

"You really want me to answer that? You haven't listened to me since the day we married. You won't let me get close to any friends. Not one friend." Her voice rose in volume. "I have plans. I always wanted to open the plant nursery. You know that. I have a distributor lined up in Homestead. I have a place in mind, around four acres. I have all these plans ready to go but each time, you just poo-poo everything." She stood up. "Everything Parson. The absolute only thing I had in this world that was really mine to claim was Gibby. And now he's gone. If I could, I'd kill you myself."

She stormed off in the direction of the house holding the photograph.

"You don't mean that."

Parson Manor stood by himself in the garden of plants and watched her slam the door shut.

40

Runy Drucker waited by his phone for a response after making a call to his handlers. Five days had passed, and he had heard nothing. When he made an inquiry, he was told everything was put on hold for more than a month. Drucker was edgy. He looked in on Parker who was still asleep and would not wake up until sometime in the afternoon after coming home just before 3 a.m. from the night club. Drucker let her fall into bed. A bad feeling permeated his mood, like death itself had marked him.

He had returned to his own home just a couple of times since he moved in with Parker. He retrieved some clothes and left. She didn't seem to mind, and Drucker spent the time laying out his grand jury testimony. He didn't want to reveal anything to her just yet. The delay in the grand jury probe signaled a problem to Drucker. The last time he was home, he wrote down things wearing on him about his role and working with Cain Stocker. In Drucker's notes, he put down concerns raised by the hackers who contacted him. Concerns there was some kind of relationship between Stocker and Parson Manor. He also wrote the mere mention of a relationship was troubling and maybe the case was being scuttled somehow, and how his very life might be in danger if Manor found out about his role in the investigation.

Drucker's moving about caused Renla Parker to come out of her heavy sleep, stretching and yawning. "Morning, baby. You must like being around ole Ren."

"Morning. I didn't mean to wake you up."

"It's okay. Sometimes I only need three hours of sleep."

"Want some breakfast? I can't cook but I can buy." Drucker searched around in his pocket for his car fob.

"Sure, that would be nice." She searched his face like she was going over the fine print in a mortgage. "You still don't look right. Something is really bothering you. And what gets me is you won't tell me about it."

"I can't get into it. Not just yet. It's something I gotta work out. And the less you know, the better."

"You sure? Renla can help." She walked over to him, letting her robe open and close in the process. "I've got an idea. Maybe I can convince you to come back and work with me. Notice I didn't say work *for* me. I mean, we could work something out. Make you a part owner."

"That's very generous. To be honest with you Ren, right now that sounds like a great idea."

"Comes with very few strings. I want you close to me and I mean close." She reached out and put her arms around his waist. "You come with me, be my co-manager. No bouncer. I just ask that the only fragrance you wear comes from my body, me, is that clear?"

"Sure. I'm clear."

"Don't make me angry again. This little body of mine can get New York tough."

"You're not in New York anymore."

"I know. I might be in Florida, but you get my scruff riled up and my bad side comes out. You don't want to see that."

Drucker leaned down and kissed her, long and hard. When he stretched back, he looked in the direction of his phone.

"You expecting a call from someone?"

"Naw. I just want to stay with you."

Parker closed up her robe and for the next twenty minutes, she detailed her vision of expanding the night club. Breakfast was a memory. She told Drucker about bringing in top name talent, renovating the dance floor. She showed him a sketch to resurface the bar top, and possibly blow out a wall and build a V.I.P. section. "I've been saving," she beamed. "I got some money to burn and time to make it happen. I don't have enough cash, but soon maybe."

"If you let me, maybe I can help with the build. I know a bit about construction."

"That would be great."

"Maybe it's time for me to move forward, like you said. You've given me some things to think about. I can see what you have planned. I have one big thing to do on my agenda and I think I'm all yours."

"Well, do this one big thing and join me, Runy."

"I think I'm gonna disappear from my other life. Start something with you."

After talking for two more hours, Drucker left the apartment, got in his car and headed home. A mile before reaching his place, Drucker stopped and parked in an empty lot. He found a storm drain and carefully, making sure no one was watching, Drucker dropped one, then a second burner down into the opening. He spoke to the dashboard when he got back into the car. "If they can't answer me, make delays, I'll drop off the grid."

Drucker got back into his home and started packing two suitcases. One suitcase for clothes, the second for important papers he wanted to bring with him. He bolted around the house like a man ready to do away with the past. No Parson Manor, no grand jury investigation, and no Miranda. He made phone calls to shut off the power and close down the cable. Letter drops, he left intact. "Let them find me," he said to the walls. He was so busy doing the last-minute things, he didn't notice the smallest amount of noise coming from the front door and the knob slowly being turned.

41

Drucker was head down deep into his closet looking for a bag when he stood up to take a short break. Drucker's world changed in the next second. He didn't feel the swipe toward his midsection until it was too late to move out of the way. Drucker jammed a hand to his side, then raised his hand to his face to find his fingers covered in blood. The attack was a surprise since the house was kept quiet, not even any music playing or the television on. He didn't see anyone and staggered out into the living room and looked for his gun, which was normally placed on the coffee table. The gun was missing.

He swung around, searching for the assailant and found nothing. In a snap movement, Drucker jerked his head, first left, then to the right checking for the person with the knife. He only saw the flash of the blade a millisecond before the next swipe ripped across his side, just inches above the first cut. His hand again slammed against his side, pushing on the dripping wounds. The person with the blade attacked then retreated each time.

"Who are you?" He yelled into the cavity of his house. "C'mon out and fight."

There was nothing. Drucker took his vision away from his focus on the attacker and inspected his injuries. Definitely something he could survive, the cuts looked like they would just need stiches. The pain of his body being sliced was intense and growing rapidly. The walk toward the living room was a jolt to his body and he winced in the movements. With no gun, he hunted for a letter opener also kept on the table. The sharp opener was not in the same place he left it, causing him to repeat the process of looking around for the person responsible. He whipped his gaze around checking for a weapon to protect himself. A sense of helplessness swept over him since he had just dumped the only two phones in his possession.

He tried to yell. "You're making a big mistake." The yell didn't last long since the pain took over and his last two words were going down in volume. All of his experience taught him to hold down on the wound, keep pressing until he could find a way to bind up the cuts.

"I meant this to take as long as possible." The voice came from somewhere in the house, a place Drucker couldn't place right away. The other man's words were a bit muffled like something was covering his lips, so he could not recognize the voice.

"What do you want?"

"I want you. What do you think?"

Drucker struggled to move in the direction of the voice, find out who was attacking him. "I am connected to some big people. You're making a big mistake."

"Take all the time you need to die. We got more to do to you. This is supposed to last a long time."

Drucker searched the room like a man positioning himself to fight rather than give in. He had knives in the kitchen drawers. Maybe something he could use as a weapon in the bedroom closet if he could make it there. Everything in Drucker's next few steps had to be calculated in measured quantities. Escape meant ways and means to protection. He scanned the room once, twice and a third time, taking in the distance to the door, how many steps to the kitchen knives, a possible wounded man's run to the bedroom where he started a few minutes earlier. The front door now was perhaps twenty feet away, far too long a jaunt to get away from the armed man. And what was still in the equation was whether a knife was the only thing to address. A gun might be there.

Drucker shook his head like a man who just tossed two perfectly good burner phones, a safety net to anyone on the quick call list. That option was gone. By keeping the pressure on his side, the bleeding was subsiding. Now would be the time to mount some sort of resistance and plan his own attack. He took three steps in the direction of the kitchen. When he got within four feet of the drawer, a shadow moved across the back hallway wall, coming in his direction. The shadow was quiet, stealth-like and only the sight of a man's image on the wall gave him away.

In the next few seconds Drucker made a dive for the drawer. Too late. The shadowy something turned from the hallway and showed all of himself. The man was wearing a thick mask covering his face and mouth which would cause some distortion in speaking. Tiny holes over the nose and lips allowed the uninvited guest to breathe.

"Runy Drucker you are a marked man."

Drucker jumped with all available strength toward the kitchen drawer. He got his hands on the handle and was about to pull the drawer open when the butt of a gun came across the right side of his head sending Drucker sprawling backward in a heap on the thick carpeted floor. From his new prone position Drucker saw the man was wearing thick socks over his shoes. The socks on carpet was a way to stay quiet.

Tendrils of pain shot through Runy Drucker from his head to his toes like water droplets dancing on a red-hot skillet. The gun butt was quickly followed with a series of three kicks to Drucker's face and neck. An attempt to get up was met with a fourth kick to the head.

"Stay down there. That's where you belong."

All the calculations and measured movements were gone and done. Drucker used his hands and arms to protect himself against more punts from the man with sockshoes. Once the barrage stopped, Drucker curled up into a fetal position and openly groaned from the pain. If he wasn't allowed to stand, unless there was something to use against the attacker, there was always the option of pleading for him to stop.

For Drucker, pleading for anything was not in his D.N.A. He opened his hips and moved across the floor with a right leg whip, putting all the power left in him to knock down the stranger. From there, he might be able to grab the weapon and reverse the attack. Drucker whipped his leg through the motion and with some difficulty, he stood up. The man lost his balance for a moment, then regained his upright posture of being the one in charge. Drucker was no longer facing a knife. A gun was pointed at his chest.

The shot tore into Drucker's upper left chest, knocking him back to the kitchen floor. He felt like his shoulder was on fire. An effort to get up now was becoming less of a choice.

The man stood over him, aiming the weapon down on Drucker's face, the barrel moved down into point-blank position.

Outside the home, on a perfect Florida day, with slight breezes and just a hint of noise coming from a quaint neighborhood, no one heard the distinct two pops and flashes inside the home near the curve in the cul-de-sac.

42

Parson Manor got into his Mercedes and drove to the security gate near the entrance to the development where Cain Stocker lived. He went up to the guard, told him he was a friend of Stocker and that he would wait in his car until Stocker came out to meet him and no, he did not want to drive into the complex.

Three times during the meetup with the guard, Manor asked him for the time, even though it was evident Manor was wearing an expensive watch. After getting the time, the guard called the Stocker residence. Four minutes later, Stocker drove out to the guard shack, pulled just outside the entry gate and looked around until he saw the Mercedes and, inside, Parson Manor.

For the next twenty-eight seconds, Manor just stared at Stocker. No conversation, just the long stare. When Manor was satisfied on the length of time, he pointed to his watch, put the car in drive and pulled out of the bricked driveway. He was gone.

~

Sana Bolton was one of the best detectives on the force, earning commendations seven times in her career for major crimes solved. The impressive resume was a reason she was hired by Cain Stocker. She left the police department and within two years was named the lead investigator for Stocker's statewide grand jury. Her day always started the same way, with the cup of coffee loaded with three sugars and just a tap of cinnamon. She hesitated before she made the phone call.

After four rings and with voicemail signaling her to talk, she reached out to her boss. "Cain, it's Sana. Sorry to bother you and hope your son is doing okay, but I need a phone call from you as soon as you can. Our asset is off the grid again. He moved from his last location, and we don't have an address. We can't get in touch."

That was all she was able to fit in the time allowed. Bolton wanted to say more. This wasn't the first time Runy Drucker went among the missing and he was not the best C.I. but he was, by far, the most effective. Since he was so close to the target, the discussion was to let him drop off the grid sometimes. Afterall, he was undercover. Her job now was to find him.

Bolton's day was spent going over other cases while Stocker was taking a few days off to be with his son. Everything seemed normal until the afternoon when her office got a call. There was a message called into the statewide hotline, a message specifically for her office. She was told something of value was placed on the door of a gas station. After more checking, the place indicated had been closed for a year. Since the station was not part of her jurisdiction, she contacted the police chief's office. They had an officer meet her at the location. Bolton looked around and if there were any surveillance cameras, they were disabled long ago.

She also dispatched a crime tech team from her own office. All of them met up, had a short discussion about what to do and before anything else happened, the crime techs got out cameras and started the process of taking photographs.

The envelope in question was stuck in between the doors. Graffiti was painted in one small section of the place. The glass doors themselves were coated with a heavy amount of dust. The station was left to the elements and the doors and the glass went unwashed.

The abandoned gas station was not close to any homes. In this area, the power lines were above ground and in two places, someone had thrown a pair of gym shoes up on the line. The grassy spots were filled with tall shafts of weeds. If needed, she could put in the paper and phone requests for any street surveillance video along the roads leading up to the empty gas station. The person or persons who put the envelope there must have known the right place to put something and leave behind few pieces of evidence. The techs could dust for prints, yet even that might not turn up anything valuable because the well-worn doors would have hundreds of partials.

Given the okay to move in, Bolton, wearing gloves, pulled the envelope out of the doors. She felt a small object was inside. More photographs were taken. The envelope was placed on a table set up by the techs. After they determined the packet was safe enough, Bolton was ready to look inside. The top of the small brown envelope was not glued shut. With all those assembled looking on, Bolton spilled out the contents of the bag onto the table.

One tech looked confused at first, then started a series of photographs. Bolton recognized the confusion on the part of those standing next to her, although Bolton knew exactly what it was and the person who wore the item.

She ripped off her gloves and reached for her phone. Bolton was shaking her head and getting ready to press the contact number for Cain Stocker. She knew all about the item since he always used to adjust the thing on his finger.

On the table was a jade ring.

43

Going on past conversations, Bolton recalled Drucker liked to change living locations more often than everyone else would change their password. Usually, she was given all the details of the move. Not this time. An hour after the envelope drop, a search of rental truck companies turned up the name of Runy Drucker. This company used trackers on all of their trucks and without needing a search warrant, Bolton was able to find his most recent home residence. The rental home was surrounded, the streets shut down and within a few minutes, they found Drucker's body.

Crime tape was stretched in front of the house. Bolton gave up the investigation to the local authorities and sat by in an unmarked. She tried four times and was not able to reach Cain Stocker. Bolton opened a laptop and started taking notes on everything that happened and what she was doing now.

Neighbors were out of their homes, looking and pointing, not knowing what was going on.

~

Claire Stanley was working on her third piece of gum. She stood up and yelled the name of Booker Johnson. He walked up to the desk with his notepad out. Stanley had some urgency in her voice like there was something major. "Looks like there's a homicide working. Need you and Coffee. I got Yang as a backup but she can only stay a bit 'cause she worked the morning shift.

Booker wrote down the address and moved toward the door. He expected Coffee to be waiting for him outside. While enroute, Stanley and others on the desk were sending out emails to everyone in the newsroom. A few scant details were emerging. Channel 27 started getting phone calls from residents about police units converging on the house. Those actions were followed by unmarked units and detectives wearing ties and carrying notebooks. Once Booker arrived, there were problems with the location. The suspected murder house was in a cul-de-sac and police had blocked off all access to the homes in the curve. Booker, Coffee and the other arriving news units were kept far away. He also saw uniformed officers going door-to-door, presumably looking for any witnesses and surveillance video.

All of the factors before him amounted to a problem getting any information until much later. The noon newscast had ended an hour earlier so Booker aimed for the 5 p.m. newscast unless the station wanted him to do a live cut-in. The cut-ins usually lasted a minute or less and could be inserted into programming any time the news director wanted to do so. For now, he was free to observe and gather information.

Coffee broke out the equipment, put up sticks, snapped the camera into the tripod head and started recording. Seven minutes later, everyone in the area, including police, heard the familiar whirr of helicopter blades. Channel 27 sent the chopper and the ground noise increased once it was overhead. Booker knew from many other scenes, the pilot always stayed back, not wanting to disturb any potential evidence on the ground. And by staying back, the general viewing distance was easily three blocks away or more. The camera on the helicopter would be able to zoom in and get video of the scene. Ten minutes later, the helicopter moved off and headed in the direction of the airport. Quiet returned to the area.

Three houses were near Booker and the reporters. The crews checked and no one had seen anything. And no, they did not know the person or persons who lived there. One person said on camera that he moved to the spot because of the quiet nature of the place, and the scene of police and investigators was out of the norm.

Booker stepped back and made more observations. He saw no indication of any children, no toys in the front yard, signaling to him the home was in an older community. The lack of any children meant no school buses coming down the road. The address was given to him when he left the station. Booker confirmed the address was correct and called back into the desk.

"It's Booker. I need you to check on this address. Find out what you can. Ownership, any past news stories we might have done here." He put the phone away and continued to watch. Crime techs in all-white outfits and booties walked in and out of the place. Booker knew once the initial victim was found and determined to be deceased, the long process of the investigation started and speed was not a factor. Here, the rule of slow and meticulous was followed. There would be hours before much happened.

Yang had arrived and was looking for some direction on what to do. Booker had an idea. He let Yang set up and she stayed in place. He turned to Coffee. "Pack up. Yang has us covered here. We're going to take a short trip."

"Okay."

Once Coffee had all the gear put away, she backed up the van slowly, not bringing a lot of attention to herself. "Where we going, Book?"

"The next block up and around."

"Got it."

While they were moving to another location, Booker got a call from the desk. "Booker you there?"

"Go."

"From what we can determine, your house is being used as a rental. I've done some checking, and some Internet searches show the place has been rented a few times in the past five years. No idea who is renting, but I think the owner is out-of-state."

"Okay, thanks. Anything else?"

"We haven't done any stories in that area in a long, long time. Really quiet."

"Thank you."

"Later."

Coffee left the cul-de-sac, drove to the very next block and turned left. More houses and no cul-de-sac. Coffee slowed down. "I know what you want." When both of them passed a house, they looked in between the locations until they were exactly in back of the house where the investigation was taking place.

"Here." Booker got out. He left Coffee in the car, walked up to the front door and knocked. Booker found the homeowner was a widowed woman who watched the news, including Channel 27. She knew who Booker was and, yes, it was fine with her if he walked to her back yard. Booker took one look and went back to the van to get Coffee. "Get your stuff."

Once Coffee was set up, they had a view all the other news crews did not. The camera was set up in the back yard. From there, they were able to see figures moving behind curtains. They were not able to see into the home, yet this was an angle where Booker could get video much different than the front side, and down the block.

Six or seven minutes later, two crime techs walked out into the back yard. They were looking at the sliding glass door and dusting for fingerprints. All the video they were getting was far better than the other location. Booker checked his watch and decided it was time to move back to the front of the house so Yang could go home.

He worked things out with the homeowner to come back if needed. They drove back to the front home location and took up the space being vacated by Yang and her photographer.

"Not much happened." Yang kept her eyes on the front door while she gave Booker a rundown. "A car pulled up and I swear I've seen that detective before. Someone who used to be here local but left for the statewide grand jury."

"Is she still around?"

"No, she left. See ya later, Booker."

All of the video captured by Yang was sent to the station. An editor there could always insert any of the video in the video package Booker would send in later.

Three camera crews remained in position, lenses aimed at the front door. Inquiries were made with the officers watching the scene and so far, no P.I.O. yet to provide information. The wait continued.

Booker was checking his phone for any new emails when Coffee whipped her camera around and was recording in the other direction. She waved hard and got Booker's attention. He turned around.

A woman, petite in size, was trying to close the door of a red and black Thunderbird, only to find she couldn't get the driver's side closed in two attempts. She slammed the door shut and started running down the street, arms pointing, bracelets jangling from her arm. She said something no one heard, then she began yelling. Booker could just make out the word she was saying was ruin or runny. No, it was possibly Runy. Booker wasn't sure about the spelling of the first name. She made a steady jaunt all the way to the first line of police officers who first caught her, then it was everything they could do to keep her from breaking through their grip and past the crime tape. Tears were streaming down her face and the name she kept repeating loudly in the once very quiet neighborhood echoed against the walls. She kept twisting and trying to angle her body yet she could not break free. Two more officers ran to the woman and stopped any forward movement. Unable to get to the house, she stopped and just stared at the house. Next came the barrage of questions for the officers. Questions they were not able to answer.

When Booker took full stock of the situation, he noticed one of her tall heels had snapped in the soft scrum with officers and she stood there, single shoe on and barefoot. They tried to calm her down, a move seemingly impossible to do. A female officer kept talking to her until the woman looked like she was the one now answering questions. The officer took down her name and she was moved to the large truck called out on major crime scenes. She stood under a tarp and looked like she was offered a chair but refused to sit down.

The entire time she was there, the woman never, not for one instant, took her eyes off the front of the house. A few times she pointed to the front door and continued to verbalize things Booker could not understand with all crews several yards away.

For now, no one knew who she was or her connection, just that clearly she knew someone in the house named Runy. Booker turned to Coffee. "I can get the desk to start a search on the name Runy or Rooney and this address, but I don't think we'll get much."

Coffee stopped recording and looked away from the camera eyepiece. "Has to be a girlfriend or wife, ex-wife."

"The other thing. Yang said she recognized the detective from the statewide grand jury."

"Yep. Now that I think about it, you probably remember her, too. What are you thinking?"

Booker wiped a thin line of sweat from his brow. "If she was here, the person in the house, whoever it is, was somehow connected to the detective. If the victim was an employee of the grand jury team, that detective would still be here."

"She could be monitoring everything from another location." Coffee again pressed her face up to the camera eyepiece and started recording more video of the woman.

Booker stepped back from Coffee and called Claire Stanley and gave her an update on the woman arriving, the name Runy or Rooney, and the possible connection to the statewide grand jury.

"Claire, how do you think that woman found out about this scene if we haven't been on the air yet?"

"Booker, we've been running video of that house for close to two hours now, teasing the story for the 5 p.m. Maybe she saw the video, recognized the house and drove there."

"Gotcha." Booker paused. "Gotta go. The medical examiner van just pulled up along with a P.I.O. Maybe now we'll get some facts."

44

Booker watched Brielle Jensen, P.I.O., drive to the house and an officer raised the yellow crime tape allowing her inside the perimeter. All the television crews knew Jensen wouldn't be walking their way immediately. She had to take a lot of notes, then filter out what she could say to the three crews waiting for some word on what happened.

The upset woman decided to sit down. She had removed her good shoe and was now barefoot talking with a detective. Jensen moved from one spot to another, careful to stay away from the few evidence markers in front of the house. The many times Coffee zoomed in, there were no shell casings. One marker was placed by a spot looking like a tire track. Another evidence marker was by a piece of clothing. From what Booker determined, most or all of the evidence was in the house.

The two people from the medical examiner's office got out and waited for instructions. A representative from the M.E. was there earlier, went inside and emerged twenty minutes later. Booker knew the order of things. The M.E. would check out the body, provide valuable details to detectives then leave. Once the M.E. cleared, the van would be called and the body removed. Jensen disappeared behind the back of the tech truck. The truck itself was massive and used for the base of operations for a major crime scene event. The fact the truck, or Crime Scene Response Unit, was here cemented for Booker the gravity of the situation.

He got a call back from the desk. A person on the assignment desk told him nothing came up in searches for the name and the location, and yes, they would keep trying. Booker took a moment and sent a text to Misha, saying he would be late, start dinner without him.

Seconds after Jensen arrived, photographers from the three stations started construction of the microphone podium. The field podium was built using a light stand with a device connected to the top. The device had slots and holes where microphones were placed. When Jensen was ready, she typically just walked to the podium.

Podium constructed, everyone went back to their respective camera and continued recording. The two from the M.E.'s office went inside the home, escorted by a detective. They walked a gurney to the door, then rolled the contraption inside the house. Booker had no idea on when the possible victim was attacked so the condition of the body was not known. There were no smells emanating from the door, like the many times when a body wasn't discovered for several days. In this case, Booker only estimated the event was recent.

Forty-seven minutes later, the body of the victim was removed. Coffee recorded and Booker took notes. By the look of the covered body, Booker believed it was a large man being rolled by gurney to the M.E. van. Within seconds, the gurney was slid into the van, the men got inside, and the TV crews got video of the vehicle leaving the cul-de-sac. The upset woman who arrived earlier was not outside. Booker guessed she was inside the crime truck.

Ten minutes after the M.E. left, Jensen checked notes and made her way in front of the make-shift podium. While the 5 p.m. newscast was still an hour away, everything Jensen had to say would be sent live to the Channel 27 website.

"Afternoon. I'm P.I.O. Detective Brielle Jensen. I won't be able to give you a lot of information, but I will tell you what I can, as we are in the early stage of this investigation. At approximately 11:29 a.m. our office received information of a possible deceased male at eleven-sixty-six Brockton Avenue. When officers arrived, they noticed the front door was open.

Inside, they found a male deceased. A homicide. As to the exact nature of the injuries, we are not disclosing that at this time. An autopsy will be done. Next of kin has not been notified so we will not be releasing a name on the victim. We are asking the public for any surveillance video or any information that could help us in this investigation. We will have another update when we are able."

She turned to go back toward the crime truck. Booker's question stopped her. "Is there anything the public needs to know? Is this someone who might have been targeted? Or is this a random thing?"

"We are concentrating all our investigative efforts in a lot of directions. We won't be saying right now if this was a targeted attack. I'll take one more question."

Another reporter asked, "Can you tell us anything about the victim?"

"Not yet." Jensen turned and left. Interview done, Coffee left the camera on the tripod. She had parked the van so while editing the story, there was a quick and direct view of her camera. Most neighbors had returned to their homes.

Booker had the story written in fifteen minutes, editing would take another twenty. Once the story was fed to the Channel 27 feed room, Booker prepared words he would use in front of a live audience.

Coffee said to him. "So, no question for Jensen on why someone was here from the statewide?"

"I'm keeping that in my hip pocket for now. Why let everyone know? When I get a bit more information, I'll put it out there."

With the station TV audio coming through his earpiece, Booker also heard from the producer. For now, all he had was a straight homicide report. Without any connection to other aspects, Booker stayed with just what facts he had. After the taped portion ran and he heard the outcue, Booker started talking again. He made the plea for information from the public and closed it off. "Booker Johnson, Channel 27 news."

He would repeat the process for the 6 p.m. newscast. A second, slightly different version was edited and sent to the feed room. He saw Jensen driving her car away as the night reporter arrived. The reporter would stay on the story for the 11.

In between the newscasts, the woman who arrived was eventually walked to her car by two officers, one of them gave reporters a hard stare as if saying stay away. She drove off in the nice car and was gone. Another item for Booker's hip pocket.

During the drive back to the station, Booker wrote and sent in a story for the website. He mapped out what he could do for a day-two news story. Tomorrow would be the second in the three-day story window. He thought about the statewide grand jury and all of his thoughts concentrated on the connection to the victim in the house on the cul-de-sac.

45

Once Booker was finished briefing the night assignment desk, he sent another text to Misha. He had one more thing on his plate before he headed home. The homicide unit worked out of a large complex some four miles from Channel 27. Booker chanced his move and drove to the parking lot and looked around. Three minutes into his search, he found the black and red Thunderbird. He waited in a well-lit area of the lot. Booker wanted to be in the light and in doing so, he made sure the surveillance cameras would let everyone know inside he was there.

He didn't have to wait long. The woman, wearing a pair of running shoes, walked out of the police station. She looked worn down and a bit frustrated. When she got close enough Booker waved his right hand and made sure she saw him.

"I'm Booker Johnson from Channel 27. I saw you at the scene today. I don't have a camera so I'm not pushing a microphone at you. I have a business card."

"Let me stop you right there." Her eyes seemed like they looked through Booker. Without the heels, her height diminished a bit. "I really can't say anything right now." Booker didn't say anything and waited for her to speak.

"We watch you all the time." She stifled a sniffle, looked down at the ground for just a second, then back up at Booker. "I should say we watched you on the news. He liked your work."

"If you were close to him, I'm sorry for your loss."

"He's a loss. No one knows him like I did. A big loss."

He again extended the card to her. "I know you're not ready to speak tonight. All my contact information is on the card. Cell phone, everything. If you change your mind and want to contact me, I'm ready to listen."

"Thanks."

"Can you say at this point, what was his name?"

"I can't. Not yet. They're still doing a bunch of stuff. A lot of things they can't tell me about. I think they're gonna have more to say tomorrow."

"Can I at least get your name?"

"Sure. It's Parker. Renla Parker. Everyone calls me Ren." She stepped off the yards to her car in a few seconds. Booker used his phone to write down notes.

By a phone call arrangement, Booker brought take-out dinner home with him, consisting of grilled salmon, asparagus and rolls. He also filled a request from Misha for shrimp cocktails. They shared the meal and discussed what each other did for the day. Booker listened to her list of exploits, then she asked him questions before he had a chance to talk about the murder.

"Book, you miss your brother, Demetrious?"

"Haven't talked to him in a while. He might be out here in a few weeks."

"I only saw him a few times. He looks like you."

"For now, he's out in California with my mother. He wants to get back here." Booker's thoughts rolled into the stack of memories of Demetrious. They shared the same mother but not the father. The father of Demetrious was a street hood thug who sold narcotics like they were groceries and once took over part of an apartment complex to run his operation. How that man met Booker's mother was a long, horrible story.

"What made you think of Demetrious?"

"I just know he really liked Florida."

"He's a good guy, thanks to my mom. His father, not so much."

"You were on that murder case today?"

"Not a lot of details. In fact, we had a lot less information than usual. Police are a bit hush-hush."

"What does that tell you?"

"The victim is someone right now they don't want to talk about. The question is why?" Booker forked the remaining portion of salmon on his plate. "You want any dessert?"

"Just you."

"You trying to make a black guy blush?"

"Yep." Her smile turned serious. "Do the murders wear you down?"

"You mean covering them? Not really. No one wants to see murder happen. My favorite stories to cover are always where a community comes forward to help someone. Murder. That's different." Booker got up and took away the dishes, headed for the sink. "The thing about murder stories is, first, is there still a threat out there that people should know about?" He started getting the plates ready to load into the dishwasher. "After that, maybe your reporting moves someone to come forward, call police, get the thing solved. And lastly, be there if the victim's family wants to talk."

Dishwasher loaded, Booker headed for the large screen television and a conversation on what they wanted to watch. "Thanks for letting me talk about my stories. Sometimes, when I talk about them, hash it over with you, it helps me organize what I need to do next."

46

By the time Booker sat down at his desk the next morning, police had emailed an update on the murder from the previous day. Renla Parker was wrong about one thing: police did not say much about the death.

The entire news release from Brielle Jensen was just a few lines:

In the death of a male discovered at 1166 Brockton Avenue, the name of the victim is Runy Drucker. We will issue another update when more information is available.

"Not a lot, is it?" Junice Coffee looked over Booker's shoulder and read off his computer screen.

"Almost nothing. They didn't list his age. I have to make a call. No cause of death. Was he shot, stabbed to death? What?"

Booker got a busy signal on the first dialup. He waited three minutes and tried again.

"Jensen."

"Morning Detective. Booker here."

"Trust me Booker, I know your voice. What's up?"

"Are you going to be releasing more on the death of Runy Drucker?"

"No."

"What about his age?" There was a short wait. Booker heard the shuffle of papers. When she came back on Booker was given a date-of-birth. "So that makes him forty-three. Was he shot?"

"That's part of the investigation."

"Have you taken anyone in for questioning?"

"We can't comment on that just yet."

Booker heard the sigh on the phone like Brielle Jensen was about done talking. "Okay. Are you planning a news conference time to give more details?"

"Not at this time. Take care, Booker."

"Thanks, Brielle."

Coffee was sipping from a cup. "That sounded like you got a ton of information."

"Can it, Coffee." Booker's next move was not going to be easy. Since he had almost nothing new, no one would be interested in a day-two story. No one. Booker had just one angle he would push. When he approached Stanley, she was in crunch mode, preparing the long list of stories to present during the pitch meeting. She never looked away from her computer except once to check the time. "Whatcha got, Booker? I saw the police release. Is that it?"

"For now. I have an angle, but it's a long shot and it might not turn up anything."

"Man, you're really doing a bad job of selling this Booker. I got some other things I could put you on. We could move on from the murder."

"Tell you what. Can I just make a few more phone calls?"

"Where will that get you? His girlfriend isn't talking, right? I don't see much of an advance."

"I think I can advance the story. Maybe."

"Booker Johnson, your pitch gets weaker the more you talk about it." She checked her watch again. Her fingers were digits of lightning, hitting the computer keyboard. "I got three minutes to get ready. You stay out of the meeting and make some calls. If the others hear you have zip, you'll move on."

"Got it."

"Just between us. Give me a hint on this angle?"

"Bolton was out at this crime scene yesterday."

"Bolton?" Stanley hit a button to send her story list to all concerned.

"Bolton is Sana Bolton. Lead investigator for the statewide grand jury. She didn't stay very long but she was there at the crime scene."

"What?" Stanley stopped all her movement. "And we don't have any possible connection yet, is that it?"

"Correct. This could be nothing or it could be a lead story. I just don't know right now."

Stanley put a fresh stick of gum in her mouth. She had that faraway look like she was going over all the places the story could lead. "And you want to see if this guy was connected to..."

"The grand jury. That's it. Maybe they won't say. I know police are pretty quiet. But there's something going on."

"Damn, Booker, you buried the lead again. Okay, make your calls. I won't say anything in the meeting, or they will expect that story for the noon."

"Thanks."

Booker went back to his desk and the group of reporters and producers moved into the conference room. Stanley settled them into a conversation of the list. Booker looked down his phone contact list for the spokesperson of the statewide grand jury. Unless there was an announcement of an indictment or a grand jury report, trying to get any information from a secret judicial body was going to be almost impossible. The spokesperson was a former reporter so Booker relied on her past life and hoped she would be receptive to his call.

The secretary to the spokesperson was as far as Booker got. No, the spokesperson was not available. No, there was nothing being released at this time. No, they were not accepting any questions from anyone. Goodbye.

Booker saw Coffee walk out the door, gearing up to work with another reporter. He took out his reporter pad and started marking up a profile of Runy Drucker. A Google search turned up nothing. Next, he checked the online court filings of cases. A Runy Drucker with the same name and age came up with one arrest for six counts of distribution and sale of controlled substances, Oxy and fentanyl. The more Booker checked, the more information on Drucker became scarce. There was no trial date and no reporting date. Reporting dates were set by the judge on when all parties would come back to court and update on where the case stood. For now, the case looked frozen.

Next, he looked up the arrest affidavit. The case was almost four years old. Booker printed out the one page of information and sent a copy to his email. The affidavit said Runy Drucker was arrested after an investigation at the Romantix Night Club. An undercover police officer made seven buys in and around the club, all through Drucker. An eighth buy was set up and Drucker was arrested during the money and drug exchange. Booker searched for more information after the affidavit was posted and found nothing. The case just looked frozen.

Booker tried one more thing. He checked into the website SunBiz and did a search on the Romantix Night Club. There was the usual info the site gave on any business, and when he came to the owner's name, Booker had to look twice. The ownership of the Romantix was Renla Parker.

Runy Drucker was arrested at her club.

47

Sana Bolton called an emergency meeting. Around the table were four people, all respected investigators now working in Bolton's office. More than eighty years of combined law enforcement experience. Stocker walked in and sat at the head of the table.

Stocker came in to listen. Bolton doled out the information. "He was shot up close twice. Initial word from the autopsy is Runy Drucker was cut twice on his left side, presumably as torture cuts. There are multiple abrasions on his side and head. Our C.I. was executed." Her eyes scanned more of the notes in front of her. "The question is what does this do to our case against Parson Manor?"

Stocker ended the several seconds of silence. "We're dead in the water. We almost have no case."

Bolton tapped her fingers hard on some paperwork. "We still have the tapes."

"You already know what I'm going to say." Stocker let his eyes roam over the group. "His lawyer will say in court that he doesn't have the ability to cross examine Drucker now that he is deceased. And without him in person to testify, the tapes can't come in. And the judge will agree with him."

More silence. Bolton made her plea. "We reinvent the wheel. Plan B. We bring in the F.B.I. and their experts to help us identify the persons recorded on that audio as being Parson Manor and Runy Drucker. You have me and our tech who can testify on what we heard. Every single word of it."

"Not good enough." Now Stocker was standing. "We're screwed. Plain and simple. No Drucker, no case."

For the next fifteen minutes, one by one, different ideas were tossed around on how the case might be revived. Stocker dismissed all of them.

Bolton jammed her hands against her head, pressing down the brown locks. "Three years of work can't just disappear. This guy needs to come off the street."

Stocker sat back down. "Any prosecutor will tell you we only get one bite at the apple. One. We have to find Drucker's killer. However, that part is not our investigation."

A secretary poked her head inside the room. She looked directly at Stocker. "Mr. Brewer is here to see you."

The meeting broke up with Stocker headed to his office. Percy Brewer was facing the window when Stocker walked in. Brewer was the Apton County, Florida prosecutor. He stood almost six-foot-four, with large ebony hands, now affixed firmly to his hips. The one-time college football player tore ACL's in both legs and turned his attention and studies toward a law degree. Now elected three straight terms, Brewer looked impatient. Brewer, who was Stocker's boss, directed his words toward the glass.

"Hope you don't mind me taking over your office." He turned and faced Stocker. Brewer still had the chest and arms of a linebacker. "Sit down."

Both men sat with Stocker looking uncomfortable sitting in the visitor's chair in his own office. "Cain, it was what, two weeks ago you came to me saying this case had to be pushed back?"

"Yes. Just about two."

"At the time I thought the move was justified. You said you needed more time. Go over witness statements. Recheck some of the recordings before the grand jury heard them. Then, last week, you wrote me saying another delay was needed. You remember all that?"

"I do. And I sent you a detailed brief outlining the reasons for the pushback."

"I don't have to tell you, this is a very big case. High profile. The kind of case that you have to bring to trial and win. Back a year ago, you promised me a win, that the case was the strongest you ever had."

"I remember. We had some problems."

Brewer pounded the table, his fist looked like a mallet, fingers moving across the desk mat, knocking over a delicate arrangement of carefully stacked gavels. "This, Cain, is a big, big problem."

"I know, sir. The case just needed more time and now we have this situation."

Brewer pulled gently on the size eighteen shirt collar and sat for a second as if to calm himself. "Our voters, the people we serve, we owe it to them to deliver guilty verdicts. Is there something you want to tell me Cain as to why this thing fell apart and our key witness goes off the grid then he's slaughtered on your watch?"

"I've been distracted, I won't lie. Been taking care of my son."

Brewer tried and failed to restack the six gavels in the same formation he found them, with one mahogany gavel rolling off the desk and landing on the carpet. He stared down Stocker like he had a witness on cross-examination.

"It all falls on me. Not my team. They were prepared. I messed up. I still feel we had to put things off. I got distracted and lost a good connection to the C.I. That shouldn't have happened."

"Where do we stand on the shooter?"

"He picked up the casings, left no prints as far as we're being told. There was some witness who thought they saw a beat up van in the area, but we have no plate numbers."

"This is really a messed-up situation which can only get worse if any of this is made public."

"We're keeping it tight."

Brewer got up, adjusted his tie and picked up the errant gavel off the floor. "We'll talk in a few days."

Cain Stocker moved around to his seat and put the gavels in the proper formation. Brewer walked down the hallway and before leaving, he looked back as though he was making sure he wasn't seen and walked into Sana Bolton's office, voice kept low. "Ya got a second?"

48

Booker's car rolled into the lot and he had his pick on where to park in the empty lot. Daytime meant almost no one was there for any festivities of the Romantix Night Club. Booker called first and Parker agreed to speak with him under one condition. Nothing on camera. Booker arrived alone.

The inside of the place was adorned in black. Walls, ceiling, the fixtures, all painted in the dark hues, making Booker feel like he had dropped into a disco time portal. There were long splashes of purple cut into the darkened box. And with no windows, Booker just hoped the few lights in the place were not suddenly turned off. Far off to the right, sitting at a desk facing the front door was Renla Parker. She had on reddish brown heels, matching outfit and fingernails painted the same color.

"Sit down, Mr. Johnson."

"Everybody calls me Booker."

"Okay. Booker. Have a seat."

There were two desk lights on the table. Up above him four rows of lights were pointed toward the dance floor. "Thanks for taking time to see me. Again, sorry about your friend."

"Runy? Yep, we go way back."

Booker imagined the place packed with people, sharp clothing, music blaring through a wall of speakers, sipping drinks and wearing out shoes on the dance floor. This was his first time in the place. He had to get used to a spot so large with no windows. Out of habit, he searched until he located the emergency exit doors.

Booker had a way of sizing up what people told him on and off camera. A B.S. meter that was very accurate. Over hundreds of stories, he had people who lied about age, marriages, city projects and, importantly, crimes committed. If needed, people would tell a lie quicker than reaching for another kernel of popcorn. The task for Booker was weeding through the verbiage and getting to the truth.

He cut right in. "Were you here the night he was busted for drugs?"

"Wow. You don't give a girl a chance, do you? No foreplay questions?"

"What was that, four years ago?"

"Four years, two months and six days. Yes, I remember it."

"What happened?"

"I always believed he was set up. At least that's what he told me. But I knew better. He would take off for a bit, reappear. It was a problem because he was my bouncer. I needed him on the door."

"What did you do?"

"I went against my own rules, and I set up cameras out there." She pointed a rusty colored fingernail toward the front door. "And I told him, baby you got to clean up your act. I'm watching."

"And did he?"

"No. Just peddled that crap in and out of a large car parked out there. He had everything goin' real rosy until the 5-O arrived." Her phone hummed with an incoming call, which she ignored. "Why are you here, Booker?"

"I think we both want the same thing. Who killed Runy Drucker and why?"

She rapped her nails softly on the table. "Shoot, I don't want to know why. Just who. I leave all that why crap to you reporter types."

"The last time you saw him, were things okay?"

"Police asked the same question. And no, things were not okay. He was bothered by his boss. I'm sure he was thinkin' someone was coming after him. Somethin' was goin' down."

"The something. He didn't say what?"

"The D-tectives asked me about that a hundred ways. I just don't know. He wasn't sleeping right. I almost got him to talk about it." She sat back, sinking into deep thought. Booker let her get collected. "What's your channel again?"

"Channel 27."

"Well, I can say a few things on camera, just not today. I need to think about it. Just 'tween us, he was seeing somebody else."

"Was he worried about that?"

"Let's just say he was worried about me. I told him I'd kill him if he didn't stop seeing her." For the first time she laughed. Hard. "The police had the same look on their faces like you have now, Mr. Booker."

"Just Booker. You threatened him?"

"A play threat. He was my Runy. I don't like a crowded room. I'm an only girl. Ain't no room for anyone else. Or else."

During the entire time Booker heard Parker tell him things, he felt she was saying the truth, rock solid. The information was valuable, yet without any confirmation from police, there wasn't much he could put on a television newscast.

"Renla, did police say exactly how he died?"

"They didn't want to at first. I think I scared them into thinking I was a suspect. Did a G-S something on my hands and everything."

"G-S-R. Gunshot residue."

"They saw how upset I was, and I got just a tiny—and I mean tiny—bit of information from them. My Runy was shot." Her eyes were covered over in a clear sheen, getting heavier until a tear formed in the corner of her left eye. She cleaned up the droplet with the soft swipe of a finger. "Runy got himself killed. I don't know why. I just want that person to get caught. And if I find them first." She picked up her purse two inches off the ground and let it drop back down. "I'll take care of it myself."

"Thanks for talking with me." Booker started to hand her another business card.

"I got one of those. I know how to find you, Mr. Booker."

"Booker."

"I came in here early 'cause staying at home was not working. I can feel Runy in the room. Had to get in here, do some bookwork."

"I'll be in touch."

In the parking lot, the red and black Thunderbird was parked in a designated spot. Booker knew in south Florida, Apton County, sometimes there were problems in and around the night clubs. He could not remember a single instance for a crew being at the Romantix. Maybe she ran a clean club, except for the night a bouncer took things too far and stepped over the line.

49

Four seconds after walking into the newsroom, Stanley cornered Booker. "Please tell me you got something."

"Not yet."

Over Booker's shoulder, two producers who put together the newscasts were up by the assignment desk. "What do you have working?"

Stanley looked across the room. "Take Dominguez, head to Crater Park. We've got a three-year-old missing. Walked off. We got a helicopter up, and a ground crew on the other side of the park."

"No problem." Booker checked his watch. An hour till sundown. He ran out the door and Dominguez was pulling up in the van.

"Afternoon, Book."

The drive to the park was fifteen minutes away. Booker found an email blasted to the entire newsroom, with details. The boy walked away from a birthday party, where more than thirty party-goers were celebrating for a nine-year-old. "Hope they're checking the water. That park has gators." Crater Park was known for its waterways connecting to the Everglades and nighttime meant prime hunting for alligators.

When they entered the park, the place was lit up with police lights. Volunteers worked in grid patterns, walking the four paths lining through the park. Booker and Dominguez took the east side of the park. Overhead, the loud whirring noise of two helicopters made talking difficult. The chopper noise sounded like they were inside a dishwasher. One chopper belonged to Channel 27, the other was a police helicopter.

Booker rolled his eyes left to right and back looking for any sign of the toddler. Dominguez was recording video and both of them were trying to stay out of the way of those searching. The search group was spread out, some of them calling out the name of Ricky. Another email from Stanley indicated the reporter on the west side of the park would do the live broadcasting. A few minutes later, a picture popped into Booker's email inbox. The child looked younger than three. His photo showed him hugging a plush tiger. Police issued an email of their own with precise details of the boy's height, weight and where he was last seen.

The sun was settling lower in the sky, with fingers of shadow creeping longer with the passing minutes. Back in the station, Booker guessed the police scanners were turned up a bit, and still no sign of the little one.

Dominguez turned back to Booker. "I think I see some movement. Check out something on your right."

Booker looked in that direction. A swarm of people were converging on a spot near three downed trees. Booker and Dominguez took off running toward them. Halfway there, Booker got in a quick phone call to the desk, letting them know they should move the helicopter.

Everyone, it seemed, in the entire park ran toward the mass of people gathering near the tree spot. Dominguez stopped and took up position, aiming his camera toward the general area. A police officer, carrying the child, was running toward a fire rescue truck. The tiny one looked half-asleep, arms dangling, head bobbing during the rush to the truck. A woman who looked like the possible mother was close behind them. After a short checkup in the rescue, the child was off to the hospital for a longer checkup, lights flashing, siren blaring.

Booker and Dominguez were able to get the video. The other crew was too far away. Thirty minutes later, Booker had interviews with relieved parents from the party. When he was done, Booker assisted and had all of the video set up for use by the other reporter.

Once the video handoff was done, they drove back to the station with Booker leaning back in the seat. By looking at websites, he checked the newscasts of the two competing news stations for any updates on the Drucker murder case. During the trip, Booker texted Misha, then concentrated on what he could do the next day. Without any new leads, the story would be stagnant. Police would be working hard, yet in Booker's case, he might be relegated to GA. General Assignment. And GA meant starting the day roaming the courthouse, then back on the street primed for the next lead story.

50

Miranda Manor had taped all the news stations she could regarding the death of Runy Drucker. She watched the coverage over and over, looking for any aspect on what happened. During the first day of news stories, the public didn't know Drucker was the victim. Miranda didn't start taping until the next day when the name was released.

When Parson entered the house, she started peppering him with questions. "Runy is dead? Parson, please tell me what you know."

"Not much. I haven't talked to him in a couple of days. After we shut the business down, we all kinda separated."

"C'mon Parson. He was close to you. Everything went through Runy."

"We don't have a lot of facts."

Miranda studied his face. "I saw the news. Somebody took him out. If he was executed that way, are we in danger?"

"Naw, we're safe. Runy just got mixed up in something. I don't know what he was doing."

"Is there a way you can find out? You always have a way of finding out everything."

"Why does it matter to you so much?"

She still kept a picture of Gibby in a pocket. "People keep disappearing around you. Your guy Pendon. Gone. My son Gibby. Now Runy. It's not right."

"He was my son, too."

She turned away from him for a moment like she didn't want him to see any tears forming. Miranda dabbed at her eyes and when she turned back, she was angry. "Aren't you doing something to find out who killed Runy? He would do anything for you."

"You're right. He did. Runy was a good man. The police are handling it. If they come to me, I'll cooperate and tell them what I can."

She moved through the house, moving in the direction of the back door.

"Where are you going?"

"Just to the garden."

"You spend a lot of time back there."

Miranda slipped on some sandals and reached for the back door. "I like it back there. Maybe someday you'll pay more attention to my plans for what I want to do. When I tell you, you just brush me off. I do have plans."

"You don't need to work anywhere. I provide for you. I can do or get anything you need. I just need you to be right here."

"Here doing what? I can't take care of my son anymore. There is no one I can talk to about anything. At least Runy listened to..."

"Listened to what?"

Before Manor had a chance to ask again, Miranda was out the door, heading down the brick paver path to the patio. Her walk was steady, and she did not look back. Halfway to the sun-protected chairs, she heard the hard stomps of Manor following her.

"Listened to what? You were talking with Runy? Where was I during all this listening?"

"Don't worry. You were around. We didn't talk much, thanks to you. But Runy knew I wanted to open a business. He was all for it."

"Is that right? And what else did he do for you?"

"It doesn't matter anymore, does it Parson? Runy is dead."

She sat down hard in the chair. Just like on many other occasions sitting in the same spot, she stared hard at the rear gate and the path leading to meetups with Runy. The conversations in the car and the couple of times she actually got to hold him, were memories. She kept her stare there, impervious to the one making a move in her direction. Manor ducked his head to move into the shade, even though he was short enough and didn't need to dip his head. "That's why you keep asking about Runy. Behind my back. And I didn't see it."

"What's dead is us. Everyone around me is dead. There's just you and me and that ain't much." She leaned back in the chair and stared away from him, focusing on the long rows of plants and the butterflies fluttering on milkweed plants. For the next minute, Parson continued to suggest things through a series of questions, only to have Miranda ignore each one. Her lack of body movement gave the impression she really didn't care about him anymore. Not the big house, the shiny collectable automobiles in the three-car garage. Nothing. Miranda kept her quiet composure as if nothing would stir her emotions.

After the long series of questions Manor stood with his arms folded tight. He stayed in the position and finally stepped off the concrete and back on dirt. His walk to the back door was quick, the steps long and fast. Just when he was about to turn the knob, he was surprised to look back and Miranda was right up in his face. He never heard her following him. She had a certain look of strength in her face, like nothing he could do would hurt her now.

"I just have one question." She looked into his eyes like a person yearning for the truth. "I made some checks. I called the office of Gibby's doctor, and I went there yesterday. Just call it curiosity. I went over the organ donation papers. All of them. Mostly they looked right and then for the last one I noticed something odd."

Parson turned the knob. Miranda stopped him. "Don't go in just yet. I have to know something. I checked those papers, Parson, and I looked at the signature."

There was an actual tremble in Manor's right hand. He again tried to turn the knob and an emboldened Miranda spoke up so he could hear loud and clear. "You know what, Parson? That wasn't my handwriting on that last page. Someone forged my signature."

He finally managed to turn the knob and walk into the house without answering her.

51

A nurse stood next to Camden Stocker, making sure he didn't lose his balance. He looked like a child taking his first steps. The nurse on the left looked down the long hospital hallway. "We've been through this before. Just getting the heart transplant is one step. Now, you've got to walk."

He had been through a lot. There was the series of blood tests, tests to make sure he was a match with the donor. A long operation. Camden was still in the hospital, doing more tests, making sure there were no complications with the new heart. And there would be even more tests done daily. Just like a toddler, Camden made tiny steps. He had graduated from the days of just standing and taking steps with an IV pole, all connected to tubes. Now, he was moving down the hallway with a rolling chair in case he got tired. "You're doing great," she urged.

"I think I can do two laps." Camden Stocker's proper tint had returned to his cheeks. The grip on the walker was stronger with each day. He was walking with a smile, talking to people in the hallway, showing a growing confidence. "When can I run?"

"Well, that's a big step. Why don't you save that question for the doctor?"

He kept moving with the roller chair.

Several yards behind him, leaning against the wall, was a beaming Lace

Stocker. Her face was locked in a smile nothing could break. The slow pace didn't seem to matter with her. She stood outside his hospital room waiting for him to return. Every step Camden made, even when he twitched with hesitancy walking, was an event.

He turned around and progressed down the hallway, followed closely by the nurse. She cheered his steps, matching his movements in case he needed help standing. Camden made his walk back into the room and settled into the bed. Lace pulled the nurse to the side.

"I know what the doctor said, but he looks okay to you?"

"He's doing great. You see how happy he is."

For the first time in days, Lace felt comfortable leaving him and getting some work done. She was now up to managing seventy rentals. Her inbox included two proposals to leave the management game and accept a position with a large apartment complex, one overlooking the Atlantic. She would run the entire place, a job offer with the enticement of a penthouse suite. There was another job request from a major hotel. She was given a ten-day window to accept, a window Lace demanded since all of her attention centered on Camden.

"He's come a long way," Lace said. "We got a miracle. And now look at him. I've never seen him so healthy looking."

"Yes, he's doing fine. We'll keep checking him and the tests, but I'll leave that to you and the doctor." She left, headed back to the nursing station.

Lace couldn't hold back and leaned down, kissing Camden on the forehead, then hugging him as best she could in the bed. She took up a seat. "Cam, I've been in this seat for so many days, my butt is carved into it."

"The nurse is really nice. I like her."

Lace went into her purse and pulled out a get-well card. "This is from Innocent. She wants to see you but the doctors say we have to wait just a bit longer." She handed him the card. Once he got the envelope open, the card read, "Hope You Are Doing Great." The word great had seven e's, making the word a long great.

"Tell her thank you."

"I will." She placed the card on the table next to four others.

"Is there space for one more in this room?" Cain Stocker entered and stood near the foot of the bed. "How's the Cam man doing?"

"Fine dad. Can't wait until I can leave."

"That might take a while."

"I know. I'm working hard. Mom saw me walking."

They shared conversations about school, boring TV programs, and the hospital food. After twenty minutes, Stocker let them know he had to get back to the office.

"I'll go with you downstairs." Lace left with him. "I'll be back in a minute." She threw Camden a kiss.

They walked out the lobby doors and into the bright sunlight. She pulled on his arm. "I have to ask."

Stocker looked up into the hot sun and guided her back under the shade of the hospital entrance. "Cain, I'd really like to thank someone. Any idea on the identity of the heart donor? This is a gift of life."

"We went over this. The donor is anonymous. We just don't know who it is."

"There must be some way to find out."

"Not if they don't want to come forward. Let's just be grateful we got the call. We got Cam down here right away, tests done. Operation was perfect. We really should be thanking the doctors."

In the years of their marriage Lace had grown to learn all aspects of her husband and his behavior. Any wife, after time, collected information about her spouse known only to her. She garnered enough about Cain, she might step into any game show and successfully answer probing intimate questions about him. Under the metal and brick canopy of the hospital, Lace stared into him hard like the probing look of a TSA agent.

"You're sure you don't know about the donor?"

Stocker stood rigid, his feet sealed to the walkway like he was facing a human lie detector. There was so much he could tell her. The foul deal, hatched by a criminal, insured the safety of Camden, yet the arrangement left Stocker getting up nights retching his guts. Guilty feelings poured into him without any warning, opening up holes in his own well-being. He stood there, as if mounting a battle within himself, and showed a practiced calm around Lace and Camden.

"I just simply don't know. Do we want to go there? Let's just help Camden get better."

Lace shifted her weight from foot to foot, and finally she gave herself balance like she was bracing to ask a tough question. "We thought Camden wouldn't be able to find a donor for a few years and now we get this gift. Tell me straight Cain, did you do something to speed this up?"

"Now how could I do that? You know I don't have that kind of power." Now the shifting was apparent in Stocker. He brought his hands up and folded his arms on his chest, only to drop them back by his side. His eyes moved from the entrance, down to the ground and back up to Lace.

"Lace can't this wait? I don't know what to tell you."

"I can read you, Cain. I just know something is off." She slapped the side of her leg. "You know I got the call the other day. The real call."

"Run for office?"

"If I'm going to do this, I have to get in my filing papers, get a staff, round up some people to start a phone bank. There's just an awful lot to do."

"That's good news. I'm happy for you."

"Really? The way this all went down, so sudden-like. I just kept thinking, what if something comes out?"

"Lace, please. Nothing is going to come out."

"I told them no, I wasn't going to run."

"Why?"

"Just a gut feeling thing. Saying no right now is, I feel, the best thing. I don't want to be that person who later thinks, I shouldn't have run for office."

In her nearly twenty years of marriage to Cain, they had only had a few arguments. The discussion into where to plant a bottle brush tree went on for more than a year, going from small talk to open shouts of disagreement. In the end, Lace won and the tree went where she first wanted. Like any marriage, there would be disputes and compromise. Lace questioning him like this was different. This just might be, if not already, a monumental change in their relationship. The talk under the canopy of a hospital seemed so calm yet a giant iceberg of a problem could be just below the surface.

People walked by them like they were interrupting an intense battle of words between husband and wife and they had no intention of getting in between them. When anyone passed, they took notice of Lace and Cain, then they stepped up their pace to move on.

"You're just acting different Cain. Can't put my finger on it but I wish you would tell me."

"There is nothing to tell, believe me."

Her eyes roamed over him, like she was hunting for any hints of being deceived. "Okay. I'll leave it alone for now. We'll talk again."

He walked off in the direction of his car. Lace watched him. A woman's gut instinct was always true and powerful. There was nothing on her face showing the impact of his words. Lace looked like she was not believing what she heard. She turned to go back to her son like a person empowered to find out more.

52

Booker stayed out of the pitch meeting and sat down in front of his computer, determined to find out all he could about Runy Drucker.

A photographer went by the house in the cul-de-sac and found a police officer was still assigned to watching the place. Red crime tape was over the door jamb. The photog also made another attempt and looked for any surveillance video. No one had any. Booker again went over all the paperwork about Drucker's arrests. He checked twice and still the police P.I.O. had not released any new information. There was an online check of bloggers and the newspaper only to find nothing was updated. Booker kept going, knowing any second Claire Stanley would walk over to him with a fresh assignment and take him away from the murder case.

"You don't give up, do ya, Book?" Junice Coffee sat on his desk.

"There's something there, I just can't prove it."

"And your thought is what?"

"The way his case just froze like that tells me Drucker might have been in the middle of something else, much bigger."

"He was flipped?"

"Maybe. If he had some good information on someone, he could use that to stay out of prison. I just can't locate anything."

Coffee had a satirical smirk on her face. "You can always come with me.

I've got the news conference on the items confiscated at the airport over the past year."

"You go right ahead. I'm sure they'll match you with a reporter for that."

Coffee slid off the desk, headed for the photographer's room for her camera and gear. The pitch meeting was breaking up and Booker knew his time for working on Drucker was about to end. Stanley actually walked past him and didn't say anything. He kept tapping the keyboard.

In his search, something seemed to bolster his thoughts on Drucker. He found Runy Drucker had moved several times in the past fifteen months or so. Different addresses in a short span of time added to his speculation. If he was connected to a case, Booker theorized that would be a reason so little information was being released.

He looked up any work history beyond Drucker's time with the Romantix Club. His efforts were failing him, and Booker was close to giving up for the moment and volunteering for a news story assignment.

Around him was the clatter of small talk and bits of laughter between reporters and producers. What people always saw was the one person in front of a camera. When Booker made public speeches, he always talked about the large group of people on the other side of the camera. The producers took giant amounts of information and turned them into logical, easy-to-understand stories for the various newscasts. The assignment desk folks all devoured rapidly moving facts and took action putting crews in the proper places. Hundreds of emails were sent to the desk from public relations firms. Each email had to be read carefully by every person on the desk. Emails from police, city officials, national and local were given a priority. In between the reading, were dozens of phone calls each hour. Reporters, producers and the desk, all working in a cohesive effort to tell a TV audience what was important and how it impacted their lives.

Once the room emptied, leaving just producers, the place got quiet like a library. The soft typing went on with some more scattered talking. The main direction now was writing news stories and fitting them into a newscast. Booker was the lone reporter in the room. Stanley didn't say a word and left him to continue searching. His no-story status made him the prime candidate for covering any breaking news.

Booker was about to start another online search when Jenny McComb, the person who worked the front lobby desk, walked into the newsroom. She was escorting a man dressed in a blue business suit, white shirt and sparkling gray tie. Booker looked back down at his keyboard. With the soft carpet, he didn't hear anyone approaching.

"Mr. Johnson."

"Please, Jenny, just call me Booker."

"Okay. This gentleman says he can only see you."

The man in the suit extended his hand and card. He was holding a brown briefcase. "My name is Kenneth Mackey. I'm an attorney, mainly handling living trusts and probate cases."

Booker stood up, shook his hand and took the card. "What can I do for you?" Booker looked at the card again. "Mackey."

"Maybe there's a place we can go and talk?"

"We're fine right here."

"Sure. I'm here because I am the attorney for Runy Drucker and I was instructed shortly before his death to speak with you."

"Me? For Runy Drucker?"

"Please, Mr. Johnson, er, Booker. Runy Drucker left me instructions in case he died. In this case, was murdered. He left me with clear directions to give you something. I urge you, we need to go somewhere we can talk."

53

Booker invited Claire Stanley to sit in on the meeting. Mackey was a thin man with brown complexion and short fingers. His shoes were shined to the max. Stanley sat down with a yellow legal pad, chewing gum at a slow pace.

"Again, I'm Kenneth Mackey and my client Runy Drucker was in fear of his life at the time of his death. I met and spoke with him by phone on several occasions but recently he came to me with his list of what he wanted done in case he wasn't here."

Mackey put the briefcase on the desk and snapped it open. "I have to admit I wasn't prepared for what he was about to tell me. First, let me give you this." He took out two pieces of paper. "You'll recognize this as a copy of Mr. Drucker's driver's license. And this one is his birth certificate." He pushed them forward so Stanley and Booker could examine them. "I will help in any way you need to insure the person I represent is, in fact, Runy Drucker."

Booker pushed them back. "I believe you."

He put them back into the briefcase. "Okay, here goes. For the past three years, Runy Drucker worked undercover for the statewide grand jury being run by Cain Stocker. Drucker did so after his arrest for narcotics distribution. He promised authorities at the time he had something big as he described it to them. Please know, Runy Drucker liked your work, Booker. He wasn't a fan, but he respected how you did things. Of course as a C.I. he had concerns about being found out. That's when he first contacted me. I kept his secret."

Mackey stopped for a moment and watched the two others in the room quickly writing down notes. "Now what I'm about to tell you is something you and your station will have to decide on what you do with the information. Drucker did both audio and videotapes for the investigative team from the grand jury. They were building a case of money laundering, extortion and murder."

Booker interrupted. "Murder. Do you know who the victim was?"

"No. That part was never given to me. Just that there was a specific discussion to murder someone."

Stanley asked, "You know when this murder would have taken place?"

"I just know recently. I don't have an exact date." Mackey pressed down his short hair. "Like I said, Drucker participated in dozens of secret tapings on a person named Parson Manor."

Booker wrote down the name Manor and underlined it three times.

Mackey continued. "All of the tapes, both video and audio are in the possession of the statewide grand jury. But what Drucker did not tell them is that he also recorded his own tapes. Five video and more than a hundred audio tapes."

Mackey reached into his briefcase and pulled out two thumb drives. He looked at his watch. "At exactly 11:10 a.m. I am handing you two thumb drives which contain all of the secret recordings made by my client, Mr. Runy Drucker." Mackey took out his own pad and wrote down the time and the two people in the conference room, Booker and Stanley. "Up until he was killed, Runy talked with me a lot. He really wanted his past case to be dropped. That was the agreement. Now he was looking at his drug case going on forever, maybe never being dropped by the prosecutor."

On the other side of the glass-walled conference room, people walked by with an obvious look of curiosity. For them, the conversation must have seemed serious since they all moved on. Booker was fighting off a multitude of questions, and centered attention on the massive job of reviewing so much information.

"In case you both are wondering, I have copies of my own. Please know at the end of the first drive I gave you is a video message from Mr. Drucker himself. He will say on the tape, which was made in my office, that he was concerned for his life when he noticed the grand jury proceedings were being slowed down and possibly stopped. He did not know why, but Mr. Manor in his own way is a powerful man. He owns an import-export business, but it's his secret dealings which are under investigation."

Booker put down his pen. "So with the death of Runy Drucker, then?"

"Most likely the case is also dead."

Stanley looked like she had a dozen questions. "But they still have the tapes."

"They have the tapes," Mackey responded, "but any defense attorney will tell you they have the right to cross-examine a key witness at trial. And if Drucker is not available to testify on cross-examination, the evidence that would go with that witness could be out. Maybe they can convince a judge otherwise, but probably not."

Stanley chewed hard on the gum. "Wow."

"I know." Mackey sat back. "There are a couple other things. You will most likely have to get with your station attorney on how to proceed. You will, of course, try to get a statement from Stocker's office and Mr. Manor. The decision for you both is what to do with the information and tapes I have given you. The decision on whether to air them rests with you, but Runy wanted this information to get out."

Booker picked up one of the drives. "I thank you for coming in. Along with the thumb drives, are you also prepared to go on camera?"

"Yes, I can do that." Mackey snapped the briefcase closed. "There is one other thing. There is a time limit. If Channel 27 does not air any video or any portion of this information I have given you, I am instructed by Mr. Drucker to offer his tapes to every news outlet in the county or even nationwide. You have exactly three days from the time I handed you the material." He sat, waiting for another question.

"You'll be available?" Booker was thinking in five different directions on what to do next.

"Over the next three days, I'll be available twenty-four-seven. Again,

Drucker wanted this information out. He worked hard to get Parson Manor arrested. It was his tip that got them going. Now, it's up to you."

Booker stepped toward the door. "One more thing. Does the statewide prosecutor know about these tapes?"

"No. The only ones who know these tapes exist are myself and now you two. That's it for now."

Booker said, "If I can ask, how did he get these to you?"

"Well, he kept all his recording gear and the drives in this wooden box in his house. Right out where anyone could find it. Days ago, he brought me the box. It's in my office."

It was Stanley who offered to escort him. "Again, thank you for coming in. I'll see you to the door." She tucked her pad under her arm and walked Mackey to the front door. When she returned, her jaws were in quick movement chewing the gum. Stanley got on the phone and made two phone calls. Then for fifteen minutes she went behind closed doors in a meeting with the news director and the executive producer. When she came out, she motioned to Booker to join her at her desk.

"Here's what we're going to do." She took her pad and drew down three lines. "We're going to split this up. Booker you will take the drive with the statement from Drucker. That one also has the five videotapes. You review them. When Merilee Yang gets here she will go through the audio tapes. I've got Sam Kinder coming in on his day off. You three will sift through all of this as soon as possible. Three days isn't giving us much time with all the stuff we just got."

"We need more people?" Booker asked.

"No, we've got too much other news to get on the air. You three just drop everything until this is done. As the drive is fed into our system, everybody will be able to pull it up on their computer. We also want the attorney on the air tonight. One portion of this can't wait."

"You mean the part about being a C.I.? And fearing for his life?"

"Yes. We're going to tease that we have all these tapes. Tonight will be part one, that this man, Runy Drucker, thought he was about to die. And that he's been working undercover for three years. For now, no mention of Parson Manor on air until we get it confirmed. The rest of this will take some time but we need that first part right away. And we need to call the prosecutor."

Booker said, "So, even though we're not naming Parson Manor, we still have to get him to respond. I will call him anyway even though he won't be mentioned in part one."

"Got it."

Booker went into a video edit booth and waited for an editor to start importing the video into the system. The first thing to come up for Booker was the message. "Ready?" the editor said.

"Go."

A homemade video appeared on the monitor and the face of a man who looked tired. "My name is Runy Drucker. For years now I have been cooperating with the statewide grand jury to investigate Parson Manor. If you are seeing this video, it's because I am dead. I am taping this as a backup to what I would have said on the witness stand. Manor had me laundering money, hired hackers to intimidate shop keepers in the business sector and steal private information and even ordered me to kill someone. On the tapes, if you hear me talking about conversions, that means a money laundering deal. I am sure Parson will deny all this, but the tapes don't lie. Please listen to them. No sympathy for me. It's my own thought that Cain Stocker, the prosecutor, made this case slow down. Yes, I deserve to be sentenced on the things I've done. But if I was murdered, please don't let this rest."

"Man, heavy stuff, Booker. Are we going to air this?" The editor and Booker made note of the next bit of video about to come up on the monitor.

"I'm going to do everything I can to make sure this gets on the air."

54

Three edit booths and three reporters going over audio tapes. Stanley walked past the booths checking periodically, checking on the progress while not interfering. Yang, Booker and Sam Kinder were out of the news mix, off-limits to being yanked out and sent on breaking news. After one hour, Stanley poked her head in Booker's edit bay. "Let's all go another twenty minutes at this, then we'll convene in the conference room and compare notes."

"No problem." Booker's task was the easiest since he was reviewing just the videos. The task was made somewhat tougher with all the videos going about forty minutes each. He made copious notes and marked down time stamps. Each reporter was also told to write a detailed memo to everyone involved. The note would list exactly what was being viewed. Stanley would produce a separate note and email for distribution throughout the newsroom.

The operative word was communication. No matter the story, crews, the desk, and producers all made sure information was shared. A missed piece of information, a press release not passed on, a phone call tip not going to the right person would mean a news story missed. The other equally key word in a newsroom was deadline. They only had so much time before the lights would be turned on in the studio.

When they got to the conference room, the aroma of pizza greeted them. Stanley nodded toward the pies. "I ordered out. Take a plate. We're going to be here awhile."

They sat down to eat a slice before the briefing. Booker took one quick second to text Misha he would not be home until late.

"Okay, who wants to go first?" Stanley put a half-eaten slice of sausage pizza on a paper plate.

Kinder wiped his mouth. "Well, at one point on the audio tapes, I guess this is Manor, he says 'How we doing on conversions.' Now, it probably means money laundering but it's not clear." Kinder was a three-time Emmy winner. He had a reputation for getting himself noted. Once, when he got a ticket for speeding, he told the officer he was under the limit and lost the argument. In court, acting as his own attorney, Kinder showed pictures and claimed there were no speed signs for almost two miles. It was his contention a storm must have removed them, that he was doing thirty miles per hour. The judge sided with Kinder.

Kinder ran his finger down the notepad. "Drucker responds 'seventeen new accounts.' What's hard is we're not clear on what conversions are?" Kinder wiped some crumbs off his paperwork. "At one point, looks like they want to send a warning to someone, doesn't say who, and Drucker tries to talk him out of it."

Stanley grabbed another slice. "And the response?"

"The response is 'Can't do it. Make him change his mind.'"

Stanley bit into the pepperoni. "Nice guy, this Manor."

Yang moved her notepad in front of her. "Not sure what happened on the threat but this guy they sent, looks here like it didn't go well. That this guy was a mess-up and like you said Drucker tries to stop Manor from doing this, but he says 'No, Runy. I want him gone.' And later, 'I want him dead. Is that clear? Dead.' That is a clear murder conspiracy." The words were helping the four draw up a picture of Parson Manor. Import-export dealer, developer, extortionist, murder conspirator. They were also crystalizing a profile of Runy Drucker, the man who was once dealing drugs and now on more than one occasion, tried to convince Manor to avoid taking a criminal turn. "I've got one more piece of video where, and this has to be a phone conversation taped in the car. I can hear street noise in the background. Drucker says 'I did what you said.' And Manor answers back, 'Good. Glad he's dead.'"

It was Booker's turn to talk. "I can clear up one thing. I watched the video of Drucker and, by the way, we can compare the video voice of Drucker to the audio tapes. But he says point blank, that when he talks about conversions that means money laundering."

Stanley was writing down what Booker said to the group. "That does help." She looked up and swept her gaze left to right. "A couple of things. Since we have this much, the boss wants us to contact Manor's attorney as soon as possible. Booker I'm putting you on that. The desk has been working on phone numbers and you should see all that info in your emails. Second, we've been in touch with the station attorney." Stanley let out a deep sigh. "He warns us this could all end up in court. If their attorney wants to fight this and try and stop us from airing this on television, then this might take a while."

Booker was shaking his head. "If this goes to court anytime soon, we lose our exclusivity. Everyone would get the lead on what we're doing."

"True," Stanley said. "But for now, they don't have the tapes. They don't have the videos. It would, I think, just stay with us. But that's if this goes to a courtroom."

Booker the reporter tried to be Booker the lawyer. "These are materials that did not come from the statewide grand jury. This is information coming directly from someone who did his own recording and gave us the material. To me, there's a difference."

"Good point, but we'll see. Tonight, the boss wants us to air the video statement from Drucker and comments from his attorney. No audio tapes just yet. We can tease them, that we have tapes, but these tapes have to be checked out before anything goes on television." Stanley got up from the table. "And that will give all parties a chance to respond." She wasn't finished. "Yang and Kinder go back to listening. Booker, call Manor. You know what to do. Or his attorney."

"On it." Booker raised his hand. "One other thing. And yes, this is delicate. Drucker, on the tape, is alleging the prosecutor, Cain Stocker, committed possible misconduct. I don't know what he's talking about exactly, but I think we have to call the statewide grand jury folks and get them on the record."

"Go ahead Booker and do that, but call Manor first. Also, they want you to stay for the eleven."

The four left the conference room. Booker got to his desk and pulled up the phone contacts for Parson Manor's business. He also had the name and number of the attorney.

Booker called the listing for the import-export business and got a message to leave a voicemail. He got the same response from Manor's attorney's office. Booker left voicemail messages for both of them saying he really needed to reach them for comment on a story that was about to air that night. He then called a second number the desk found for Manor.

"Who is this?" The woman asked.

"This is Booker Johnson from Channel 27 news. It's very important I reach Parson Manor. Is he there?"

"I'm his wife. What kind of story?"

"I'd really like to speak with Parson Manor if I could. It's very important."

"He's not here right now."

"Tell him it's regarding Runy Drucker."

"Runy?"

"Yes. When do you think Mr. Manor will be home? Or can you give me his cell phone number?"

"I can reach him. You say this is going to be on TV tonight?"

"Yes. 6 p.m. I can't stress enough that we'd like for him to contact us."

"It's terrible about Runy. I'll call right away."

"Thank you."

Booker noted the time. Less than two hours before airtime. He needed to make more calls, interview Drucker's attorney when he returned, write and edit the story. Two hours would go by fast when a deadline was approaching. Again, he called Manor's attorney, Scott Loson. After speaking with two desk assistants and a four-minute wait, Loson answered. "What is this in reference to?"

"We have a story we're airing tonight regarding Runy Drucker and his death. The story also involves Mr. Parson Manor. We would really like to speak with him before our story goes on the air tonight."

"Do you want to submit questions in advance?"

"Mr. Loson, we want to speak with Manor, if we could, on camera, on the record."

"I will try and reach him, but we would really like to know more about what you're going to say."

"I can do all of that if we can meet. Is that possible?"

"Let me get back in touch with you."

"Okay. I'll give you the number to the assignment desk. They will reach me right away. Thanks for your time."

Next, Booker dialed the number for Cain Stocker's office. He was able to reach the media contact for the statewide grand jury and left his name and number. When he was finished with the call, Drucker's attorney was back. Coffee had her camera and sticks set up in the conference room. Booker walked in and taped a fourteen-minute interview, going over a wide range of subjects, including the recorded videos and tapes. The attorney described sitting down with Drucker and letting him do a play-by-play narration of the tapes for the attorney so he was clear on what he was hearing.

Once the interview was over, Booker decided to write his story, then contact everyone all over again, one by one. He planned to keep contacting them right up until seconds before he went on the air at 6 p.m.

55

Booker sat down at the computer and began writing. He went short on the words he would say in the edited story with the intention of letting Drucker's death statement remain the meat of the story. When he finished writing, no one had called him back. Another round of phone calls would be needed.

He started with Manor and his attorney. No one picked up and he again left voicemail messages. The media contact for the grand jury called back and needed clarification on what would be on TV. And again, Booker explained he needed to speak with Cain Stocker. Conversation over.

Next, Booker spent time showing his script to the executive producer. The process took fifteen minutes. Script okayed, he went into the edit booth. Booker leaned into a microphone and recorded his voice. The script was already in the hands of Coffee, and she proceeded to match words with video of the murder scene.

While she edited the story, Booker sat by the phone waiting for a response. From anyone. Less than one hour till airtime.

The first phone call returned was made by Scott Loson. "I understand you have something we need to see. Can you explain more?"

"I can meet you right after the 6 p.m. newscast. I can meet with you anywhere you like. Can Parson Manor be there as well?"

"I can't assure you of anything until we know more."

"If I don't hear from you, please watch the 6 p.m. newscast. Thank you."

Channel 27 management decided not to put on any tease information about Booker's story. Booker sat in and watched the finished and edited story. "Looks good, Coffee. Thanks. I hear you're planning to work tonight?"

"Wouldn't miss it."

"See you later."

Booker made last minute checks on his shirt and tie, standing in front of the mirror in the talent dressing room. He walked into the freezing cold studio. What viewers never knew by watching, television studios were always kept cold to offset the warmth of the intense bright lights. Booker sat down behind the anchor desk, clipped on his microphone and waited for his cue to speak.

"Good evening. Tonight Channel 27 begins with a break in a case we reported on, the murder on the cul-de-sac. We were given the victim's name and now Booker Johnson has exclusive details about that death. Booker?"

"Thank you. Runy Drucker was murdered. Police released his name, however, we really didn't know much about what led up to that murder. Tonight, Channel 27 has learned Runy Drucker was a confidential informant, working for the statewide grand jury. And from his attorney, we've learned Drucker was set to testify in a case going back three years. What we're about to show you is a statement made by Drucker and given to his attorney who says Drucker feared he would be killed. You will hear what Drucker himself had to say. Please know, Drucker also mentions the name of the person under investigation. Channel 27 will not name that person in this broadcast. For now, the name will be removed from the statement as we are getting responses from all parties involved."

Booker's edited story was aired to the people of south Florida. They heard and saw Drucker explain his role in the investigation, a confidential informant, and making recordings. When the tape was over, Booker picked up live in the studio.

"We have a lot of information that we are going through, and we plan to air a lot more tonight and in the coming days. We have tried several times for comment, and we are still waiting to hear from the statewide jury spokesman. Booker Johnson, Channel 27 news."

By the time Booker unclipped his microphone, the newscast had moved on to other subjects. He walked back into the newsroom to await a possible onslaught of phone calls.

Miranda Manor watched the newscast and when she saw Drucker's face and heard his words, she started punching the large couch pillow next to her. "Why didn't he tell me?" she whispered to herself. She called Manor for the tenth time. This time he answered.

"You hear this about Runy? Did you know?"

"I honestly didn't know anything. I didn't even suspect anything, Miranda. How could he do that to me?"

"That's what you meant about your attorney and something legal you were worried about?"

"Yeah, my guy has been trying to keep me updated."

"Parson. They didn't mention you by name, but he was investigating you, wasn't he?"

"Yes, it was me."

"Parson, answer me honestly. Did you kill Runy?"

"Me? No. I had nothing to do with it. I will tell you soon where I was. Anyone could have killed him. A guy like Runy probably had a lot of enemies."

Miranda Manor listened to her husband, listened to the intonations in his voice, matched the wording with other times when he lied directly to her. "Are you coming home?"

"I hate to tell you this. I have to make myself unavailable for a while."

"Even from your wife?"

"It won't be long. I need to just make myself scarce. I'll contact you soon and we're gonna make a new home, I promise."

"One more thing before you make yourself scarce. What happened to Gibby and the organ donations?"

"What do you mean? There's nothing wrong."

"I bent some arms, especially on the signed forms. I know what you did, Parson."

"You don't know what you're talking about. I have to go."

He hung up.

Parson Manor leaned up against his parked Mercedes and continued to wait. Cain Stocker drove up in his car, lowered the window and did not get out.

"Parson, this is the last time we're meeting like this."

"Don't worry. Way ahead of you. I just wanted you to know I didn't kill Runy Drucker, and I have an alibi."

"There's a lot you have to account for."

"Me. Mr. Prosecutor, the maker of the so-called brick wall around defendants. You have a lot yourself. The moment Runy was killed I have the best alibi ever. I was with you, Mr. Stocker."

"You drove up outside the guard gate."

"That was me. Timing is everything. Have the police bring me in if you want. I'll gladly tell them exactly where I was when he was killed. Standing next to you." Manor let out a taunting, shrill laugh. He opened the door to the car and got inside. When the car took off, spitting dirt and rocks, the haunting laugh stayed in the air.

56

In the comfort of the beat-down ramshackle van, the figure had the satellite phone pressed up against his ear. He had a dirt smeared piece of paper on the console where he was writing down information. On the paper, he had the name Booker Johnson, an address for the apartment and exact location of Channel 27.

"Got it. So, he won't be there. Go for the other one. Okay." He put the phone down and drove to the spot where Booker Johnson lived, scoped out the exact apartment and went back to the van. Eleven minutes into the stalk, he saw movement on the second floor. Four minutes later, Misha Falone walked out the front door and got into her car.

"Gotcha," the figure said. He took out his camera and snapped four or five good photographs. Through the dust-caked and cracked windshield, he put his van in drive and followed the yellow Toyota. The female driver went two blocks north, then three more blocks east until she entered the parking lot of a restaurant. Again, the figure waited. When she went into the restaurant, he checked his camera and retrieved what he needed. The figure smiled. She was in the place almost twenty minutes. He glanced back and, like other times, checked over the display of weapons and knives at his disposal. No matter what happened, he was ready for her.

She came out and stood by her car, opening the bag like she was checking to make sure the order was correct. He snapped off seven more photographs.

"Perfect," the figure said to the dirty windshield. He reached down and picked up his 9mm handgun and aimed directly at the woman. His lips were cracked from dryness and he had to keep running his tongue over them. The piss jar rolling around in the back was half-full. The gray van was parked yards away from a tall royal palm tree. He pointed the gun toward Falone. A practice aim. The figure made adjustments to the aim like he was lining up angles, taking the aim down for the height of the target. For the next minute, he aimed, took down the weapon, then snapped the pistol back up and into a firing position. He looked down at the paperwork and stared at the last line telling him to wait until he got the signal. The woman got into her car and drove off. The van followed.

NEWHALL, the night assignment editor spotted the message first. He stood up from his computer, looked around the newsroom and finally saw Stanley. He waved her over to his desk. When she got to him, he pointed to the computer screen.

"What is it?" She stared at the monitor. "Oh, my gosh." She looked around. "Booker! Come up here."

Booker was about to grab his sport coat, then put it down and went to Stanley. She pointed to the computer screen. Now, six others in the room were pointing at their monitors after getting the same message. "This just came into our general email feed. Anyone know who this is?"

On the screen was a woman's face standing next to her car. And below her were the words in big red letters: DON'T AIR ANYTHING OR SHE DIES

"That's my girlfriend, Misha." Booker was dialing her cell number while Stanley called the police. Newhall went to the news director's office. When he came out of the office, Newhall went to the front lobby desk and informed them of a threat outside the building and to watch for anything in the parking lot.

There was frustration in Booker's voice. "I can't reach her. Tried her phone six times."

Newhall offered, "Maybe let's wait a couple of minutes and try again." Stanley was finished speaking with police. "They're sending a unit here." She called out to Newhall. "Any word from the prosecutor's office on our story?"

"No," Newhall replied.

"Manor's lawyer?"

"No."

Booker stood near the assignment desk, staring down at his phone. Stanley grabbed his arm. "I'm sure she'll turn up."

"I recognize where she was, that's a restaurant we go to all the time. Someone is following her." He sent a text for the seventh time. "She has left her phone at home before. Maybe that's why I can't reach her." He called the restaurant and found she had already left.

Stanley waited until she had Booker's full attention. "Look. Someone is obviously trying to get us to shut down and not air anything tonight. This very well could be a life or death situation. The decision is yours, Booker. We can stop it and put something out that we're not going to air another story. What do you want to do?"

"I'm going to put some faith in the police. I know Misha would not want me to give in to a threat. For now, let's move forward."

"Okay. We can change that anytime you want. Just give me the word. What do you plan to do?"

Twenty minutes passed. Booker remained in-house and worked on a new version of the story, one for the 11 p.m. newscast. Police arrived and Stanley assured them they did not need to stay. Booker gave them all the details he could about Misha and tried to concentrate. All he thought about were ways to contact her or where she might be now. In the newest story, Booker used Drucker's videotaped message again.

A woman entered the newsroom. When she walked among the desks, all heads turned. She was Allison Stewart, the general manager of Channel 27. Everyone's checks were signed by her. She walked directly to Booker Johnson who was working at his computer.

"I'm staying here tonight and I'm not leaving until I hear your girlfriend is okay."

"Thank you, Allison."

"I know what Claire told you, but I want to also say it. There is nothing more important than the people in your life. This threat against you threatens all of us. If you want to stop the story tonight, no one will say anything. I want your friend to be safe."

"I appreciate it. But if we give in to threats, I don't want to be a party to that and I know Misha wouldn't either. I'm trusting everything will turn out fine and I want to go on the air and do this story."

"Okay. Carry on." Stewart left, headed back to the elevator. Booker looked at the clock. Ninety minutes till news time. Still no word about Misha. He went into the edit bay and watched Coffee's edited version. Booker flashed a thumbs up.

THE VAN FOLLOWED the Toyota down busy I-95 Expressway until the car turned off and went east. The van followed. The smaller car pulled into a large lot and the woman in the driver's seat handed the meal to the security guard.

The figure parked out on the street, staying back from the surveillance cameras. He stopped and pulled his 9mm, taking another aim. The figure could take the shot and explain later there was no need to wait for a go signal to shoot. The woman was quick and she turned around and went back to the main road, turning left toward I-95. The van did the same and went after her.

The security guard left his post and brought the food into the lobby. A front desk assistant carried the food bag and handed it to Booker.

"Where did this come from?"

"Some woman brought it for you. Said you'd be working late."

"This woman?" Booker showed her the email photo.

"Yes, that's her."

"Well, is she still here?" There was excitement in Booker's voice.

"No. She left."

"Left? How could you let her leave?" Booker was shouting now. "She's in trouble."

Stanley stepped in. "Booker, they didn't know. If she got to here, maybe she's headed home. Safe."

"And maybe she could be dead by now."

"Concentrate. What do you want to do?"

"Okay, okay. I'll make another round of late calls for a response."

"Okay." Stanley looked sullen. "Booker, part of this is my fault. I sent the police away to help look for your friend. It was just the guard out there. He didn't know."

"It's nobody's fault. We'll find her."

Booker's eyes worked the room and the clock. There wasn't much time left until he went on air. Stanley must have sensed something and walked a quick pace over to Booker. The words poured out of him before she reached him.

"I can't just sit here and do nothing. I've got some time. I'm going to look for her."

Stanley pointed to the other side of the room. "If you don't make it back, Kinder will do the live stuff. Go find her."

Booker patted his pocket to make sure the cell phone was not on his desk and ran to his car.

57

Booker first drove toward his apartment. Even though she never answered all the previous times, he continued to call her. Nothing. There was a neighbor on his floor and Booker called him.

"Hi Steve. You got a sec?"

"Go ahead Booker. What do you need?"

"Could you knock on my door. Maybe a few times. See if my girlfriend Misha is there? If she is, tell her to please call me."

"You got it."

Steve kept his cell phone on. Booker heard the unclicking of a locked door, the steps in the hallway and the four hard knocks on the door four down. "Misha, this is your neighbor Steve. Booker is checking on you. Are you there?"

Booker heard him knock six more times and got no response. "Sorry. I don't think she's there."

"Thanks."

Booker was driving fifteen miles over the speed limit. He arrived just outside the apartment complex and looked upward toward his kitchen window facing the street. The place was dark. He sat in the car, watching approaching cars, watching people walk by and his watch. A deadline was near, and he wasn't in the studio. All of the possibilities of where she could be flashed through him. He mentally tracked her movements as best he could and retracked them again. He drove off, torn between staying and heading back to the station. Booker called Stanley. "I'm headed back. As soon as I'm off the air, I'll go back out and look for her."

"No problem. We'll be ready for you when you get here."

Booker drove off, his car pointed for Channel 27. Just when his car turned the corner, Falone's turned onto the street. The two just missed each other.

Misha Falone parked her car, got out and checked her watch. She stood there, seemingly enjoying the night breeze outside the apartment complex. She reached in for her purse and slipped the strap over her shoulder. The street was quiet, no one around, no traffic. That's when she saw him.

The man, wearing a mask, was standing twenty feet from her, hands holding the gun and the aim was directly at her midsection.

"Don't move," the figure said. "Your boyfriend didn't do what he was told and now you have to die."

Misha looked around, her eyes darting from the apartment complex doors, the street and the space in between her parked car and the Audi in front of her as if she should run for safety.

"Don't think about moving. I'm giving you a wound shot first, then I'll put you down." His words were somewhat muffled coming through the face covering.

"You don't have to do this. Here, let me call him." Misha jammed her hand down into her purse and could not find the cell phone.

The figure was yelling. "Stop moving. You move again and I start firing. Take your hands out where I can see 'em."

In a slow and deliberate movement, Misha pulled back and lowered her hand to her side. "I don't know what you're—"

"Stop talking!" He took three steps closer to her, gun now pointed to her head. "All of this could have been avoided." Misha's eyes widened, a sign that if she was going to do something, this was the moment. She turned sideways like she was trying to make herself a smaller, moving target.

He took a final aim.

The shot tore into a shoulder and blood spurted in a spray. The sound of the blast echoed hard against the walls nearby. A few lights were turned on. Blood streamed across the sidewalk and turned the concrete crimson. A loud groan was heard, brought on by the hole in the flesh.

Misha Falone stood there not knowing what to do.

A woman ran past Falone's right, moving toward the gunman. "You okay?" The question came from Renla Parker. She kicked the gun away from the figure on the ground.

"Thank you." Misha appeared emotionally drained and sank to the sidewalk in a heap. Parker walked to her, lifting up Misha while keeping her Glock 19 aimed at the man's head. "I'm here. You're safe. Now, here take my phone and call the police."

Renla handed Misha the phone. Before she tapped numbers, she asked, "Who are you?" Misha kept staring at her, then the person bleeding on the ground. "I've never seen this man before."

Parker went back to him. "Don't move or you'll get bullet number two." She pulled the mask off his face. Parker looked startled. "My, my. Well, I've seen him before. This piece of crap is Marcus Pendon."

"Who?" Falone was dialing.

Pendon pressed his hand into the gunshot wound. Parker said, "The word on the street was you're supposed to be dead."

"Dead?" In the excitement, Falone almost dropped the cell phone.

Parker kept a sharp aim on him. "Yep, that's Pendon alright. My Runy brought him to the club many times. I know this guy. And he's still driving that piece-a-crap van."

Police sirens were heard in the background, the sounds were moving closer to them. "He was supposedly a friend of Runy, but I'm guessing you're the one who killed my Runy, aren't you."

Misha held on to the phone. "How did you find me?"

"I was headed to Channel 27 to see Booker Johnson about the video with Runy talking. I had some questions."

"Booker is my boyfriend."

"Your boyfriend? Okay, now I get it. Turd face here was probably threatening your Booker by using you. I saw you delivering food and this guy was following you. I knew he was up to something so I followed both of you here. He was so focused on you, he didn't see me sneaking up on his left."

"Thank you."

"No problem." She leaned down to Pendon. "Keep pressing on that shoulder. I coulda shot you in the head. Now listen, I got two minutes before police get here. You tell them everything you know and I mean everything. If you don't, I swear I will get to you in prison, or out, I don't care. You got that?"

Parker turned to Misha. "I'm putting my gun down and when they get here, I'm gonna raise my hands in the air. You just tell them the truth."

"You saved my life."

"Just the truth. They'll figure it out."

Four police cars pulled up, sirens blaring.

BOOKER STARED AT THE CLOCK. Twenty minutes until airtime. Then he got the phone call. When he was off the phone, he clapped his hands. "Just talked to Misha. She's safe. Someone was there at the right moment."

The speed of Stanley's gum chewing picked up. "I got two night reporters headed there right now. They'll have a sidebar piece to yours. We just got word. The prosecutor's office confirmed, Runy Drucker was working for them undercover. They will have a news conference tomorrow. You ready?"

"Let's do it."

Seconds after 11 p.m. after an intro by the anchors, Booker sat on set and talked to an unmanned studio camera.

"Channel 27 is taking you inside an investigation and the murder of Runy Drucker who was working undercover, according to his attorney. Drucker, we're told by those who knew him, was shot to death. Here is Drucker in his own words."

The videotaped and edited story ran three minutes and fourteen seconds. Extremely long for a local TV newscast. In the 11 p.m. version, Booker again used Drucker's statement. On set, Booker wrapped up his story.

"Channel 27 is going through audio tapes we are told were made by Drucker himself while working undercover. There is more to come tomorrow. And we will also hear from the statewide prosecutor.

Booker Johnson, Channel 27 news." There was no mention of Parson Manor.

Booker left the studio, entered the newsroom, went to his desk and sat down, exhausted. He watched the reports from the field on the shooting just outside his own apartment complex. He watched video of Misha standing and talking with police. More video of a man being transported to the hospital. And Renla Parker in the back of a police cruiser.

"Nice job, Booker." Stanley tossed the spent gum into the wastebasket.

"Who was this guy trying to hurt Misha?"

"From what the P.I.O. told us, the guy's name is Marcus Pendon. And that he worked for Parson Manor."

"Any word on where Manor is now?"

"We hear they are looking for him."

"And no word from Manor's attorney?"

"No. But we're getting tons of calls from all over. The network took your story, four wire services called. I gave them permission to use the link to the website stories. Are you up for tomorrow?"

"I'll be in early. I'm getting her away from everything. Staying at a hotel."

Stanley picked up her briefcase. "Be careful. We don't know where Manor is right now."

MIRANDA MANOR WAS STILL CLUTCHING the same couch pillow, smashing the thing with her fist when Parson's name was mentioned. Gibby's photograph was always somewhere close. When the newscast was over, she grabbed the double M necklace and snapped the jewelry from her neck and threw the gold chain against the wall. She picked up a newly purchased chain with a heart pendant. Miranda carefully cut Gibby's photograph and pressed the tiny face into the pendant and closed it shut. She kissed the pendant and put the chain around her neck. The giant wraparound couch swallowed her up. She leaned back and stayed there in that position, lights on, the entire night, alone in the house where her son once played.

58

Booker waited until past midnight before Misha was cleared by police. She gave a statement to a detective, then waved off a smattering of reporters, saying she was too tired to talk. Once they checked into a hotel and got to their room, she grabbed Booker, burying her head into his chest.

"I was so scared. Didn't think it was real at first, then when he started talking..."

Rather than ask any questions, Booker just listened and held on to her. She pulled back from him. "I want some water."

He went to the mini fridge and grabbed two bottled waters. They didn't even want to go into the apartment for any clothes. Misha insisted on just getting away. "I just remember all of his blood on the street and thinking that could have been my blood."

"But it wasn't. I'm glad she was there."

Misha's eyes were expressive. "She came out of nowhere. One second, I'm looking at a gun barrel, the next he's going down, shot." She pulled her purse open and pulled out a business card for the detective. "I've got to call him when I wake up. They warned me."

"Warn?"

"Parson Manor is still out there. He could have hired other gunmen. We don't know."

"I won't let anyone get near you."

She laughed, softly. "I never thought being your girlfriend would be so dangerous." He tried to laugh with her. Misha sipped the water, her eyes jumping from Booker to the dark skies out the window. "The thing about Ren is when I got over the initial shock, I noticed she wasn't wearing any shoes. She's tiny enough, but without shoes, she's really small. In those few minutes before the police got there, I asked her why she didn't have any shoes on." Misha downed more water.

"And?"

"No shoes? She said her tall heels would make too much noise and she wanted to sneak up on, well, I won't repeat what she called him."

"That sounds like Ren."

"I like her."

"You know, my station, when they found out you were in trouble, they let me know I could have killed the story and given in to the threat."

"You didn't, did you?"

"Misha, I thought about what you would have wanted me to do."

"I would have wanted you to go ahead. Don't give in to them. You didn't, did you?"

"No. I just kept telling myself you would be okay."

For the next thirty minutes, Booker just hugged Misha. He ignored three phone calls and let them all go to voicemail. He was beyond tired.

While Misha went to sleep right away, Booker's mind was stuffed with the tasks still ahead of him. There were many avenues to check with the audio tapes that could air the next day. The station attorney was ready and prepared for a legal fight. He couldn't sleep. There was too much going on and the adrenaline was making his energy surge. By 4 a.m. he was asleep. Just in time to get up at 5:30.

59

Channel 27 had three crews at the news conference. Booker was assigned to the main story. Merilee Yang was given the angle of the shooting of a suspect in front of the apartment. The joint news release stated the county police agency would handle the arrest of Pendon.

Coffee was in the middle of three photographers. Arrangements had been made by Stanley for a hard-wired setup to Coffee's camera for a feed back to a satellite truck, and from the truck a signal would be beamed back to Channel 27. Everyone, including the website would get the live signal.

Drucker's attorney also put out a release indicating the audio tapes would be released providing there was no legal challenge by prosecutors.

Brielle Jensen, the police P.I.O. walked out in front of the cameras and sat down. The next person in the room Booker only knew from past news conferences.

"Hello. I'm Brielle Jensen. I am only going to brief you regarding the arrest last night. After arriving at the apartment complex on Parnell Avenue, our officers found one man with a single gunshot wound. This individual was shot by a private citizen and is hospitalized in stable condition. Evidence so far shows the private citizen prevented this man from shooting an unarmed victim. Under arrest is Marcus Pendon, age forty-five. Mr. Pendon has been cooperating with our investigators and he admitted to his involvement in this attempted shooting. He has also admitted his role in the murder of Runy Drucker, who was an undercover informant working for Parson Manor. Pendon told our detectives Manor ordered the hit on Drucker and the shooting of a Misha Falone. Mr. Manor, at this time, is a fugitive and there is a warrant for his arrest for murder. It should be noted, Manor also told Drucker to kill Pendon, but instead Drucker let Pendon go. Only to come back and kill the man who freed him. Since this case overlaps the investigation by the statewide grand jury, I am turning this portion over to them."

Jensen moved away from the microphones. The man next to her scooted over until he was directly in front of the mics.

"My name is Cain Stocker. I am the prosecutor overseeing the statewide grand jury. I was disappointed last night to see the case I have been working on in full display on the news on Channel 27. We have been working hard to develop a case against Parson Manor. We have learned Pendon won back his standing by promising to kill Drucker. We will not be discussing anything else on the death of Runy Drucker, except to say he worked fully with our office to bring charges against Manor."

"Are you sure you worked hard enough?" All eyes turned toward the back of the room.

Stocker craned his neck around, looking for the source of the question. "I'm sorry madam, I don't think you're a member of the media. Will you please hold your comments."

The woman stood up, her voice full with emotion. "I am Miranda Manor. My husband is the one you mentioned, who is on the run right now."

Every camera in the place whipped around and zoomed in and focused on Miranda Manor. "Before Parson ran off, he told me some things, Mr. Stocker. Things I am sure you are not proud of. I am saying here, in front of all these people that you, Mr. Stocker, arranged to get my dead son's heart for your boy. Now, isn't that right?"

The cameras now whipped back to the front and zoomed in on Cain Stocker. "I ah, I, I don't know what you mean?"

Miranda poured in with her directives. "My son died in a car crash along with another boy. My son was on life support. Parson said you agreed to drop the case if your sick son got my boy's heart. I find that despicable, Mr. Stocker. Absolutely despicable. How can you live with yourself. A deal over an organ! That heart probably could have gone to someone else, but you two worked out a backroom deal to let Parson off. Terrible, Mr. Stocker. Terrible."

When her comments were all driven toward Stocker, he was lost in a cloud on how to respond. The room was silent. Stocker's lips moved slightly but nothing came out. Every reporter and photographer in the room waited for him to say something. Before Stocker had a chance to speak, another person entered the news conference and stood behind him. Stocker looked utterly surprised by her appearance. "What are you doing here?"

"Cain Stocker, please stand up."

"Sana what is this?" Stocker stood up, eyes jumping from the cameras to the woman now holding handcuffs. "What's this all about?"

"Sana Bolton from the statewide grand jury. Cain Stocker, I am arresting you for obstruction of justice. You have the right..." The handcuffs were snapped on his wrists. "To remain silent." While she finished giving Stocker his rights, she attempted to lead him back and out the door away from the reporters. Stocker turned toward them. "I just want to say I know what I did was wrong. To think about it now, it sounds just the worst thing you could do as an officer of the court. A person who helps enforce the law. But this was my son's life. My son. You can understand that, can't you? I couldn't just let him die one day. If I faced the same thing tomorrow, I would do it again."

Bolton led him away and they all went through the door leading to the inside of the police building. When they were gone, genuine shock moved through the room.

After they left, a tall man stepped out. He did not sit down at the microphones. "This will only take a minute. I'm Percy Brewer, county prosecutor. Cain Stocker answered to me. I can't say much right now, but it came to my attention the case was in jeopardy because of the alleged actions of Cain. No one in my office is above the law. No one. The case against him is not over and other charges are pending." Brewer looked directly at Booker. "Our current older case regarding Parson Manor has been terminated. Our office will not be challenging the station or any station for airing the audio tapes." He stepped off in the direction of the door and was gone.

Coffee started waving at Booker. "Get in front of the camera. They want you live now!"

Booker had his microphone ready for questions. Now, he had to summarize what just happened. He saw Miranda Manor walk outside to a moving group of reporters and cameras with Yang who moved with her. Yang was right there in the midst of the questions.

"I'm Booker Johnson. If you were just watching, just like the rest of us, we had no idea there would be an arrest of a presiding prosecutor. We witnessed a lot of developments in the last few minutes, in what was supposed to be an update on the murder investigation and a response to the release of dozens of audio tapes given to Channel 27 from the murder victim through his attorney."

For the next four minutes Booker summed up the minutes leading to the arrest of Stocker. He was full of cross-thoughts. While he was talking to a camera, he wanted to be elsewhere, following up on the many new sides of the story. When he finished, Booker went outside and witnessed Miranda Manor willing to speak to any reporter there.

She repeated what she'd said inside, without mentioning the name of Stocker's son, only that her son's heart went to him in a deal worked out between Parson and Cain Stocker. Yang was doing all of the questioning, and Booker stayed back and made notes. He studied Manor. Her posture was straight, eyes clear, she spoke with a certain confidence of a person relieved to be heard, really heard for the first time. Her words sounded unafraid, almost bold in the delivery.

Booker stepped away and called Claire Stanley. "I'll be sending out story assignments. I gotta tellya Booker, I've never seen anything like that. Not live on TV. Everybody's jaw dropped."

"With the cameras whipping back and forth between Manor and the others, I wasn't sure how it would play out on television."

"It was fine. We were glued to it."

"So, I'm staying on just the tapes?"

"Yes. The way it breaks down is you continue to go over the audio tapes. You will also use the clip where grand jury prosecutors will not go to court to stop us from using the tapes. Yang will handle the arrest of Cain Stocker and use all of the interview she got with Miranda. A third reporter will concentrate on the shooting last night, how the gunman planned to kill. Let me stop. Is she okay?"

"Misha is doing fine. I can't thank Renla Parker enough."

"Glad to hear she's okay. I know that must have been traumatic. The third reporter will handle the arrest of Marcus Pendon. And, of course, the world is looking for Parson Manor."

"Hope the world finds him."

Booker stuffed the phone in his pocket. The room was still a cacophony of noise with reporters on the phone to their news stations. Like Stanley, Booker had the task of figuring out how all of the events would fit together. He imagined the combined reports of himself, Yang and the search for Manor would take up the first five to eight minutes of the newscast. He also thought about Runy Drucker. He wanted the information about Manor to get to the public. If he figured he might die before he testified, Drucker put in his course of action.

Booker and Coffee headed back to the station. There were no stops for food. He moved on pure adrenalin, nothing more. Coffee drove without saying anything. This was her way of letting him think it out. Booker had all the audio tapes locked in his own memory. An edit booth awaited them. Booker put himself in the place of Cain Stocker. What would he do if faced with a moral dilemma, what was ethical versus the life of your son? He couldn't answer. Just not right now.

The one thing he faced was the task of meeting the deadline. Granted permission to publish the audio tapes, over the next two days Booker and Channel 27 aired most of the tapes given to them by Drucker's attorney.

60

Booker walked up to the club and didn't see the big sign out front. He also didn't hear the blare of music or a packed lot, just the red and black T-bird. The door was locked so Booker knocked.

"Who is it?"

"Booker. Booker Johnson."

Renla Parker opened the door and showed him to the large room of empty tables and chairs. "Pick one."

When he walked in, she locked the door and walked to a table, heels clacking on the hard floor and sat down. He joined her.

"I'm here to thank you."

Parker said, "Busy day, huh?"

"Yes, busy. I have to ask. How did you end up at my apartment and then stop Pendon from killing my girlfriend?"

For a moment, she didn't answer. "Police still have my gun. They say it's part of the investigation. Don't know when I'll get it back. That's why the door is locked. Feel naked without Little P."

"Little P?"

"What I call my pistol."

"The apartment?"

"Did what I had to do, simple as that. I've known Marcus for a long time. Not a good guy. Would steal his mother's last meal." She examined her nails like they needed a touchup.

"And you being there?"

"I explained to your friend. I got a visit from Runy's attorney and after he talked to me, I wanted to see you and not on the phone. So I drove to your station. That's when I saw Marcus eyeing your friend. I had no idea she was with you, nothing. I just saw Marcus was up to something bad. So I followed them. When he got to your place, and he came out with that gun, I grabbed Little P. Took off my bracelets, my shoes, and moved in all quiet. And that's it."

"What did the lawyer say?"

The hard exterior of Renla Parker started to melt. Her eyes glossed moist, and she started tapping her nails on the table. "The lawyer told me Runy left me some money. Not dirty money, it's stuff he saved up. His salary built up over years. Told the attorney it was for the renovations I wanted to do. All of them."

"That's why there's no sign out front?"

"Got some people to take it down. This is going to be called Drucker's Place." The nail tapping stopped. "Lawyer told me Runy gave money to one other person. He wouldn't tell me who, and I'll probably never find out."

"After last night, are you okay with police?"

"I'll be fine. Under some portions of Florida law, I'm allowed to use my weapon if I'm trying to save the life of someone else. They did that thing on my hands again and took my piece."

"G-S-R."

"Yep. After your friend told them what happened, they took my statement and they let me go."

Booker's phone rang. "Booker."

"Turn on your television." There was an urgency in Stanley's voice.

"What's up?"

"We got a special report in four minutes. You need to see this."

Booker put away his phone. "You got a TV someplace?"

"Back in my office." He followed her through a short maze of hallways to an office with no windows. She turned on a large flat screen. "What's going on?"

"Don't know. I just got a call to watch."

Parker watched the screen come to life and stood back so both of them could see. The familiar booth announcer voice used by Channel 27 broke in. "We interrupt scheduled programming for a Channel 27 special report."

Booker recognized his colleague. "This is Sam Kinder, Channel 27. Just moments ago police announced the arrest of Parson Manor, who was captured as he was about to enter the state of Georgia. A Florida Highway Patrol Officer spotted Manor getting gas and getting into his car. We're told the F.H.P. and several agencies moved in on the car and made the arrest. We have video of Manor being put into a police car."

Booker and Parker watched video of Manor, head down, being walked down the highway and placed into the back of a police vehicle. Cars were stopped along the road, people out and staring at the arrest.

Kinder filled in more detail. "Police say Manor was headed north and had plans to try and enter Canada. Manor is now facing obstruction of justice charges. He is also looking at murder charges in the death of Runy Drucker, the man who was working undercover with authorities. And we're told it was Parson Manor who instructed Marcus Pendon to kill a person outside an apartment. Pendon is cooperating with police and is giving full details on a wide range of crimes including money laundering and extortion. And there is an active investigation into a deal with prosecutor Cain Stocker in an organ donation scheme. We will have more on this and will update as we get more details. This is Sam Kinder, Channel 27 news."

"Wow," Parker patted the side of her leg. "Justice for Runy. I like it."

"I better go. See if I can help at the station."

She walked him back to the front door. "The sad part for me is what Marcus did. I'm on the outside with nothing official but Runy was supposed to kill Marcus and let him go. Then Marcus, only looking out for himself, convinces this Manor guy to take him back so he can kill Runy."

Booker stepped outside. "You can lock the door."

"No need. Manor is under arrest."

Booker's face moved into a half-smile. "Thank you for saving Misha. You're an angel."

61

Miranda Manor sat in the lobby and waited there for more than an hour. A woman passed her and stopped. "Mrs. Manor, how are you doing?"

"Please, it's just Miranda. The Manor part is going away."

"Sorry to hear that."

"Not me. I told myself I was never going to enter this place again. Too many sad memories. But this is important."

"Well, wish you the best." The nurse went back to her routine.

Miranda looked around the place where people entered with anxious or hopeful faces. The visits here were painful, where her hope was lost. Four times she got up, ready to leave and go home. She gently pulled on the locket around her neck and just merely touching it seemed to give her strength. Miranda opened the tiny locket and kissed the photograph. Another ten minutes passed until someone came to her. "Hi, I'm the nurse up on the floor."

"I remember you."

"When we get up there, if you could, please wear a mask and I'll take you to the room."

"Thank you."

They rode up the elevator in silence. When the doors opened, Miranda walked out with the pace and direction of someone who had been there before, recognizing all the familiar paintings on the wall. She picked up her pace when she passed the room where Gibby had been hooked up to a machine. Miranda didn't even look in the direction of the number on the wall. She just kept moving. They stopped by the nurse's station, where she ripped open a clear plastic wrapper and pulled out the single medical mask, adjusting it to her face.

"Now the hard part," Miranda told the nurse.

"It's okay. They're waiting for you."

For a flash of a moment, Miranda looked down at her feet, like they were suddenly heavier than sandbags.

"You okay, Miranda?"

"I will be in a minute." There was a struggle with the first step. A woman popped out of a hospital room, and walked in Miranda's direction until she was next to her, taking her hand.

"I'm Lace Stocker. You look like you need some help."

"Don't know what's wrong with me. All of a sudden I can't walk right."

"It's okay. I got you." The usual harsh hospital lighting was still kind to Lace's face. Her honey-toned arms had a certain glow.

By the third step, Miranda was in full stride. "You're much prettier in person. Saw you on TV."

"Thanks. Like everyone else, I got interviewed."

Miranda stopped just outside the door. "Please, tell me the truth. Is this okay? I mean, okay with your son. The doctors?"

"Please. Your son Gibby gave my son the gift of life. I'm telling you here and now. You are okay to come visit Camden anytime you want. Here's my card. My cell phone and address are on the back. It's just Cam and I now. You can come anytime you want."

"Thank you." She took the card, placed it in her purse and pulled out a card of her own. "Here. This is a card for my new business. I haven't opened it yet, but it will be called Miranda's Garden. A lawyer came by, and I found out someone I loved left me the money to start my dream. I had to share him with someone, but I didn't mind. Then I lost him. Lost him and Gibby within days."

"Miranda, I'm sorry to hear that. My ex is still around, and I don't think he will get jail time. First offender stuff but he's no longer in the picture. Are you ready?"

"No. But I'll go in." Miranda stopped again. She reached up and held on to the locket. "I think I'll go home. I'm intruding."

"You're not going anywhere. I promise you, we're going to stick together. Now come on, he's right through that door."

Miranda entered the room slower than her walk in the hallway. A teen stood next to a bed. "It's okay. I won't break." Camden Stocker had his hand out, waiting for a handshake. "I wanted to be standing when you came."

"I just want." She stopped and started again. "I just wanted to see how you were doing."

"I'm on the right path, thanks to Gibby." His hand was still extended. "I'm about to leave here in a few days. So far, there are no signs of rejection. My tests are all coming back fine, and I feel great. I don't lose my breath after taking five steps. My skin color almost matches mom." He laughed and brought his hand back down.

Lace gave her a gentle push. "Go ahead."

Miranda Manor stepped forward. "If it's okay, there was this thing I did with Gibby. I would say 'you know the routine.' And then I would hug him until he got tired of me."

"Can I call you Miranda? I promise, right now I won't get tired."

She stepped forward, arms out until she wrapped and hugged him. "I don't want to let go but I have to give you back to your mother."

Lace interceded. "Miranda, it's okay. Hug him all you want. He's a part of both of us now."

She unwrapped her arms and stood back, admiring Camden.

Lace approached her. "Okay, I'm giving you this and I think you know how it works." She handed Miranda a stethoscope. "Just press it up to his—"

"Mom, I think she knows how to do it."

Miranda put the stethoscope around her neck, raising it to her ears, then she stepped into Camden until she was an inch from placing her hands on his chest.

Camden whispered. “It’s okay. Listen.”

She moved the end of it on his chest, closed her eyes and took in the sounds of a beating heart. Her son’s heart. Gibby’s heartbeat. “Oh Gibby, I love you.” The tears came down in a torrent. She was shaking. Camden put his arms around her and let her cry.

Investigation Con
Book #1 of the Frank Tower Mystery Series

They thought he'd be an easy mark. They were wrong...

A con gone wrong sends two women running for their lives in this sizzling thriller about lust and power.

After meeting in domestic violence therapy, two women decide to change their lives in a radical way. Reinventing themselves as the Pearls, they establish their con. Flirting with single men in bars. Slipping drugs into their drinks. Stealing valuables from their unconscious bodies. They won't be victims anymore.

Until they steal a locked briefcase from the wrong man.
Now the girls are running from a trail of death following them across South Florida. A private investigator by the name of Frank Tower is their last hope for survival.

As you follow the Pearls through a "Fugitive" style chase, you'll be desperate to uncover the dark secrets behind the briefcase...and you will never believe what's inside.

AUTHOR'S NOTE

I want to thank the always-hard-working editors and staff of Severn River Publishing for helping make this book happen.

Please know, Apton County, Florida, mentioned in the book, is the creation of the author. Apton would be located next to Broward County and Miami-Dade.

I based my character's medical condition on Arrhythmogenic Right Ventricular Cardiomyopathy. The condition is very rare and does impact young people.

I urge anyone to consider organ donation as it does save lives.

ABOUT MEL TAYLOR

For many years, Mel Taylor watched history unfold as he covered news stories in the streets of Miami and Fort Lauderdale. A graduate of Southern Illinois University, Mel writes the Frank Tower Private Investigator series. He lives in a community close to one of his favorite places – The Florida Everglades. South Florida is the backdrop for his series.

Sign up for the reader list at
severnriverbooks.com

ABOUT BRIAN SHEA

Brian Shea has spent most of his adult life in service to his country and local community. He honorably served as an officer in the U.S. Navy. In his civilian life, he reached the rank of Detective and accrued over eleven years of law enforcement experience between Texas and Connecticut. Somewhere in the mix he spent five years as a fifth-grade school teacher. Brian's myriad of life experience is woven into the tapestry of each character's design. He resides in New England and is blessed with an amazing wife and three beautiful daughters.

Sign up for the reader list at
severnriverbooks.com

Printed in the United States
by Baker & Taylor Publisher Services